AMERICAN BOURBON

A NOVEL

JENNIFER JENKINS

NORTHAMPTON HOUSE PRESS

Some portions of this novel have previously appeared in
The Canopy Review, Up North Lit, and *CommuterLit* in different forms.
First edition 2021 by Northampton House Press, Franktown,
Virginia USA.
Jacket design by Naia Poyer.
Jacket photos: table by kwasny221/iStockPhoto; glass jug by
Shablon/iStockPhoto; distressed American flag by carterart/
Vecteezy; hundred dollar bill by rightmeow2/Vecteezy.
Title page illustration © Antonina Bevzytska/123RF.

ISBN 978-1-950668-09-0
Library of Congress control number: 2020925572

10 9 8 7 6 5 4 3 2

For

Emma and Joy

Nora and Carla

And Dad, who was nothing like Caleb

CHAPTER 1

Caleb McKinsey smelled the smoke before he saw it. He jerked his head up, shading his eyes and scanning the cloudless summer sky over the imperial range of the Blue Ridge Mountains in Virginia. There it was, a black cloud shooting up, curling in on itself and thickening. The smoke flew upward, expanding into the sky before bursting forth with an explosion that rocked him from his feet.

"Son of a ..." he grunted, catching his balance and unable to look away. Fire on the mountain could only mean one thing. He hoped to hell it wasn't Seamus O'Hearn's stills burning, but the flames were roiling forth from that direction.

Caleb high-tailed it toward his truck to help his friend. Another blast shook him, and a third knocked him to his knees. He understood, with those three well-timed detonations, that this was self-sabotage. Seamus had been hinting about it for weeks, swearing to blow up his own outfit before the Feds could have at it.

Caleb rose slowly. O'Hearn was beyond his help now. All he could do was hope Seamus was not near the stills when he'd triggered the charges. The bright green leaves of the sugar maple trees and the lush spear-shaped foliage of the yellow birches shimmered in contrast to the treacherous alcohol fire blasting into the sky. Solid yellow flames shot into the air as the stills blew, one by one, all that white dog blazing into the heavens. Nothing burned like a fire fueled by moonshine.

Caleb reached for a cigarette in the pocket of his overalls. The swivel head wrench he'd been using was still in his hand. He turned suddenly and flung the tool hard, wincing at a pull in his shoulder as it struck his tractor with a dull metal clang and fell to the ground.

"Don't need ya," Caleb said, flexing his sore shoulder muscle and turning his back on the old John Deere parked in front of the equipment bay of his pristine white cow barn. He lifted a ragged gray fedora, wiping sweat from his forehead and smoothing long silver hair back before replacing the hat. With a slight tremor, he lit his cigarette while watching Seamus O'Hearn's life go up in flames. Seamus would be smart enough to get out of the way, Caleb hoped, but this was an act of desperation. Many moonshiners had supported their families on bourbon for generations, and there was a lot of pure 140 proof going to waste today. Instead of sorrow, though, Caleb felt a prickle of envy.

Lonny Allan shuffled up behind him and coughed. Lonny had been with Caleb since his hill-trash parents took off one day when he was seven and forgot him. Over the last thirty years they'd both stopped waiting for someone to come looking for him. He coughed again. Lonny worked hard, but he had trouble with conversation.

"You seen the fire." Caleb nodded toward the sky.

"Seamus? You think it's all gone?"

"Hell, I know it is."

"We have to call him." Lonny pulled his cellphone out of his pocket.

"No. We don't know who might be listening." Caleb grabbed Lonny's phone before he could connect. Wasn't hard for the government to tap a phone. Almost everyone had a cell in his pocket these days, waiting for that important call. The old shiners like Caleb and Seamus preferred to be unreachable.

"You think Seamus's all right?" Unlike Caleb, Seamus had not bought licenses, built warehouses, or given in to the tax man. He didn't brew as much as Caleb, but he didn't have to, without taxes. This was always the gamble, and Seamus had not drawn aces this time.

"Sure as hell hope so," Caleb muttered.

"You going up to help him?"

There was nothing he wanted more than to jump into his pickup and fly across the dirt country roads to his friend's house, but he knew better. "Me being there'll only make it worse."

"Well," Lonny was quiet. "You, uh, you got that doctor appointment."

"Piss on that," Caleb said, bending to pick up the wrench.

"Third one," Lonny said.

"Don't care if it's the thirty-third. Ain't going."

"Well. Insurance company cares if you go." People often took Lonny for a dimwit, but he never missed a thing.

Caleb dropped the newly dinged wrench into his toolbox. Jesus H. Christ on a cracker, the things you'd do to protect your liquor. Used to be you'd have to threaten to shoot someone; now you had to bend over and grab your ankles for the board of directors. Hell of a thing, that. Caleb didn't know which was worse. Add that to Seamus's disaster, which was just the beginning. He wished Seamus had told him it was going to happen, but he also knew why he hadn't. The less you knew, the more honest your denial. Maybe now they'd leave Caleb alone.

Bourbon Sweet Tea was the McKinsey claim to moonshine fame. The old family mash bill, going back more than two hundred and fifty years, had started with corn simply because that's what they had the most of on their land. Adding a small amount of wheat made it smoother, and the juice from Virginia's native peach trees made it "nectarous," as one of the first Irish immigrants had christened it. The mash was cooked in spring water filtered by limestone and collected in jars, numbered for the output by purity.

This process had been passed carefully down through generations of McKinseys, from legal to illegal to deadly when the government stuck their hand in. Prohibition revenuers had forced most of the old shiners to close down operations, then the government got ruthless about throwing people in prison for the vicious crime of tax evasion. Old Popcorn Sutton had been well into his sixties when the feds decided to pop him for a two year stint even though he'd just been hit with cancer. Before being fitted for prison issue breeches, Popcorn had locked himself in his garage one day and swallowed a tailpipe. The government always underestimated the bullheaded moonshiners.

Caleb had taken note, though. More than twenty years before, it had taken nearly every cent he had to buy the federal licenses and give in to the Department of Justice. More money to build the warehouse for the stills that were up to code; codes which changed every couple of months, just when Caleb had met them. He made sure the product was at least 51% corn as the government required, though his was 75%, and aged in brand-new charred white oak barrels. This earned the legal name of bourbon. Congress had declared in 1964 that bourbon was purely America's whiskey, and had to be produced in the United States to bear the name. There was a pride in producing it, as opposed to any other whiskey. Of course, every year the tax man took more than he let Caleb keep. That's what it was really all about, from the beginning—chasing the almighty dollar.

Today, Bourbon Sweet Tea was no longer made with spring water or peaches. In a spotless warehouse lined with thousand-gallon copper stills, a cheap synthetic sucrose-based flavoring was mixed with chemical-filled city water from Charlottesville. The bourbon didn't taste the same, but it sure did fly off the shelves with a label featuring a sexy, juice-dripping peach. There were enough idiots in cities like Seattle and New York who wanted to appear to live dangerously on hard liquor, and Caleb was happy to sell them that illusion.

He'd incorporated as the company grew, and now a board of shithead directors sat around all day drinking six-dollar coffee and making up rules. Caleb was the chairman and majority stockholder, looking at every business proposal and showing up in his overalls when there was a vote. The newest rule they'd caffeinated their way into was mandatory annual physicals. Caleb got it. They were looking to get rid of him. It wasn't just his age, but he suspected Constellation Brands was sniffing around with an offer. It wasn't the first time a mammoth company had come gunning for Bourbon Sweet Tea. Caleb had fought off a Molson-Coors Brewing takeover attempt right after he went legal. That had been a good fight. But that had been years ago, he was younger, and the board was still on his side then. They tried to keep things from him now.

There were also rumors his daughter, Brigit, had talked to the board about ideas for expanding Bourbon Sweet Tea. She wanted to build a fancy tasting room and a high-class restaurant that featured bourbon recipes. Even a resort hotel, partnering with golf courses and horse farms to create some sort of exclusive destination. There was even a hushed-up notion of adding new flavors to Bourbon Sweet Tea, like ginger and jalapeño, for Christ's sake. She had a bit of stock, not enough to swing anything, but she was coming into her voting rights on her next birthday, in a few days. Course, she didn't tell *him* any of these hare-brained ideas, no sir. He'd be goddamned if anyone was going to take his company away from him, not while he still had fire in his belly.

But to protect the company, he had to go along with the rules. Caleb honestly couldn't remember the last time he'd been to a doctor. All the old sawbones he knew had long since retired or died, and these new young jackasses were bound to make him run on a treadmill or some happy horseshit like that. He had no time for it. He came from good Irish stock, strong people who worked hard and didn't whine. To prove the point of his obvious good health, he barked out a long, wet cough, then ground out his cigarette.

"Well, shit. Best get it over with, then, so's I can get back to work," he said, walking to his truck. Lonny gave a long sidewise glance at the ground near Caleb's feet.

"I don't need ya to drive me, Christ's sake. Day I can't drive my own self I might's well roll down the mountain and let the water moccasins have at me." When Caleb had been just five years old he'd come across a nest of writhing water moccasins near a stream. Coiling furiously around each other, their black scales glistened. Angry white-fanged mouths had struck at each other as they battled over a man's severed hand, puffed with venom and discolored by snake bites. Whoever had tossed the hand into the creek, and where the rest of the unfortunate soul had ended up, was just another cautionary mountain tale.

Caleb rumbled down the gravel road in his new Dodge Ram 1500 quad cab pickup, his one concession to wealth. He'd walked down this unpaved road alone with frozen winter gales whipping at his head too many times as a kid. Sometimes now he let Lonny drive him, but that was for Lonny's sake. The boy went almost nowhere by himself, and if Caleb didn't bring him along, he'd never leave Bucks Elbow Mountain. Wasn't good to keep too much to yourself. There were still hill people back in the hollers who never came to town. Every so often one of their kids would pop up for supplies, pulling dollar bills soft with age out of dirty hand-me-down pants, suspicious of strangers even in the small town of Touraine. Usually mountain families only hit the news when there was a house fire or a hunting accident. Then town people would tsk and say, *I didn't even know anybody still lived back there.*

The thick Virginia woods, blessed green with recent rain, burst with the sweet fragrance of wild winter honeysuckle vines. Patches of delicate white flowers waved gently as Caleb drove by, filling his head with their sweet perfume. The foliage thinned as he got closer to the blacktop. Though he could well afford it, Caleb had never paved the roads out to his house. As a child, he'd been trained not to invite too much attention to their home, and for good reason. Old habits died hard. His wheels grabbed pavement as he turned onto Sans Valeur Drive, a dusty two-laner pocked with crumbling edges and crusty potholes and a skewed street sign listing at a forty-five degree angle. Though these back roads had been here for generations, they'd only been officially named in the last fifty years. This one had been tagged by a right-wing farmer in response to a young Democratic governor who'd subsidized industrial dairies while bankrupting family farmers. The disgruntled farmer was long gone, with just a few weathered boards of what had once been his silo poking out of a patch of sweet-smelling clover. He'd left behind his opinion of the area by using his French heritage to name the road for what he considered it to be—worthless.

The road improved as he got closer to town. There wasn't much to Touraine, just two proper blocks for the two thousand residents, but its elegance belied its size. A sparkling new firehouse sat at the welcoming western edge, and a fully-restored Art Deco library perched on the eastern side. One bank, two Southern restaurants, and three dive bars rooted the town, with a few small artisan boutiques scattered here and there. Caleb had had a lot to do with the beauty of the town, though he'd growled at anyone offering to name something after him when he wrote a big check. He insisted on anonymity. "They know you got money, they'll come asking for it," he'd barked at a town council member. Still, in a small town everyone knows your business; everyone in Touraine had learned to never ask Caleb for a cent.

He pulled into the ugly strip mall on a side street. He'd been vocal in his opposition to this cinderblock eyesore that now housed his doctor's office. Hell of a thing, to have your medical professional next to a frozen yogurt shop. He pulled open the heavy glass door and strolled in, ready to turn his head and cough and get back to his day. He gave his name to the cute young front desk gal with the blond ponytail and almost smiled at her slightly startled reaction to his name, wondering which stories about him she'd been told, until she handed him two entire pages worth of medical history to fill out. Caleb wrote in his name, then drew a straight line down the "no" column for the inventive menu of diseases he might have. Maybe he did, maybe he didn't, but it was the doctor's job to figure that out.

They finally called him to an exam room, and doctor college-boy with swarthy skin and thick black hair came bounding in with a smile and a clean white coat. "How are you today? Mind if I call you Caleb?" he chirped.

"Mind if I call you Jack?" Caleb snarled.

"That's not my ... right, Mister McKinsey." The smile faded as the lad straightened. "What seems to be the problem today?"

"Have to get this damn physical for insurance. Healthy as a horse so if you can just poke the places ya need to and be done I'd appreciate it," Caleb said.

He'd give the doc credit, the lad went right to work. Dr. Marwan—that was how his name tag read—seemed to know what he was doing, even if he was clearly from one of them Middle Eastern countries. Caleb gave him points for learning English without an accent. He prodded and peered until Caleb was about to lose his patience. Long as he got to keep his pants on, it was fine. The doc frowned when he got the stethoscope out, though, and listened to Caleb's chest. Then his back. Then his chest again. And his back.

"Maybe you need to squirt some Windex on that thing if you can't hear out of it," Caleb murmured.

"Have you had the flu recently, or bronchitis? Any respiratory illnesses?" Dr. Marwan asked, peering at Caleb's chart.

"Nope. Healthy as a horse, I told ya. We done?" Caleb buttoned his shirt and re-hooked his overall straps.

"It sounds like you've got some fluid in your chest. Not even a cold lately?"

"No, sir. I'd like to get on back to work now if it's all the same to you."

"You need a chest x-ray." He scribbled on a long yellow form and handed it to Caleb.

"What the hell for?"

"Just to make sure your lungs are clear. Come back on Friday. The imaging center is just a few doors down. It won't take long, then we'll be certain you are healthy."

"Goddamn it, I told ya I was healthy. This is what you do, order up all these expensive tests thinking us damn rednecks won't know no better," Caleb barked.

"Mr. McKinsey, you don't *have* to have the x-ray. It is entirely up to you. But then, I don't *have* to sign your physical." He clicked the pen and put it back in his chest pocket. "You have a nice day, sir," and out the door he went.

Caleb sat on the examining room table, slightly stunned. People didn't usually talk back to him, but this young doctor didn't know that. He had to respect that; man had a job to do, after all. People didn't usually make him wait, either, but two days before he could have the damn x-ray? He shoved the form into his overalls pocket as he left the office and walked outside into the sunshine.

"Mr. McKinsey?"

Caleb looked up, shading his eyes once again. Two cheap black suits, clearly government agents, stood in front of him. They'd been driving around all week, dusting up the town, about as subtle as a pair of African elephants. He was surprised it had taken them this long to get to him. One was a tall drink of water, strands of blond hair plastered against his forehead by the midday heat. The other was shorter and round, jacket straining to close over his middle. He'd be the one with something to prove, Caleb figured.

"Caleb McKinsey?" said the tall one.

"What do you want?"

"I'm Agent Mark Peterson. This is my partner, Julian Miller. We're with the Bureau of Alcohol, Tobacco, Firearms, and Explosives." Peterson held out a badge. He nudged his partner, who grudgingly dug his badge out of his coat pocket and flipped it over too quickly to see anything.

"So?"

"Do you have a few minutes to talk?"

"No," Caleb said as he continued to walk to his truck.

"Seamus O'Hearn had time," Miller called after him.

That stopped Caleb, and he wheeled back. Seamus would never talk to these agents except to tell them to go to hell. "You got what you wanted, now why don't you hit the road before the stink gets too bad."

"Mr. McKinsey, we just need…." Peterson started.

"We know there's more, McKinsey," said Miller as he wiped his brow. "And we'll find it."

"Talk to my lawyers. Mine's all legal. I've got the permit and the distillery license."

"Do you?"

Caleb turned to Miller. "You got a problem with me?"

"If we could sit down and talk I'm sure we could clear this up," Peterson said.

"Even if it was legal, regulations change. Laws are updated. Licenses revoked," Miller said.

"I had this good old dog once," Caleb walked slowly up to Miller and stood nose-to-nose. "Bit by a rabid raccoon. Shame. Had to shoot the cur myself."

"Are you threatening me?" Miller said.

Caleb cleared his throat, hawked up a gob of mucus, and thwocked it to the ground near Miller's left shoe. He turned and walked back to his truck, climbed in, and blew a good cloud of exhaust in their faces as he screeched out of the lot.

He wailed out to the street, barely missing old June Hunnicutt waddling back from her chicken and biscuits lunch at the cafe. She raised an angry fist until she recognized Caleb's truck, then quickly lowered her hand and looked away.

Caleb drove straight toward the river, halting abruptly at the banks of the blue water and throwing the truck into park. Seamus hadn't said a word to the Feds, he was sure of it. But this was what the ATF did, planting doubts, watering them with gossip until they grew into suspicion and accusations. He needed to keep quiet now, no matter how much he wanted Seamus's reassurance.

Caleb jammed a cigarette into his mouth and reached into his overall pocket for his Zippo. A sharp slice nicked his thumb under the nail and he withdrew his hand. A drop of blood taunted him as he carefully extracted the offending x-ray form which had cut him.

"Son of a bitch!" He crumpled the form in his fist and tossed it on the floor of the truck. He stuck his thumb in his mouth. They wanted him to have a goddamn x-ray and waste more of his time and money, those bull hockey board members. Did they really think this would stop him? Did they think it would be so easy to take Bourbon Sweet Tea away from him? Hell no! Did this board of idiots have any idea how the government was dogging him, with these god-damn federal agents? They did not. He was the only one who could save Bourbon Sweet Tea. He'd done it before, he could do it one more time.

He leaned down and snatched up the yellow form. He'd play the long game, by their rules. He'd get his x-ray. He'd get it right this damn minute.

The engine roared to life as he slammed into reverse, narrowly missing a mail jeep that swerved around him at the last minute. He pulled into the same parking lot again, relieved to find the federal nut-munchers were gone. Into the radiology office he stormed, up to the brightly lit reception desk where the scrawny intern in blue scrubs, a friend of his son Mack's from school, swiveled around in a cheap office chair trying to escape Caleb's thinly-veiled fury.

"Don't you go running away there, Ian Shaughnessy. Need this x-ray, and I need it now."

"I'll see what I can do, Mr. McKinsey. What is it for?"

Caleb tossed the crumpled yellow ball at him. Ian unfolded it carefully. "Let's get on with it, then, I ain't got all day." He strode through the interior door, down the hallway of radiation rooms.

Ian scrambled up after him and just managed to bar him from a collarbone x-ray in progress. "Over here, this room. I'll get you started."

"Don't you run off for a half-hour like all you medical people do. You don't want me to come looking for you."

A young girl in the same blue scrubs came in less than a minute later, wiping her mouth and bringing the smell of tuna with her. Eating her lunch, probably. "Mr. McKinsey?" She smiled at him. "I'm Krystal, and I'll be taking your x-ray today. How about if we get those overalls off and put this on." She handed him a flat plastic-wrapped package. "Then we can get some nice pictures of your chest. You go on in the restroom and change and I'll be right here."

Caleb unhooked the overalls and dropped them to the floor without bothering to step into the restroom. He yanked his shirt over his head and dropped it too, standing there in his socks and boxers, trying not to smile as the girl turned away. He unwrapped the little paper dress and shoved his arms through the holes, tearing it down the side in the process. They were really pulling out all the stops on this humiliation train, but he wasn't riding it.

"If you could just back right up against that wall for me."

She shrugged a big old lead apron on, so she wouldn't get the radiation poisoning she was about to pump into him. She settled the machine against him and went back into the room that was safe from all this nuclear nonsense and started clicking away.

"My, but you sure have some great muscles there for your age, Mr. McKinsey."

Caleb snorted. *Piss on that, I got great muscles for any age. Spend your life lifting gallon jugs in and out of cars, hauling equipment by hand into the woods, building troughs and welding copper pots, you're gonna have muscles. Dumb bitch. Nice tits though.* What he really wanted to do was tear off this paper robe and wave his good-for-nothing at her before bolting out the door.

Something buzzed briefly, then she returned. "We're done, you can go ahead and get dressed. We'll send the results to your doctor and he'll give you a call."

"I don't think so, sweetheart. You can just go ahead and give them to me right now and I'll take care of it."

"Oh, no, Mr. McKinsey, that's not what we do."

"They are my x-rays and I'll take 'em with me."

"But you see—"

"I ain't got all day!"

The booming voice brought Ian down the hall. "We'll get them right out to you, Mr. McKinsey."

"Ian, we don't—"

"Just this once, Krystal, we do."

Caleb stood in front of the door, prepared to go nowhere without his pictures. They were his, paid for with his insurance, he'd take them with him. He did not care that he'd have no idea what they might show. That's what the doctor was for.

When Ian handed him the envelope, he pounded down the sidewalk toward the doctor's office. Nice of them to be in the same complex, only separated by the frozen yogurt shop, in case hunger set in between getting a picture of what was going to kill you and an explanation of how. He marched in again, past the other patients, past the receptionist, straight toward the back.

"You can't go back there! Sir!" the receptionist yelled. Caleb continued down the hall. She came running after, ponytail swinging.

"Where is he?" Caleb asked. Blondie was cute; no reason not to be nice, none of this was her fault, after all.

"You can't just walk in here," she said nervously.

"Well, I guess I just did, sweetheart. Now why don't you go back there and answer the telephone which is apparently all you are good for and let me be."

Her eyes grew huge as if threatening to pop out and roll away. A nurse stepped out of an examining room.

"*What* is going on out here?"

"I need some x-rays looked at. Your little panic rabbit here thinks she can tell me what to do, but I don't have the time or the crayons to explain this to her."

The nurse gasped, then narrowed her eyes. "Joanna's doing her job. *You* need to apologize."

"Listen here, Nurse Ratched, he's gonna look at these for me right now." Caleb squinted at her.

"The doctor is with a patient. You will have to make an appointment like everyone else." The receptionist was backing down the hall now. The nurse blocked Caleb's way forward.

"Piss on that," he raised his voice. "I didn't wanna be here in the first place, but the goddamn insurance company's gonna hold me hostage. Marwan's probably sitting in their pocket as well, look at all this fancy-ass equipment; can't tell me there's not some kickbacks going on here."

Heads were turning, rumblings beginning in the waiting room.

"And who's paying for it all? We are, the working people stuck sitting here waiting with our crappy insurance. Last time I checked this was still America. Make me sit around all weekend wondering what the hell's going on when it won't take him but five minutes to tell me. Now, you can go get him, or I can just start opening doors until I find him. Hopefully not with somebody that's naked."

Dr. Marwan marched out of an examining room, shutting the door firmly behind him and stopping directly in front of Caleb.

"Doctor, he insists—" the nurse started.

"I heard him," he said sharply. "Everyone heard him. In here, Mr. McKinsey." He led Caleb into a room, snapped the envelope roughly out of his hand, slammed the images up on the illuminator and flicked the switch.

Caleb could see his spine, and the ladder of his ribs. The doctor pointed to some opaque white spots, floating like small jellyfish throughout his chest.

"There. And there and there. These are nodules, probably lung cancer, and there are a lot of them. This is what's making you cough, though you didn't admit to that. You should quit smoking, though you didn't admit to that either. You might want to have a biopsy, which is a long needle inserted into your lung, then find an oncologist and work out a treatment plan. If you don't want to die. Now, is that what you were looking for?"

Caleb nodded, reduced for once to silence. The x-rays were returned to the envelope and shoved into his hands. Dr. Marwan held out Caleb's physical form, now signed, and he was shown the door.

Driving back up the mountain, Caleb began to steam. Doctors got shit wrong all the time. This mouthy pup didn't know what he was talking about. He wasn't sick, never had been. They had no idea how strong he was. Whatever was wrong, he could fix it. They didn't know what his considerable fortune could buy. Hell, wasn't this what all that money was for? Caleb hammered the wheel, infuriated. Strong men had tried to kill him and failed. He would not give in.

He would not cave in to the ATF clowns, either. In the old days, he'd have seen the feebs sniffing around for illegal stills from a mile away, but he hadn't been paying attention this time until it was too late. He felt responsible for Seamus's downfall; Caleb had helped Seamus build his illegal distillery in the first place, years ago. Caleb needed a snort with his buddy right about now, but the owner of Bourbon Sweet Tea showing up at the O'Hearns' would only make things worse for them both. There'd be alphabet boys crawling all over Seamus's land now, barking out orders like armchair commandos in front of TV cameras and newspaper reporters. The slightest tingle ran up Caleb's spine, like the old days. He wasn't afraid, but he needed to stay aware.

Instead of continuing up the road to Seamus's place, Caleb took a dirt turn-off that led into the woods. After a few hundred feet, he drove slowly off the road and stopped behind a stand of scotch pines. He covered his truck with pine boughs and climbed up the mountain, careful to avoid the barbed wire traps he'd set in case anyone decided to ignore the "No Trespassing" and "No Hunting" signs and visit his mountain uninvited.

He wiped his brow; even under the tree cover, it was hot in August. He hadn't been out here since May, and the incline seemed steeper than he remembered. A tall rock formation jutted almost straight up through some oaks. A small cave within the rocks was covered with moss, cobwebs and critter nests. Past that was the well-camouflaged heavy wooden door to Caleb's pot of gold.

This was where his secret stills lived. In addition to his government-approved warehouse full of huge copper pots, he also brewed his own bootleg bourbon. He'd stopped for a while, while he was getting the licenses. But once Bourbon Sweet Tea was on its feet, he'd grown restless. Moonshine was in his blood, and there had to be a bit of danger in it. Building this underground concrete bunker deep in the mountain had taken the better part of two years. But in this hidden lair lived twenty blackpot submarine stills, large enough to mix in the mash directly, propane fired and virtually invisible. This was pure shine, illegally cooked and bottled at 140 proof.

Caleb did just one secret run per year. It was smaller than his legal operation, but it was all tax-free. His distribution and shipping expenses were inflated due to the secrecy. It was all shipped overseas, where there was a thrill about drinking underground bourbon, the only true American whiskey. Each spring he brought in a crew of ex-cons for two weeks, driving them up the mountain blindfolded and paying them more for their silence than they'd make in a year otherwise. He'd caught one young thief late last fall trying to make his way back to the still site, but all that was left of him was a steel-toed boot hanging from a tree. Whether or not there was still a foot in the boot was anybody's guess.

With all these expenses, Caleb still walked away with over two million dollars a year. This was his security money, and he figured that after fifteen years he was pretty well set and could stop anytime he wanted. He didn't need to take these risks anymore. Especially now that the spooks had invaded. Son of a bitch, if that wasn't a pain right in Caleb's behind, he didn't know what was. It was a challenge, though, and he'd never walked away from a fight; the thought of a battle put a bounce in his step.

Or at least, it had used to. Today it made him tired. His kids didn't know anything about the secret stills. He'd always looked forward to the day he could bring them up here. He'd longed to see their faces. He'd been waiting for the day they'd be old enough to appreciate it, but with his oldest turned 29, he was still waiting.

He'd tried his damnedest with his kids, raising them up all on his own after his wife, Maeve, had died when they were young. He knew what that was like, he'd lost his ma when he was just a pup, too. So he made sure to teach them country values and the merits of hard work. This had led to a lot of grumbling, fussing and fighting over the years. They'd had tussles, then they made up. But three years ago, after Brigit's high school graduation, his kids had high-tailed it away from him, the business, and even each other. They'd been mad at him before, but this time was different. This time, they hadn't come back around. There was, for the first time, no McKinsey to take over the moonshine.

His fiery daughter Brigit had loved bourbon from her first sip. Everyone had doted on her as a child, which was easy because she loved to laugh. She'd been barely two years old when Maeve had died, and her two older brothers began hovering around her like she was a baby bird. That's probably how she got so spoiled, Caleb thought. The daredevil in her emerged, running recklessly into life without a thought for her own safety. She also stood strong on her convictions, and if you doubted her, she'd turn on you like a wildcat. Brigit had a too-familiar temper; Caleb knew exactly where it came from and sometimes it worried him. She wasn't fit to take over anything, no matter how many fantasy plans she cooked up.

His oldest, Mack, was just plain stubborn. He was so goddamned certain he knew what was right for everyone. Mack was like his mother in that arrogance, but what had been sweetly challenging to Caleb in a wife was irritating in a son and they butted heads like bighorn rams. Mack used that tenacity well when it was to his advantage; so focused, so intent on winning, until he'd jumped full blast into drinking as a teenager. Caleb had hoped that was how he'd learned to respect it, and come out the other side. But Mack didn't seem to be able to keep it in check. After Caleb had bailed Mack out for his third public drunkenness arrest, Mack had quit drinking altogether and shunned the factory, preferring to mow goddamn lawns for a living instead. He'd started going to those AA meetings, and began sermonizing to convince everyone else they were alcoholics, too.

As for his lost boy, well, best not to think of Kieran. Kieran had been the sparkling golden boy. He'd kept the family together and smoothed out the wrinkles. He'd always been quick with a funny story to deflect battling personalities. He'd put his arm around you, and smile, even if you were mad as a wet hen.

Caleb winced at a quick shot of pain in his chest. He didn't like to remember what had happened with his middle son, who could no longer fix anything, wherever he might be now.

Generations of McKinsey moonshiners had come before Caleb, but he might be the end of the line. He'd produced a lot of bourbon in his lifetime, but it didn't look like he'd produced a McKinsey to keep it going. Now, with the ATF breathing down his neck, he had no more patience. There was too much at stake for his young and impulsive daughter to handle, but he would use any means necessary to force his sons to take over Bourbon Sweet Tea.

He hoped that, unlike their father, they could do it without killing anyone.

CHAPTER 2

Brigit McKinsey charged into her last illegal hangover with eyes wide open. She burst out from under a mess of tangled blankets, dirty clothes, an empty cellophane sleeve of cracker crumbs, and a scrawny gray cat that did not belong to her. At a little after noon, she banged at the insistent alarm clock that had been ringing for hours and knocked it off the stand, when it finally shut up. She glanced at an indecipherable phone number scribbled on her left hand. Swinging her legs slowly to the floor, she sat up to assess the condition of her head. Not clear, but not terrible either. Time to shake off the cocktail cobwebs of the night before.

Stumbling to the kitchen, she twisted up long, wavy masses of wild auburn hair and fastened them in a potato chip clip. A half-filled bottle of her family's famous product, Bourbon Sweet Tea, perched precariously near the sink before she tucked it safely back into the cabinet. She searched the refrigerator for a Coke and grabbed two lonely Saltines off the counter. She prided herself on her ability to get up and go, no matter how much she'd drunk. That was why she was a Master of the Party, a title she relished. None of her friends in Touraine had come to the party innocent; drinking was a hazard of small-town living in western Virginia. Either the Baptist God was going to save you, or the Devil had already taken hold of your soul. Brigit didn't think she needed her soul.

"Happy-almost-birthday!" Annamae Hamilton cried as she flung open her best friend's front door, bringing in the bright August sunshine. Her cornsilk hair flowed around her tiny shoulders like a waterfall, the coveted treasure of all the Southern belles in her family. With Annamae barely five foot one, Brigit towered six inches over her. They were polar opposites in looks and temperament, with Brigit forgiving Annamae's addled innocence and Annamae putting up with Brigit's sharp cynicism.

Brigit, with a mouthful of crackers, raised a hand to wave.

"I think I know where your birthday party's going to be," Annamae said.

"Where?" Brigit mumbled. She'd be twenty-one tomorrow, and rumors had swirled about her surprise party.

"You're not going to believe this, but I saw your brother making plans."

"Mack?" Brigit said, spraying crumbs down the front of her shirt.

"He was going into the library with a very intense look on his face."

"Wait, what?"

"Mack, your sexy brother," Annamae purred.

"Ew, shut up, you pig."

"So I think the party's at the library."

"Maybe he was just getting a book."

"Brigit ..."

"What? He knows how to read."

Brigit absently placed the crackers on the counter. She snagged a pair of blue jean shorts from a pile of discarded clothing on the floor and pulled them on. She grabbed a wadded-up T-shirt too before Annamae shook her head and snatched it away, handing her a cleaner shirt with fewer wrinkles and no stains.

"No, but seriously. Remember the bluegrass party last fall at the library? Remember how much fun it was, with the bar and band and everything? And they stayed open all night, because it was a private party," Annamae said.

"But why? Why is *Mack* doing this?"

"He's your brother."

"Look, Annamae, I know it's supposed to be a surprise and all, but you gotta come clean. Tell me what you know." Making demands of Annamae wasn't really fair. She was too honest and too convinced the world was a good place. "Shit, this one's missing a button. Two buttons." She ripped the shirt off and flung it back in the pile. Annamae sighed and went into Brigit's closet, pulling a blouse from a hanger and handing it to her friend.

"Well, I don't *know* anything. Yet. But Mack's got a lot to make up for, in the party department." Annamae picked up the discarded shirt and hung it over the back of a chair. She picked up the first shirt and sniffed it, her pert little face scrunching up from the smell as she added it to the laundry basket. "Maybe it's his gift to you."

"Did you talk to him? What did he tell you?" Brigit was now digging through the clothing pile for a pair of shoes that matched.

"No one in your family talks to me until the very last minute." Annamae said. It was true. Annamae couldn't keep her mouth shut any better than a big dog at a barbeque.

"Well, it's insane, even for you."

"What if he is, though? What if he and your dad are doing it together? Wouldn't *that* be a great twenty-first birthday present?"

Brigit watched her friend's face as she floated into the childhood fairy tale of one big happy McKinsey family and continued to tidy up the clothes on the floor.

"No. There's no way my brother's throwing me a party. Or my father, either. It's been three years since the Graduation Disaster, Annamae. Mack and Caleb have learned to leave me alone." She slid her feet into a pair of sneakers that had seen better days.

"I thought you threw those nasty shoes out."

"I just told you I did. I like them." She wiggled her feet and her little toe peeked out a rip in the side.

"They are ugly as sin and there's a hole, I can see your toe."

"Stop looking then."

"Brigit," Annamae said, "You have to forgive them sometime."

"No, I don't."

"But ..."

"I thought you had an interview at Fardowner's Cafe today," Brigit said.

"I forgot!" Annamae jumped up, dropping the shirts she had been folding back onto the floor. "I gotta go. I'll figure it all out and call you later." She sprinted out the door, leaving it open.

"You won't figure anything out, you never do," Brigit yelled after her from the doorway. She and Annamae had been friends since they could sit up in a sandbox, but my God, she was blonde.

Brigit leaned against her front door, waiting patiently for the scrawny gray tabby to make up its mind about staying in or going out. She stared into the sun-dappled Blue Ridge, the endless shades of cobalt and indigo bringing calm in the hills that surrounded her. Annamae often went off on bouts of fanciful ideas, but that didn't mean this one couldn't be real. Brigit was hesitant to admit she really wanted it to be true. She and Mack had always been close, and at nine years older, he had helped raise her. What if Mack was planning her party—or what if he and her father were planning it together? That would be a hell of a surprise. No one's twenty-first birthday went by unnoticed in Touraine. It was a big deal, the last hurdle to adulthood, and celebrations were expected.

Brigit's high school graduation had been the last McKinsey party, which her family had carefully planned for months. The entire class had been invited, and for once, Caleb had spared no expense. But the fairy tale had turned into a nightmare as Mack and Caleb had started a vicious fight that soon jacked up her whole class, the brawl growing as friends attacked friends, with Brigit caught in the middle.

The night of her graduation had been warm with a sky full of stars. Caleb had rivaled Rhett Butler's charm that evening as the perfect Southern gentleman. He welcomed the guests with a wide smile and open arms. This was unusual; he was not known for his warmth, and very few people had been invited to the McKinsey home before. At the entrance, Caleb himself offered cold bottles of ginger ale and beribboned bundles of monogrammed chocolates, soothing apprehension at the rumors of his bootlegging past. Immense striped tents had been hung with twinkling lights to usher in the guests. Linen covered tables had been laid with china and full-service waiters stood patiently attentive. A full bar with top-shelf liquor had beckoned to those old enough to drink. A popular new band with a feisty singer who was giving Pink a run for her money was setting up. All of this, just for Brigit.

Upstairs in her bedroom, she heard the laughter and cheers as her friends downed shots and pledged lifelong friendships. She reached into the back of her closet for the quart of moonshine she kept hidden there. With a hand firmly on her doorjamb for support, she threw back her third swallow of the night. Shaking the stars from her eyes, she smiled at her decision to cast off her tomboy ways this evening.

Brigit waltzed out to the front porch in a vintage 1950s dress of shimmering midnight blue taffeta with small rust-colored leaves that almost glowed. The long V neckline disappeared into a wide belt cinched over a small waist. It was her mother's, one of the few things a friend of Maeve's had squirreled away after her death, and kept safe for Brigit all these years. In the pointy-toed matching pinup heels, her wavy auburn mane flowing around her, she swayed ever so gently, warmed by bourbon and the soft glow of the lights.

Shooter Jackson stood below her in the yard with perfectly muscled arms under his gleaming tawny brown skin, the temp fade haircut with soft curls accentuating his six-foot frame. He appreciated Brigit in her own right, as stubborn as she was sweet. Shooter was not a lackey or a bootlicker waiting for the money to fall off the McKinsey tree. Not that it would fall on anyone beside her father; at least, not yet. She shivered as Shooter held out a hand to her, his amber eyes glowing. Tonight, she would let him take this dress off.

One face stood out at her carved in panic. Caleb stared as if she were about to burst into flames. Instead of proudly climbing the steps of the porch and escorting her down as Brigit had hoped, her father turned away, stumbling unsteadily back toward the bar, knocking into guests on the way without seeming to notice. Brigit frowned uncertainly.

"Brigit, you look beautiful," Shooter said, bounding up the steps to her side.

She engulfed him in a hug. "We made it, Shooter."

"Brigit!" Her older brother, Mack, stood just behind her boyfriend.

"Mack!" She hugged him as well. "Look at me! I graduated," she said, smiling.

"You did!"

"Where's Kieran?"

"I don't know, but he'll be here."

"So let's celebrate!"

"Brigit … Caleb's pounding whiskey," Mack said.

"He promised me he wouldn't." Brigit stepped back and squeezed her eyes shut for a moment. The shots from her private stash were lighting her up.

"I'll try to keep him—" Mack started, as Brigit bolted down the steps toward Caleb. People parted as if she were breathing fire, but they didn't go too far back.

"Brigit, you don't want to do this," Mack said, quickly placing himself between her and their father.

"Get out of my way," she hissed as she pushed past him.

"Step 'side, son, it's her graduation party. What the hell's wrong with you? Let the girl, 'scuse me, lady, enjoy herself," Caleb said, whiskey coaxing out his drawl.

"Please, Brigit," Mack implored.

"Let's have a drink, Dad," Brigit yanked the bottle of Bourbon Sweet Tea away from the bartender.

"Let's have a real drink, sweetheart." Caleb reached behind the bar and lifted out a clear bottle with no label, topped by a black cork stamped with an M. While Bourbon Sweet Tea was aged and bottled at 85 proof, this was Caleb's private stash; 70% alcohol and bottled at 140 proof.

"Why don't we save that for another time?" Mack suggested.

"I been saving this for a special occasion." Caleb didn't take his gaze from his daughter.

"It might go down better if you hadn't already started with something else," Mack said. Brigit felt a finger of doubt creep up the back of her neck. Maybe Mack was right; maybe she should just walk away.

"Realize yer too much of a pussy t'drink anymore, son, but I'm pretty sure your sister can handle moonshine. 'Sides, she's got herself all dressed up," Caleb said. He opened the bottle and looked down. "Someone's already been into it." He winked at Mack. "You grow a set 'n sneak into my stash, boy? Maybe you are a man after all."

"Mack?" Brigit looked at Mack. But he didn't drink anymore. Did he?

"Proud of ya, little son a bitch. But take care. There's a lotta kids here don't need to sample this."

"I did not drink your moonshine. I don't drink anymore." Mack said.

"You ain't been passing this around, have ya?" Caleb leered. "Seen some pretty girls tonight. 'Course they's a little young for you, Mack."

"Jesus Christ, stop it," Mack said.

"Nothing to be ashamed of. Let's all have a toast." Caleb grabbed three glasses, clinking them onto the bar together and pouring double shots into each. Brigit watched a smile grow on Caleb's face that didn't hit his eyes. The bourbon fumes made her eyes water as the vapors drifted upward.

"Stop it. This isn't funny anymore," Mack said.

"Wasn't trying to be funny. Why can't Brigit have a toast, a little nip, on her graduation night when you've already been dippin' into it? Don't seem fair to me."

"Don't do it," Mack said.

"You don't think she can handle it."

"I can handle it," Brigit sneered. How dare they argue over her as if she were not standing right here? She clapped a palm firmly down onto the bar.

Caleb raised his voice to the crowd. "Who thinks my beautiful daughter deserves to have a shot with her family?" There were cheers and glasses raised. Caleb hoisted his glass high, and after a moment, Brigit did the same. They both looked to Mack, who put his head down and took a step back from the bar.

"To my daughter!" Caleb yelled. Many glasses went up, and down, including Brigit's. Tears came to her eyes as she struggled to catch a breath while not showing any distress at the double shot of pure fire burning down her throat. There was clapping from the crowd, hoots for her bravery. Oh, yes, she would show him. She grabbed the whiskey bottle and poured two more.

"To my father!" Brigit yelled. She raised her glass, not waiting for anyone else. Caleb was quick on the draw and matched her in downing another shot. Brigit's friends were now watching the match with more than a little awe. Brigit coughed and choked after this one, but kept her head up. Her eyes were still tearing but she ignored them as eyeliner ran down her cheeks. Shooter slid up to the bar next to her.

"I'd be happy to help you out with that extra shot," Shooter declared smoothly as he took the glass that had been meant for Mack.

Quicker than a viper, Caleb's hand squeezed around Shooter's wrist. "Don't think so," he growled. Shooter stepped back, waiting for

Caleb to release him. "That's for my son," Caleb gave Shooter a look like he was a rival rumrunner, and finally let go after a long squeeze. Shooter rubbed his wrist as he backed away.

Regaining his jovial crowd demeanor, Caleb shot them all a smile. "You gotta be a McKinsey to ride this white mule tonight."

Brigit's vision was spotty now, and people were moving strangely, all blurry and unfocused. She missed Caleb pouring two more shots and holding one out to her. She was wobbling side to side. Annamae appeared next to her to hold her up, though Brigit thought sitting down would be better. Caleb thrust the glass in her face.

"Had enough?" Caleb snarled.

Brigit grabbed the glass and locked eyes with her father. They were even now, but she needed to win. Her head went back, the drink went down. She felt triumphant for a second before the whiskey smacked into the back of her head like a thousand pounds of granite and slammed her face forward with the quickness of a cannon shot. She couldn't put her hands out to break her fall. There was a crack as her nose hit the bar and blood gushed down her face. Her head slumped over the bar. One eye began to swell, and Brigit tasted the cuts in her mouth where her teeth had bitten into her lip. She tried to wipe her hair from her face, now wet and streaked. Her legs folded as Annamae struggled to keep her on her feet. Caleb stood jubilantly behind the bar with his arms crossed.

Mack pushed everyone aside. He took off his shirt, wadded it up and applied it to Brigit's nose to stanch the flow. She tried to tell him how much it hurt, but the words bubbled in her throat.

"Knew you'd come back for your drink," Caleb said.

"You son of a bitch. This is your seventeen-year-old daughter," Mack said. As she toppled in front of him, Mack picked Brigit up in his arms and turned away.

"Where d'you think yer going?" Caleb demanded. "No McKinsey leaves 'thout having a drink."

Brigit looked at her hands, now slick and red. Blood and bourbon spilled down the front of Maeve's movie star dress as her head collapsed on Mack's chest.

"Don't you walk away from me," Caleb warned.

Mack started off with Brigit.

"Mack McKinsey!" Caleb roared.

Mack turned just as his father flung the glass at his face, the heavy highball smacking into his brow and splitting it open. The whiskey Mack had sworn off now rushed down into his eyes. With his hands holding Brigit, he was unable to wipe his face and inhaled drops of it up his nose. He choked and swallowed a mouthful, now mixed with his own blood. He stumbled and almost dropped Brigit.

Shooter jumped in. "You sober enough to drive?" Mack asked him. Shooter nodded. Mack placed Brigit in his arms. "Lay her down in the back seat and take her to emergency. Do not leave her. I'll be right behind you."

Mack turned back to the bar. He grabbed a pitcher of water from a table and upended it over his face. He swiped the water into his eyes, flushing away the moonshine. He walked behind the bar where Caleb was still holding court as if nothing had taken place, all eyes on him. Mack seized the bottle of private stock bourbon and took a long swallow.

"Yessir, that'll fix what ails ya," Caleb crowed and clapped his hands.

Mack drew back his fist and walloped Caleb with a long-overdue left hook that dropped him to the ground. Caleb lay there in shock. Mack stood back as his father struggled to his feet. Halfway up Caleb swung at Mack with a kidney punch that almost landed, but grazed his ribs instead. He managed a groin kick which Mack saw coming and grabbed Caleb's foot, slamming him down again. He lay wheezing on the whiskey-wet grass.

"Knew you'd ruin Brigit's party! Why couldn't you let 'er have a special night, you crazy jackass?" Caleb cried, crawling to his knees.

"Me? You poured half a bottle of whiskey down her throat until she broke her nose on the bar, you son of a bitch," Mack spat, taking another long drink.

"We was having a nice time together, and you jus' force your way in here and carry her off, then you deck me for no reason a'tall!" Caleb rose slowly from the ground.

"You are not that strong, old man."

Caleb grabbed Mack by the crotch hard and twisted sharply. Mack couldn't hold back a high pitched squeal. He grabbed his father's wrist and yanked it down, wrenching Caleb's arm around behind his back. He forced it farther up between his shoulder blades as Caleb bent over grunting.

"Stop it! Stop it stop it *stop it!*" Brigit screamed. She'd fought Shooter on the way to the car as her father and brother viciously battled, and now he struggled to hold onto her.

"He's outta control, Brigit. Jus' a mean drunk, is all your brother is. Can't leave the bourbon alone. Shoulda hid it away but I wanted you t'have a nice party. Then he attacks us," Caleb moaned as heads swiveled toward Mack. This was whiskey truth. Everyone would now remember what Caleb told them they saw.

"Mack, why'd you have to go and do that?" asked Bennie Patterson.

"Mack, you're hurting him!" Brigit screeched.

Mack dropped Caleb's arm, but as he tried to step away, Caleb stomped his cowboy boot down on Mack's foot so hard everyone could hear the bones crunch.

"Please, Mack. Let him go. Help me," Brigit begged. She looked into her brother's eyes, knowing he could stop it all.

Mack caught Brigit's beseeching look but turned away. He punched their father in the chest, knocking him back into Seth, the school's star quarterback. Seth went reeling into Henry, who had been cut from the team senior year for skipping school and was feeling the resentment. Henry had indulged in some bourbon, as had most of the graduating class, and jumped up and swung on Seth, missing and smacking Seth's girlfriend Rachel instead. Although the instant regret showed on Henry's face, Seth now dived on him and the crowd broke as the brawl began. High school rivalries, fueled by moonshine, blossomed into all-out war as the crowd of teenagers jumped into the fight.

There were too many injuries for the one ambulance in Touraine, and back-up was called from as far away as Waynesboro and Charlottesville. Caleb was later sent the bills for a lot of hospital visits, including the one for Thomas Sterling, whose athletic college scholarship was revoked after an ankle was broken in four places at the party. He would always walk with a pronounced limp. Townspeople gathered their injured children and turned their backs on the McKinseys. They'd heard violent rumors from the past, and now they knew the truth. People continued to work for and profit from Bourbon Sweet Tea, the largest employer around for many miles, but they finally had the proof they needed that those people were wild, unpredictable, dangerous.

The reign of the unbreakable McKinsey clan was over.

Now, even three years later, Brigit could recall the pitying head-shakes she'd gotten all over town when she emerged with a metal splint attached to repair her shattered nose. She reflexively touched the scar on her lip where she'd bitten through it. Annamae always told her it was sexy, but to Brigit, it was a reminder of her ruthless family. These weren't her first family injuries, but she swore they'd be her last. Mack had apologized several times, but not Caleb. She still wasn't sure who was trying to kill who, but she did remember them fighting while she hung on Shooter, bloody, broken, and forgotten.

Her brother Kieran, the peacemaker who always came to the rescue, had disappeared without a trace. He'd just walked away without a word of good-bye. At first Brigit, sure he'd been in an accident, had called hospitals and then searched back mountain roads, hoping and not hoping to find something. But then a breezy postcard had arrived from New York City. Kieran was having a wonderful new life, which made it so much worse. Raised in the nest of these three contentious, conflicting men, Brigit had been coddled but never put in first place. Her graduation had been destined to be her shining moment, the beginning of her future, but instead Brigit had been abandoned by her entire family. She hadn't spoken to any of them since.

The acrid scent of smoke assaulted her nose, the slightly sweet warning of alcohol going up in flames. She hurried outside to see two thin plumes of black, dancing and twirling around each other as they rose from Bucks Elbow Mountain. It was not Bourbon Sweet Tea that was burning, she noted with relief. She'd know if that was going up. She was connected to the distillery in her heart. It was where she belonged. On her twenty-first birthday, she'd finally be old enough to vote on her stock. It was the day she'd been waiting for her whole life. She'd have her big twenty-first birthday bash, and then cut back on the drinking and get serious. She was no longer the little girl, the little sister, and they could no longer pretend she didn't exist.

She was going to take over Bourbon Sweet Tea.

CHAPTER 3

Mack McKinsey was king of the bank today. He suppressed a grin on this hot summer Friday, striding confidently into the lobby. This meeting to sign the loan agreement was a formality; his landscape architecture degree from Virginia Tech, the solidly researched business plan, and years of hands-on experience would bring him the landscaping company he'd dreamed of for years. He threw a half-smile and a nod to his old high school friend, Molly Bannon, behind the counter. Her eyes widened at the sight of him. Over ten years out of school and still working as a bank teller. Mack modified his judgment; maybe she was happy here.

Though spit-shined and in a nice new sport jacket and tie, a shadow of stubborn clay still clung under his nails. Despite his scrubbing, the dirt wouldn't let go. That was going to change soon, when he could hire others to shove their hands in the ground while he did the designs. Years of hard work and sobriety had served him well, and he was ready to bring McKinsey Landscape Designs to life.

The ding of a bell signaled a car in the bank drive-through. Clerks lounged in the corner, discussing lunch options as if there were more than two in Touraine. The ceiling fan rotated slowly, not cooling the humid air but simply pushing it around. More customers were lined up outside at the ATM than inside, a fact that probably dismayed the meticulously made-up single clerks, who were no doubt scouting potential marriage prospects.

"Nice to see you, Mr. McKinsey," the young loan officer said, walking up and extending his hand as he ushered Mack into his office.

"You too," Mack said, shaking a hand that was smooth and free from calluses.

"You have a solid business plan here." The loan officer settled into his leather chair.

"Thank you."

"Your projected growth over five years may be a little conservative, and you don't hear that often from a bank." He chuckled, his gaze still on Mack's business plan. *Joe Thomas*, the brass nameplate on his desk read.

Mack sat up straighter. It wouldn't hurt to show some respect. "I like to keep things realistic."

"You do want to show conviction in your ideas, though," Joe said to the business plan.

"Some of my gardens have won awards," Mack said. "Like the one for your bank president's wife."

"Oh, no one's doubting your work, Mr. McKinsey," Joe's face remained in the folder.

"Call me Mack. Please."

"We do have a few concerns, though."

"Concerns?" A drip of sweat rolled down Mack's left ear; he wiped it away. Jesus, it was hot. Was there no air-conditioning?

Joe leaned in. "In the matter of ..."

"Shit!" Mack shouted as pain radiated up his leg. He'd been stabbed! He leaned down to see a long ink stain on his brand new khaki pants, and a spinning pen on the floor. His head swiveled as customers frowned at his language. Dr. Kalna, the local dentist, with a fondness for Italian suits and the root canals to pay for them, glared at him. Councilwoman Jane Tipton, a trail of ammonia smell escaping her tight gray curls from the permanent she'd just received, shook her head and looked away. Neither looked surprised at a cursing McKinsey. A small boy playing with a rubber band on the other side of the glass door was smirking at him. An irritated-looking woman with eyebrows permanently scowled snapped at the kid. She yanked on the child's arm and shoved him into a dented late model Mazda with more rust than paint.

"Is everything okay?" Joe was looking at him.

"Sorry, I just, uh, you missed the flying pen," Mack answered lamely, holding up the offending weapon.

"The what?"

"Nothing. Sorry." Mack pasted a smile.

"What I'm concerned about, Mr. McKinsey, is your lack of collateral. You're asking for an unsecured loan, which is a risk to us."

The guy was right, of course. Technically. There was nothing concrete to back Mack up. Unless you counted Bourbon Sweet Tea, but he wouldn't count the family business. That belonged to his father Caleb, and all the profits along with it. Mack preferred planting things and watching them grow, as his mother had taught him. Caleb was so proud of his liquor, Mack was surprised the labels didn't feature a picture of the mountain man in his droopy hat, smiling or sneering, depending upon how well you knew him. Mack had grown up soaked in the white lightning, and had finally found the strength to walk away. He needed to wipe the taint of shine off his skin and make the name McKinsey mean something good.

"I'm willing to pay a higher rate," Mack said.

"Also, your lack of credit is an issue." Joe's face was back down in his file.

"I've had a Visa card for ten years."

"But you've never used it. It's true there are no delinquencies on your credit report, but there is also no credit on your credit report."

"So not being in debt is a bad thing?"

"Showing you can use a credit card and pay it back on time is one point of having it," Joe said.

Mack felt his previous confidence slipping. This had been supposed to be a formality, this meeting. Tom Tritter, the previous loan officer, had assured him he was a perfect fit for a small business loan. Mack had been on his hands and knees digging weeds out of Tom's flower garden while Tom sat back in the shade, watching him and drinking a beer.

"I had this conversation with Tom Tritter a few weeks ago."

"Tom's been sent to the Richmond office," Joe said. He glanced quickly to the right and leaned in. "Listen, Mack, I was thinking that maybe your father could help out."

"No," Mack replied.

"If he were to co-sign on this loan we could wrap it today."

"No."

"To be honest," Joe leaned farther forward with an encouraging smile. "I'm not sure why you aren't just asking *him* for the loan. Let him get you started, on your feet, up and running. Family business and all, you know."

"This is for my landscaping business. It has nothing to do with family or liquor."

"Landscaping. Right." A tiny smirk appeared and disappeared on Joe's mouth as if imagined, but Mack had seen it on too many others before.

"Could you speak to the President?" Mack's voice dove into his lower register. He couldn't look at Joe without wanting to smack the smug off his face.

"Your application's been on his desk," Joe said, sagging back in his chair with a squeak. Joe was turning slightly pink and drops of sweat now dotted his upper lip. The red "denied" stamp had probably appeared on Mack's application about a minute and a half after he first filled it out. Mack had detailed his landscaping proposal, with graphs and intricate renderings, but they still didn't believe him. Once a McKinsey, always a McKinsey. No bank wanted to get in bed with a moonshiner.

"So what's the answer?" Mack demanded.

"Well, as I said, if you had a co-signer...."

"I don't want a co-signer."

"Then our options are limited."

"I like the way you say 'our' options."

"Mr. McKinsey—"

"Why can't you just say no?" Mack asked.

"Talk to your father. I'd like to help you out, I really would. Look, I know—"

"You know nothing," Mack said. He shot up and snatched his proposal, months of hard, tedious work to justify his dreams, and brandished it at Joe's throat like a knife. The ding of the drive through echoed louder as a heavy silence muted the lobby.

"C'mon, Mack. I'm trying ..."

"Caleb McKinsey wouldn't spit on me if I was on fire. And if I had the chance, I'd smash every single bottle of bourbon he has."

Mack walked carefully through the lobby, head up, aware of the stares. Let them look. His mother had taught him to always hold his head up, no matter what.

The sun outside was shaded for a moment. He looked up to see a column of smoke climbing out of the side of the mountain. People on the sidewalk were stopped, watching the black plumes curl and spin like Latin dancers. The local folks shook their heads sadly. A massive, shiny new red tanker backed out of the firehouse, but everyone knew it was too late. Old-timers probably remembered when this was a regular occasion, moonshine stills blowing up rather than giving in to the government. Mack saw someone else's life going up in smoke. He took no pleasure in seeing dreams crushed, as his had just been.

The interesting thing was the frantic movements of several black-suited strangers across the street. They pulled cameras out of an unmarked white van, taking pictures and yelling into their phones. Government agents, Mack figured, IRS, FBI, ATF; Caleb had schooled him as a child on contempt for all forms of Washington bureaucracy. His father was viciously opposed to the CIA in particular, "presidential spooks and paid assassins" he called them. Mack was sure there was a personal story there, and he'd asked, but Caleb never talked about the past.

As he drove home in his old Ford truck, Mack tried not to think of Caleb and his moonshine money. It had been three years since he had spoken to his dad; three years since the last time emergency sirens had headed up the mountain, only that time, for Brigit's graduation party. That party had changed the way Touraine looked at the McKinseys. Growing up, people had been fascinated by the success of Bourbon Sweet Tea, aware of the dangerous past but drawn in by the long, secretive family legacy. Since the party, though, the gild was off the lily and Mack knew townsfolk peered down at them with a mixture of pity and disgust, while still cashing their Bourbon Sweet Tea paychecks.

As he pulled into his driveway, he listened to the pickup's engine knock before shutting down. He needed a new transmission. Or a new truck. Neither of which he could afford. The living room of his tiny rental house held a secondhand brown plaid sofa, a Salvation Army lamp, no pictures on the walls, no books, no shelves. He lived here, but it had never been his home. His life had been on hold for so long. He'd saved, worked, and planned for this day, but he'd never considered failure.

He pounded down the dim hallway to his bedroom and ripped off his money-grubbing clothes. The khaki pants and white button-down shirt now bore the stink of despair as he threw them into the corner. With a swift kick a brown loafer catapulted off Mack's foot and into the closet door, cracking the cheap plywood. "Now don't you go getting your Irish up, boyo," he muttered. What his mother would have said.

He bent to grab the phone that had fallen from his pants pocket. He took a deep breath and sat on the bed as he called up Anthony Abruzzo's number. Mack had graduated from Virginia Tech with Anthony, who always bowed good-naturedly to Mack's superior talent in landscape design. Anthony had done well, and had called a few months ago to offer Mack a job managing one of his new garden design studios in Colorado. Mack told him he'd soon have his own company, and skimmed over the brief pause on the other end of the phone. Anthony knew what Mack had been through, and wished him well.

Mack had never seriously considered the offer, but he'd never forgotten it, either. He'd been following this path for so long, he felt at the edge of the cliff now, unable to move. He wanted a drink, still, after all this time. Build a raft of bourbon and float down a river of whiskey into oblivion, like the old days. He had to keep moving. Stopping led to thinking, and thinking led to drinking. That was his mantra.

"Hi, Anthony, it's Mack McKinsey," Mack said on the voicemail recording. "I've been thinking about our last conversation, and I am ready to get out of Virginia. Give me a call back when you have a chance."

There was no reason to stay here now. He'd never amount to anything in a town that would always associate him with alcohol. Molly Bannon might be happy as a bank teller, but for him, it was time to go.

Changing back into his Carhartt's, steel-toed boots, and the ridiculous fluorescent yellow Sunshine Landscaping t-shirt with the oversized smiling sun his boss made him wear, he stood, no one's boss, but just a laborer now. He'd used up his lunch hour at the bank and he had two more yards to mulch, a dirty and precise job. Too much and it could harm your trees, too little and it could allow weeds. When he was done, specks of dirt would float on his sweat-covered skin, his unruly hair christened with tiny wood chippings. The worse he looked, the better the job he'd done, but there would be no satisfaction in it this time.

Mack climbed back into his old Ford but instead of returning to work, he headed up the mountain. There was one thing keeping him in Virginia, and although he knew the fire was not near it, he needed to check. Twisting and turning down back roads that were barely paths, he eventually steered off the overgrown dirt road and rolled to a stop deeper in the woods. He looked around out of habit before picking up some large boughs from the grove of pines and loosely covering his truck. He camouflaged no matter what time of day it was.

Mack leaned against the hood and listened to the abrupt quiet. The katydids came back first, the rhythm of the zinging chorus to and fro. The tree crickets came next with a long steady insistent bowing of violin legs, which would stop suddenly, louder in its absence, and start up again just as quickly. The short, yearning barks of a lone barred owl broke through. *Who-cooks-for-you*, the owl begged, *who, who*, again and again, until a faint, faraway reply came. The owls' evensong rose in harmony until there was a slight flutter of wings, and Mack was once again alone.

He slipped carefully through the trees. Caleb had taught him well. He took a different route each time to avoid wearing down a trail. Tree cover was vital for a still to mask the smoke from the fire heating your mash. You could only pray the sheriff's planes flying over couldn't pinpoint the exact location of the smoke. You also needed to build a solid trough near cold water to haul the water in and cool the copper worm, the last carousel ride of the liquor. You had to solder it carefully, too, because if it leaked the whole thing could blow up in your face. Mack had once seen a leaky cap explode on one of Caleb's turnip copper stills when he was seven years old. Caleb had taken him out on the mountain, but Mack was less interested in the distilling process than what was growing nearby. He had been examining a strange mushroom just a little ways away from the site when the boom of the explosion thundered, making him jump. Projectiles of sharpened metal rocketed straight up and crashed back down. Yellow alcohol-vapor flames shot to the tops of the trees in a triumph of freedom, released from the twisted cap. Mack had stood paralyzed as teenaged Lonny ran past with an old wooden bucket of water to douse the fire before it spread through the forest. Blackened chunks of riveted copper thudded to the ground like knocked-out prizefighters. Caleb had caught Mack's eye and flinched.

"Git on out to the truck, boy!" Caleb had yelled.

Mack instead had trotted over to the ruined still site, stomping out some smoldering embers. If Lonny could help, he could too. Caleb had scrambled over and grabbed him by the back of the neck. He'd turned Mack around and frog-marched him through the trees, stumbling too fast over rocks and back down to the truck, where he'd shoved him inside.

"You stay in the goddamn truck," his father spat.

"I can help," Mack had insisted.

"Don't say nothing about this to your ma," Caleb had said, hands shaking as he slammed the door and stood for a moment, then headed back to the ruined still.

Later that night Mack had heard a terrible argument between his parents. Now that Sweet Tea was almost legal, Caleb had promised Maeve there would be no more hidden stills back in the mountains. But he also insisted there was no challenge in the licensed distillery the government would allow him to run. Maeve had furiously blasted back that if he did it again, she'd leave and take the boys somewhere safe. It had been the only time Mack had ever heard his father give in to his mother.

Now, out on the mountain alone, he worked his way through dense pine branches. A little farther along in the woods was the red chokeberry bush sheltered between tall alders, his marker. As he pushed his way through thick branches, checking behind one more time, Mack's paradise was revealed. It was not a still site he was hiding. It was a garden.

As a child, Mack had spent most of his time outdoors. His mother, Maeve, had coaxed the budding trees and flowers around the outside of their house into an oasis of calm to mask the thin air of tension that always hung inside. His mother had loved the vegetable garden best, and sometimes she and Mack spent hours together planting. On the mornings after loud, late night fights, Caleb usually wandered out around lunchtime, bleary-eyed and crazy-haired, to find them. He'd clumsily compliment Maeve's newest project, but she would not hear him, not at all.

"Boy, you ought to come on out to the distillery and see how the hoppers work," Caleb said late one morning as he towered over the two of them.

"No, thanks," Mack answered.

"I want to go, Daddy," Kieran said, trotting out in Caleb's shadow.

"Don't ya want to learn about the family business?" As Caleb leaned over him, Mack had smelled last night's cloying alcohol sweating from his skin.

"Maybe he'll make his own family business," Maeve said, cutting okra and cursing the stiff leaf hairs that poked her naked hands.

"Careful there, woman. Don't turn that boy into a fruit roll-up," Caleb said. As he walked away, Kieran trailing after him, Maeve picked up a clump of dirt and lobbed it squarely into the back of Caleb's head.

One late summer when Mack was ten, he sat on the back porch separating bulbs for fall planting. Maeve joined him on the steps, shaky hands holding a cup of coffee. The worse her night, the more coffee she drank. On a good day, she had one cup. This was her fourth. Mack had heard the battle his parents had late the night before; it had even woken Brigit, who now napped fitfully on a blanket nearby.

"I have a secret for you, Mack, but you must promise me to keep it absolutely to yourself," she said.

"Okay," Mack said.

"Which means you cannot tell anyone, anyone at all. Not even Kieran."

Mack looked up; he told his brother everything, but it was true that Kieran was terrible at keeping secrets. "I promise."

"We're going to Ireland."

"We are?" Mack grinned. "When?"

"Two weeks' time. You need to meet the rest of your family."

Maeve had told so many stories about his Irish grandparents, uncles and aunts and cousins, that Mack felt he knew them already. But when he looked at his mother, there was no joy in her face. Anxiety edged out his excitement.

"What about Dad? Is he going?"

Maeve shook her head. Mack had heard them argue about Ireland many times, Maeve begging to go and Caleb flatly refusing. Mack felt a surge of pride at Maeve's trust, mingled with shame at keeping something so big from his father.

"I can keep a secret," he said. Maeve kissed him on the top of his head and walked down to the garden.

True to his word, Mack was silent as he counted down the days until the trip. He imagined sending a postcard to his best friend Lauren, all the way from Ireland. They'd never been anywhere that he could send her a postcard, though Lauren sent cards from every family vacation she took. He wanted to tell her about the upcoming trip, but he'd promised not to.

Mack's worries grew with this silence. Would Caleb yell at them on the ride to the airport? Would he even take them to the airport? What if he didn't even know—would they slip away in the middle of the night? Were they ever coming home?

This tripped him up to where his mind could go no further. Surely his mother would tell him if she planned to keep them in Ireland. She couldn't mean for him to never see Lauren. Or his father. Caleb wasn't perfect, but he was his dad. If only he could talk to Kieran. They always worked everything out together. But he had been expressly forbidden to. Kieran knew something was up, and tormented him to tell, but Mack kept his promise.

That day, Maeve was planting a row of tiny pines, which Mack thought was dumb. Who would water them while they were gone? By his count, they were leaving tomorrow for Ireland, but Maeve had said nothing more about the trip. It was hot, the trees were scratchy, and all Mack wanted to do was sit with his feet in the creek and skip rocks, alone. He dug a few holes and grudgingly thrust in some trees. A horsefly buzzed by, loud and hungry, diving at him, no matter how much Mack waved it away. He felt the sting on the back of his neck. He slapped at it, but the insect had taken what it wanted and was gone. He threw down his small sapling.

"I'm sick of these trees!"

"What's wrong with you?" Maeve stopped and looked at him.

"I don't want to do this."

"Mack—" his mother started.

"These trees are stupid!" He started to yank the last few trees he'd planted out of the ground.

"Please pick them up," his mother said in a low voice.

"No! *You* pick them up!" he yelled, full of rage and confusion

"Mack." She looked straight into his face. There were dark circles under her eyes, along with a hint of fear.

"I hate your stupid trees!"

She came over and put her arms around him.

"It's going to be okay," she said soothingly.

"You want to … you want to leave, then *you* should leave!" He slapped her hands down and pushed her away.

"You don't mean that," she said.

"Go! Just *go!*" he yelled at her.

Maeve turned away and walked out of the garden. She looked back at Mack for a moment. He watched her climb into her car, start the engine and begin to drive. She was leaving without him.

"Wait! Stop! Where are you going?" He ran after her, waving his arms at the departing car. "Stop!"

Mack began to fling the wilting seedlings. He pelted the moving car with little pine trees, but on she drove. One landed on the windshield in front of his mother, and he saw her hit the brake for a moment, but she kept driving.

"I hate these trees! And I hate you too!" he screamed. He ran to the saplings she'd planted and snatched them out of the ground to keep up the assault. Trees flew through the air toward the car until she was out of sight.

There was no family dinner that night, which was rare. Later, Mack waited at the window for Maeve to come home. Caleb paced around the house and finally sent him to bed. After the phone rang, a piercing wail echoed through the house. Mack flew downstairs to his father sitting on the floor with both hands over his eyes. The phone lay next to him, and Mack picked it up.

"… those curves are sharp around the Meachum River," said a stern, official voice. "There's a lot of clouds tonight. She hit the bridge over Lickinghole Creek, the car flipped and she landed in the water. There's some question—"

Caleb grabbed the phone away from Mack and threw it across the room, smashing it into the wall. Mack ran outside to the front yard. The grass was a battlefield of dry, tiny pines, trees sprawled on the ground like vanquished soldiers with broken limbs and brittle roots. Mack had gathered up all the forsaken trees. Their still sharp needles dug into his arms. He flung himself down and clawed open holes with his hands, planting seedlings that had no chance.

After Maeve's death, a canyon of loss swept through the house like a strong wind, blowing them all back against the walls, away from each other. Caleb was drunk more often than not. He railed against Maeve, cursing her name late at night, tromping through the house, tearing down pictures and reminders of her, as if she'd died just to hurt him.

The day of his mother's funeral, Mack had headed into the woods alone. Once he was far from the house, he collapsed to the ground. He hated these green plants, still growing while his mother could not. It wasn't fair. He screamed at the peashooters and the stream cabbage, yanked them out by the roots, and pitched them away. He reveled in the destruction, tearing the plants up, welcoming the sight of the mournful, wet brown holes they left behind. Exhausted at last, he sat back, panting, surveying the desolation he'd created. It was a war zone, torn and broken branches scattered away from blasted holes, crushed flowers next to clumps of trampled grass. But it brought him no relief.

Mack returned the next day carrying his mother's gardening tools. He raked up destroyed plants and carefully piled rocks. He gently dug around the young trees, bent but still clinging to life, and transplanted them farther out. He smoothed and fixed and filled, reversing the destruction he'd caused. He came every day, and by the end of that summer, he had an empty circle tightly surrounded by trees.

Mack knew the Native Americans believed the medicine wheel was a never-ending cycle of life, each direction flowing from the center. He wanted to plant Maeve's favorite, a gardenia bush, with tiny buds in the spring that burst into fragrant blossoms in the summer, turning to fat clusters of red bird berries in the fall, and green leaves all winter. But he couldn't just ride his bike to a nursery and buy one without raising suspicion. Nothing out of the ordinary happened in Touraine without his father getting wind of it, and Caleb could not know.

He'd seen a dozen gardenia bushes just inside the wall of an estate on the way to Charlottesville. One night he slipped out of the house after midnight and skulked through the dark, squeezing his way through the wrought-iron fence. Digging up the bush took longer than planned, and with the sunrise threatening, Mack panicked. With a last sharp thrust of his spade, he cut through a stubborn root and yanked his prize out of the ground. He anchored nineteen one-dollar bills, all he had, under a rock next to the hole and took off running.

He made it back to the garden just as the sun came up. He gently took out the bush and examined the weeping root. The gardenia went into the center of the ground and he patted fresh dirt around it, watering it with a can he kept hidden under a bush with her tools. Over the next few weeks it began to thrive, standing out in the wide, barren circle.

Mack sketched plans for the medicine wheel. The eastern quarter was fire, spirit, and rising hope, which he assigned to his two-year-old sister Brigit. He would plant pink turtleheads, their small mouths opening like Brigit's when she cried at night for her mother. The south would be Kieran and his sunny nature, filled with butterfly bushes.

Mack was to the west, and his space remained empty for a long time. The northern quarter would be for Caleb. Mack had hesitated about bringing that cold, dark, wintry spirit into his garden, but Maeve had taught him that there was balance in nature, whether we like it or not.

He called it Maeve's Garden. It was his penance for his mother's death. He had never told anyone it was here, but he couldn't just walk away. He couldn't walk away from his sister, either. He had tried repeatedly to make amends over the last three years, but she continued to shun him. Tomorrow she would be twenty-one, and he was not welcome in her life. Today's humiliation in the bank seemed to cement his destiny.

Touraine had given its answer; there was no future for him here.

CHAPTER 4

Brigit twirled in front of the mirror in an emerald green silk dress that danced off her shoulders and swirled around her hips. She wasn't usually one for dresses unless they were vintage, like this, and it was her birthday, like today. This was what you wore to your twenty-first birthday celebration. She had even bought new shoes, green suede ankle-strap pumps with tiny cherries, that she really couldn't afford. Her rent would be late again but she couldn't think about that tonight. She'd planned to go into Charlottesville for her birthday to do a bar crawl with Annamae. They'd hit all the places around the University, dance with all the college boys and let them buy the drinks. But the seed Annamae had planted about a party had grown overnight. She wanted a surprise, to be the star of the show. Tomorrow she would get down to business; tonight was just for her.

She had already been drinking for a few years, just not legally. Although there wasn't any fooling people in Touraine with a fake ID—the town was too small to pretend to be someone else—she and a few bartenders had a mutual "look the other way and tip well" policy. As long as she kept out of trouble, she was fine. The keeping out of trouble had been an issue, but now, all bets were off.

She'd been anxious yesterday when Annamae brought up a surprise party. At first, she rejected the thought of Caleb or Mack throwing her a shindig. Mack had apologized, many times, but she shivered to think that he'd rather take Caleb down than help her. She was still waiting for Caleb to apologize. She was deeply familiar with his policy on never saying he was sorry to anyone, but she was his daughter.

Caleb never apologized when townspeople complained about the whiskey fungus attacking their houses from gas vapors due to the Bourbon Sweet Tea operation. He laughed. He told them the black mold growing on their homes wouldn't hurt them. The top two percent or so of the ethanol from distilling alcohol would evaporate—the "angel's share" as it was known. But when kissed with moisture in the air, the angels sent it back down to Earth and it grew on buildings. Stubborn black spots and streaks crept up the sides of their homes like a bad Halloween decoration. The fungus was tough, resistant to scrubbing and needing a power washer to remove it, an expensive and temporary fix at best. Legal cases over whiskey fungus in Kentucky had been abandoned as the courts dragged their feet, and it seemed the big distilleries had won. But distillers in California had found a way to capture the evaporating ethanol before it could cause damage, turning it into a profitable byproduct. Brigitwanted to investigate this for Bourbon Sweet Tea, as a way of showing the people that they did care.

She knew, from talking to Seamus O'Hearn, that her mother had charmed many grizzled Southerners suspicious of outsiders when she first came over from Ireland. Maeve had been instrumental in fostering good will with the town, and that eased a lot of the rumors about Caleb's past. The Clean Air Acts in the 1980s had shut down anthracite mining in the area. Low sulfur coal was much easier and safer to mine in Wyoming, but that had left a lot of local people desperate and hungry. Caleb was just breaking ground on the big plant, and Maeve convinced him to expand the distillery to bring more jobs to the area. She created a sense of family among the workers, and people were once again proud of what they did.

Brigit could do this, too, when her expansion plans started to materialize. She could make people forget all the bad blood Caleb had spread in the years since Maeve died. She could triumph over the public display of her graduation party. She could turn it all around on Caleb.

As the day went on, though, some good family memories seemed to gang up on her. She remembered her father teaching her to sing all the verses of "Found a Peanut" and listening carefully on the porch as she did so, decidedly off-key. She smiled at the memory of Mack showing her the rules to a dodgeball game where he and Kieran let her win by pelting them with a rubber ball. She clutched at Kieran as he secretly whispered tales of the mother Brigit could barely remember. Brigit could summon up the dark times as well, but they didn't want to stick. At least, not today.

She'd heard from no one at all so far today, which had to mean something big was brewing. Everyone was pretending it was just another day. She called Annamae for the third time, but got voicemail. Annamae had probably lost her phone again, and there was no point in leaving another message. Or else Annamae was in on the surprise, and wouldn't answer for fear she'd give it away. Brigit was tormented, not knowing who was in charge. Caleb used to love to tease her, and would get a kick out of making her work for it. Mack would be sincere, but Caleb would be fun. What if … what if they really had planned her party together, and all it would take for them to be a family again would be for her to forgive them?

Annamae had already sworn to grab Brigit, around the neck if necessary, and drag her away if Caleb came near her with a jar of shine tonight. One day she'd show the old bastard what it felt like to lose your shit in public. But damn, it was the best alcohol she'd ever had. As a teenager she had happily served as his taster.

Reaching far back into her hall closet now, she found one of the jars she'd liberated from Caleb's house when she moved out. He had his private stock well-hidden, but not from her. Brigit held the jar to the light and shook it to watch the big beads that burst almost instantly, showing its high proof. She put her hand on the doorframe to steady herself, tilted her head back and took one long swallow. Her eyes watered and she coughed. She carefully screwed the led back on, and put the jar back with a longing look.

She jumped in her car, ready for a party. But when she pulled up in front of the library, there was not a car in the lot or a sliver of light peeking out. She dialed Annamae again, but again it went to voicemail. She could call someone else, maybe Margaret or Deanna, just casually. Ask them what time they were coming to the party. But what if they were already there? Then Caleb and Mack would know she hadn't been able to figure it out, and she'd lose. Mack and Caleb, working together. She liked the idea far more than she'd have thought.

She knew exactly where to go now. She fired up the engine. The perfect place for her surprise birthday party would be right there at the distillery. She pulled in to park, and walked into her future.

The building for Bourbon Sweet Tea had been built with windows high in the walls, away from "prying-eyed thieves" according to Caleb. Heavy steel doors opened into a small room with a plain wooden counter and two long metal shelves of product behind it, mainly for the retailers to sample before they placed orders. There was nothing welcoming about this room. This should be a bar, Brigit thought for the thousandth time. She would expand this first impression of Bourbon Sweet Tea, completely remodel it, with a long polished oak bar and high leather chairs and tables all around. She would hire a mixologist, offer salty appetizers, have live local music at happy hour, and decorate it with local country crafts and paintings. Make it a place people wanted to go, instead of resembling a prison commissary.

"Hi, Jeanette, sold out yet today?" Brigit asked the older woman behind the counter.

"Well, aren't you just a sight for sore eyes!" Jeanette came around to fuss over her. "Look at you in that dress, just as pretty as a picture for your big day."

"You know I had to come to my favorite place before the party."

"You go on in, honey."

"How are the on-site sales?"

"Could be better," Jeanette admitted. "Don't tell your dad I said that."

"Not a word," Brigit replied as she walked into the production room.

She loved this view every time she walked in. The distillation room was massive, with warm white walls and bright overhead fixtures lighting the space. The huge thousand-gallon burnished copper pot stills gleamed from the afternoon sun streaming in from the high windows. The long glistening tubes above carried the liquid from the caps to the spiral condenser worms that coiled down to cool the bourbon as it swirled around like a carnival ride. The stills were humming away, with workers in chambray aprons and safety glasses checking gauges as they cooked the mash to the precise temperature so it would boil but not scorch. Brigit walked down the wide main aisle, waving to the people in charge of caring for the bourbon. She came through frequently, and they were used to seeing her and not spooked as they would be if Caleb walked in. Sometimes they came up to chat, offering their suggestions as they would never do to her father.

Caleb had filled her head with the legends of bourbon as a child. Kentucky could crow all they wanted, but Virginia was the first place bourbon had been produced. Strong pioneers from Europe came over bringing their experience with hundreds of years of spirits. Using the abundance of corn in this land, they created a fine whiskey that, by an act of Congress, could only be called bourbon if it were produced in America. There was no shame in cooking spirits either. George Washington had made liquor at Mount Vernon, though, as Caleb always remarked sadly, "why he wanted to make *rye* whiskey is a mystery to us all."

One of Brigit's favorite parts of the distilling floor was the photograph of her family's operation back in Prohibition times. A line of battered old turnip still boilers with wood fires underneath and hand-soldered copper caps on top each led to their own water-cooled spiral worm condenser and finally down the skinny pipe with a coonpecker at the end to guide the liquor safely into the jar. In the background of the photo was a cow eating out of a bucket of leftover corn mash. The picture was old, grainy and creased, but Maeve had found the photo and hung it for luck, and Caleb would not challenge the luck of the Irish.

Facing the future laid out for her before she was born, Brigit decided now that she would forgive her brother and her father, after all. It was time. They were all adults. When they heard her ideas for the major expansion of Bourbon Sweet Tea, they would know she had done her homework.

She wanted to build a luxury hotel and spa with a fine dining restaurant that featured recipes focused on bourbon. It would be near the golf course in the rolling green hills with a Bourbon Sweet Tea-themed 19th hole bar, and close also to the exclusive stables featuring guided horseback rides that would point out old still sites with just a hint of danger. These luxuries would put the town on the map as a coveted destination spot.

The new flavors she'd been toying with, like ginger and jalapeño, would turn Caleb's face twelve shades of red. It had always been just Bourbon Sweet Tea, with the peaches, but there could be *so much* more. If she closed her eyes, she could smell the fragrant ginger, Bourbon Spiced Tea, she would call it. She could taste the tickle of heat with the blazing pepper, which she thought of calling Bourbon Fire Tea, replacing the peach on the label with a flaming jalapeño. After hearing her proposals there would be no doubt where she belonged in the family business.

She hadn't really expected the party to start in the distillation room, but it would have been nice to open the doors and hear everyone yell "Surprise!" Caleb kept his production secrets as hidden as a steak in a roomful of starving dogs, though. They were probably waiting in the barrel room; that would make more sense.

"Hi, Brigit," Jason Garner, the safety specialist, called as she was about to walk through the door.

"Hi Jason. I was on my way to the barrel room. Where you headed?"

"Anywhere but there. We had a leak this morning, couple of barrels just gave way. Could be old oak, but it made a mess. We're still cleaning up. I haven't gotten ahold of your father yet, so if you wouldn't mind, don't say anything until I have a full report for him."

"Oh. Sure."

Now she was let down. That would have been the perfect place. One day, she would host her own party here, but for now, she was on a mission to find it. She started back toward the front doors and back into the gloomy, institutional-looking front room.

"Brigit, I hate to bother you again, I know it's your birthday, but is there anything happening with the fungus?" Jeanette asked. "I keep scrubbing, but it's tough and comes back so quick, and I can't afford to power wash the house every few months. I know you said you were maybe going to look into it."

"I have, Jeanette, and I think there's a way we can fix it. I should have details real soon."

"Thank you, Brigit. I don't want to bite the hand that feeds me."

"Don't worry, Jeanette." She stepped out into the warm afternoon. She liked the people who worked here. With as much time as she put in listening to them, she might as well work here. The offer of a job had never come from her father, however.

"Hey, Brigit?" Robbie Turnbull, one of the local farmers who delivered corn, strolled over.

"Hey, Robbie. What's up?"

"Listen, I, uh, there were a couple of guys poking around asking questions."

"Questions about what?"

"Where else we delivered for Caleb."

"What? They must be confused. Who were they?"

"Suits. Said they were from the ATF." Robbie looked down.

She narrowed her eyes, instantly on alert. But kept her tone casual. "Must be some kind of routine check. They do that sometimes."

"Then they asked what I was going to do when Bourbon Sweet Tea shut down."

"Well, they have some bad information," Brigit said, smiling. She put on the rueful face she used as a waitress for someone who had gotten the wrong order. "Don't you worry, Robbie." She patted him on the shoulder. "We're not shutting down."

But she didn't feel casual as she got back into her car. What the hell was the ATF sniffing around for? *Was* this a routine check? She didn't know, but she hoped her saying so had soothed Robbie, who would pass it on to the others wondering the same thing.

The first order of business was, don't panic. She would ask Caleb and Mack about the ATF first thing. And the fungus, the goddamn fungus! She was going to make that a priority. She looked at the building and noted how Caleb had fixed the fungus on the distillery. He had painted the outside of the entire building black.

Now she really needed another drink. *If Kieran were here*, she thought for the millionth time. He always soothed her during the McKinsey battles. Had never let her down, until he ran off on the night of her graduation. Brigit put the car in gear, her tires squealing slightly as she gunned it. She didn't want to drive around all night and not find it until too late, when everyone was already good and drunk. Hell, by that time, they'd forget what they were there for and not miss her at all. People did love a party.

She drove to the Trickle Inn, a dive bar where she could think. Her father would never have a party there; she doubted he would even darken the door. It would be dead tonight. Everyone she knew would be at her party. Except her. It was almost comical for the guest of honor not to be there.

She sat at the bar and quickly downed a beer. With each cold swallow came more clarity. She hadn't even had to pull out her I.D., since she'd been drinking here for at least a year, and she didn't want to ruin the bartender's assumption that she was well over age already. She'd have to hit a store later for a six-pack just to flash her license.

She felt better having a plan and ordered another beer. The sharp edges of anxiety were taking on that nice, soft glow so easily mistaken for happiness.

The door swooshed open, and Bennie Patterson plunked himself down beside her on a stool. She didn't have to glance over to see who it was, she could tell from his tired exhalation, plus the odor of sweat radiating from him. All Bennie had done since graduation to distinguish himself was grow incredibly fat. He worked on the family farm and made shine on the side, or maybe it was the other way around. He used to get such delight from tormenting people; in school, Bennie had been the king of the unexpected wedgie attack, but the tables had turned now. He looked like a badly drawn cartoon character, he smelled worse, and he was aging at twenty-two.

"Hey there, Brigit," he said as he wiped the sweat from his face with his sleeve. "You look nice."

"Thanks, Bennie." She was surprised; she thought everyone she knew would be at her party. Touraine was a small town, and leaving him out struck her as mean. She was about to invite him herself, until she remembered she didn't know where it was. Yet.

"You still waiting tables at the Southern Way?" Bennie asked.

"Yes, I am."

"Gotta come over one day."

"You do that, Bennie."

"Believe I will."

They both pretended this was true. Bennie didn't eat out much, due to uncontrollable loud and potent gastric issues that could clear a room in thirty seconds.

"Is this seat taken?"

Brigit twirled around to see two men standing at the bar. They were not from Touraine; that was immediately evident. Both wearing tucked in polo shirts in an attempt at respectability, they also had the slicked back greasy hair that spoke to a lack of showers.

"No." She turned away

"May I buy you a drink, pretty lady?" As they sat, the closest smiled at her, showing a couple of brown teeth and a few missing.

"I'm getting ready to leave," she said.

"Just one quick drink. Looks like you need it tonight."

I will if I sit here with you, she thought. Before she could turn her head, a shot of Bushmills showed up in front of her. She looked at the bartender, who nodded in Bennie's direction. He also had a shot, and he raised it to her.

"Here's to ya, Brigit."

She raised her glass to Bennie and they drank.

"My 'pologies, sir, I did not realize this was your woman."

Brigit and Bennie both snorted a laugh at that.

"Brigit McKinsey ain't nobody's woman," Bennie said.

"Let me buy you the next one, in that case."

Well, this was fantastic, Brigit speculated. She could spend her twenty-first birthday in the middle of a pissing match between two-ton Bennie and a couple of tooth-challenged crackers on a midnight run to Franklin County. She stood and stepped back.

"Sit down now, sweetheart, jes' a friendly drink." The rumrunner put his hand on Brigit's arm.

She looked down at his hand, and then up to his face.

"I am not your sweetheart, your pretty lady, your woman, or anything to you. I don't want you to buy me a drink, but I do want you to remove your hand from my arm because I don't believe you want to lose any more of your teeth," Brigit said.

She quickly made her way to the ladies' room to Bennie's chuckling. This night was not turning out right at all. She hated waiting; her impatience was legendary to anyone who knew her. Maybe at one point Caleb had been trying to teach her a lesson, but she was too old for that shit now. It was him she'd usually been waiting for in the first place. And he didn't always show up, and if he didn't, it was your fault for expecting him to do things he never promised to do, like drive her to school. You miss the bus, you walk or you don't go.

This would not be happening if Kieran were still here, she thought as she splashed water on her face to cool it. Kieran would know this torture was going on too long, and swoop in and rescue her. No matter what Caleb and Mack were wrangling about, he always put her first. She'd known she could depend on Kieran, until that ratty piece of hill trash took him away.

Brigit shook her head. She needed another shot. She grabbed a waitress by the pool table and ordered a double, then sent one to Bennie as well. It was good to buy back, and he sure as hell wasn't going to take it as an invitation.

The two rumrunners were still there but had found someone else to smack on. Brigit's former classmate, Julie Hatfield, was letting them buy her drinks. Julie was a master at the hair-flipping flirt, but these runners seemed like dangerous marks. Brigit wasn't sure Julie knew what was in store for her if she went on a drive over the mountain in a car full of moonshine. At school, Julie had sometimes kept a thermos filled with vodka and coke in her locker because she said you couldn't smell it. In an attempt at friendship, Brigit once brought her a thermos of moonshine. Julie had retched all over the gym floor, and Brigit had had to clean her up in the locker room. Maybe Julie needed to be rescued again.

The waitress arrived with Brigit's drink. She raised her glass to Bennie, who raised his back, poured it down his throat, stood and waved as he lumbered out of the bar. Brigit set down her glass and stepped forward, resolved to pry Julie away from the hootch hicks for her own good. As Bennie walked out, Thad Madigan, Annamae's patient boyfriend, walked in, with Shooter Jackson right behind him.

Shooter, Brigit thought, *they've sent Shooter to get me*. She smiled and waited for his approach. She hadn't imagined this, but it was exactly right. After the graduation party disaster, Shooter had been much more attentive and protective. He was the one who sat with her in the hospital, never leaving. Brigit had believed Shooter still loved her despite her damaged face, until she heard one of his friends refer to her as a mercy fuck. From then on, all she could see was pity on Shooter's face. She dumped him immediately with no explanation, only to miss him and call him back a few months later. The off-and-on continued, but Shooter had told her the last time she broke up with him that his patience was running out. She felt now that he'd been punished enough, though she couldn't quite remember for what.

Thad and Shooter headed toward her, but stopped at the pool table. Brigit waited, but Shooter did not come up and put his arms around her. Instead he leaned over the green felt and racked the balls with sure movements. She watched the muscles flex in his strong brown arms.

"Hey," Brigit said, walking over to the pool table.

"Hey, Brigit. New dress?" She saw the smile in his eyes as he tried to hide his appreciation. "Can I wish you a happy birthday?"

"What're you doing?" She needed to remain casual, so they'd know she was in on it.

"Playing pool. How 'bout you?"

"Don't you want to go somewhere else?" Now that she knew, Brigit was anxious to get to the party.

"What's wrong with the Trickle Inn?" Shooter frowned.

"It's a fucking dive, for one thing," Brigit insisted.

"Geez, Brigit, if you hate it so much why are *you* here?" Thad asked, choosing his pool stick.

"You know why I'm here. How long have you been following me?"

"What's the matter, no date?" Julie had sidled over to them. Now she had her hands on Shooter's shoulders, and began winding her way around his body like a snake, sloshing beer from her unsteady glass all over the floor.

This was wrong, so wrong. "Where are you all supposed to be?" Brigit's voice was rising in her fury. "Thad, you have to know. Annamae must have told you."

"Brigit, I am sure I do not know what you are talking about." Thad bent over the perfect triangle of colored balls. "Annamae flaked on me tonight. I called her and it rang in my truck. You know how she is, losing her phone."

"All right, this is enough!" She slammed her palm hard on the pool table.

"Hey, Brigit, calm down." Shooter was staring at her, which infuriated her as Julie was clamped around his waist. Things were sliding out of focus now.

"You are all supposed to be at my surprise party right now!"

"What?" Thad asked, straightening.

"I wasn't invited to a party. Were you guys invited to a party?" Shooter asked. Both Thad and Julie shook their heads.

"Geez, I mean, happy birthday, Brigit," Thad offered.

"No! It's not like this! This is wrong! There's a *surprise* party for me! Don't you get it?"

"You don't have to get all jacked up about it," Julie said.

"Yeah, I mean, we can all go, if you want," Thad put his pool stick down.

"Sure, Brigit. Let's go," Shooter said.

"I don't know where it is!" Brigit screeched. Now everyone in the bar was looking at her.

"Well, shit," Julie slurred. "Can't be that good, you aren't even at your own party."

Brigit knocked the beer out of Julie's hand.

"Christ on a crutch, Brigit, what the hell?" Julie asked. "No wonder you're alone on your birthday."

Brigit slapped her across the face, hard. Julie's hand flew to her cheek. She turned and spat a large glob that landed on Brigit's silk dress. It dripped down her chest before Brigit walloped Julie hard in the stomach and watched her collapse on the floor.

"Shit, Brigit," Shooter said, kneeling down to a gasping Julie. Thad grabbed Brigit's shoulder and she elbowed him in the chest, sending him sprawling back.

The bootleggers at the bar were busting a gut. "Ah knew you was a feisty one, but damn!" said the one who'd put his hand on her.

Brigit raced stumbling toward the door. Everything in her path was too bright, like a white hot summer day with no shade. In the parking lot, she jumped in her car, fumbled with the keys and started the engine. She threw it into drive and gunned it, tires squealing as she sped away. There was no party. Nothing had changed. She drove recklessly, because it no longer mattered where she went.

CHAPTER 5

Caleb sprawled on his front porch, stewing over his succession trouble. He had to get those boys of his back in line. He might maybe have made it a little more difficult with his recent investments, but they should appreciate the challenge. No fun starting off smooth, and they sure had it easier than he had when he started. His boys had moonshine in their blood, deny it as they might.

He torched a Camel, smoke drifting up around his head as he watched the cow parade trudge back to the barn for afternoon milking. Their black and white heads slowly bobbed up and down in rhythm, udders swollen with milk swaying from side to side. Lonny would patiently milk the small herd, stroking their smooth sides as he hung the milkers around their backs. Though Caleb had offered a couple of times to upgrade the system, Lonny told him he preferred the old surge milkers, with vacuum pumps attached to the round silver buckets that you could pour with one hand. There were two milking machines, which Lonny handled with perfect precision, emptying one bucket into a milk can while the other pumped, the soft hypnotic susurration of the electric motors lulling the cows into a quiet trance. Caleb usually made it a practice to wander through the barn at milking time, taking in the sweet humid smell of the fresh hay and the grassy tang of the silage. Mostly he just liked to watch Lonny at work, flowing and precise, like a dancer, without a movement wasted. That boy really loved those cows, talking to them, asking them about their day in the pasture. The cows looked back at Lonny with big brown eyes, lashes impossibly long, so trusting, and Caleb would swear they loved him right back, if he believed in such things. Lonny was dedicated, something sorely lacking in Caleb's own offspring.

Caleb lifted the droopy, faded fedora from his head with one hand and smoothed his long straight silver hair back with the other, then replaced the hat just a little lower. He slid back in the old rocking chair that had been carved by his great grandfather out of one massive walnut tree during a long bitter winter. He liked to glide his hands down the back that curved into the arms, feeling the strength of the chair, grains burnished to a reddish brown that glowed like a fall sunset. Though the chair had to be a hundred and fifty years old, Caleb rocked it softly without a sound, rubbing his callused hands over the smoothly polished arms, almost drifting off to sleep.

A sleek blue Audi cruised by on the road, stopped suddenly, and idled for a few seconds. It backed up and crunched slowly up his drive. A blond woman climbed carefully out of the low car. Caleb pegged her a Yankee by the fancy black leather riding boots that were far too perfect to have ever seen a horse and much too hot for a Virginia summer, and the lavender silk scarf around her throat, the point of which, given the weather, escaped him entirely. She must be lost. Caleb thought maybe he'd be a Southern gentleman today and give her the right directions.

"My, what a beautiful day!" She smiled broadly toward the house. "Makes me wish I lived in such a glorious place. Your view is gorgeous," she said, shading her eyes with one hand and peering around into the mountains.

"Ma'am," Caleb answered.

"I wonder if I could ask you about your chair," she said.

"What do ya want to know 'bout my chair for?" Caleb asked as he lit another smoke.

"I was wondering how much it would take for you to part with it."

"Why would I want to do that?"

"I have been looking for a rocking chair for months, and that is exactly what I was hoping to find," she said, taking a few steps closer. "It's got to be hand carved, the lines are idiosyncratic but refined in their imperfections. It's walnut, am I right? It's got to be hand-rubbed, and it's natural, isn't it? Not a touch of stain."

"Guess so."

"Is it a Gareth Moore? It looks like his work, maybe an early piece."

" 'Fraid not," Caleb said. How he loved to string them out, these antique collectors from up north. This one was probably even a trader; in a minute she'd tell him how perfect the rocking chair would look in her living room by the fireplace, all the while calculating how much she could get for it in her shop, especially combined with the story of the dear old mountain man rocking on his porch. He snorted at the thought of being someone's marketing tool. Next she'd ask if she could possibly use his bathroom, she'd had such a long drive, so she could see the museum of treasures he was hiding in his house. This wasn't Caleb's first two-step with antique traders, but he did marvel at their naiveté for mistaking hospitality for simplemindedness.

"I'll give you two hundred dollars for it," she said, reaching into her purse.

"Don't think so."

"How about three? It's so beautiful, the more I look at it the more I'd really like to have it."

"No, ma'am.

"The thing is," she smiled, hand to her forehead to sweep back a golden lock of hair, "my daughter's about to have a baby, and I know this rocking chair would make her so happy."

"Ain't that nice," Caleb drawled. Damn, she was digging even deeper into the sob story than he'd figured. She must be used to getting what she wants.

"So I could go up to five hundred, for her sake."

"Don't think so."

"Well, what do you want, then?"

"My mama rocked me in this chair. My great-granddaddy carved it, during a particularly hard winter, prob'ly bout hundred-fifty years ago. It's all of one piece, and I'll tell ya, it's mighty comfy. There ain't another like it, hell, anywhere in the world." Caleb tugged his hat down a little further. "And that there's the truth."

"I'll give you *nine hundred dollars* for it."

"You just ain't hearing me," Caleb stood up and walked to the edge of the porch. He flicked his cigarette butt to land just at her feet. She flinched, and a shade of uncertainty finally crossed her face. "I'd chop it up into kindling before I'd sell it."

She got back in her car with a final look at the chair she'd never have. Caleb stood watching as she glided down his driveway and turned back onto the road.

Her blue Audi passed the nondescript rental car motoring slowly past again. Two pair of black sunglasses stared out at Caleb. His friends from outside the doctor's office. They didn't turn down his driveway, though, instead cruising slowly by. They wanted him to know they were there. The chatter had been the ATF boys were here for Seamus, but Caleb's suspicions were growing.

He eased himself down again, but now the chair itched at him. What would he do with it one day? There were years of rocking in it. Desperate women with colicky babies wrapped in rough blankets, coughing children turning purple from being unable to catch their breath, their mothers trying to hide the panic from their sleepless faces. Many little lives had been nurtured in this rocking chair; some who made it, and many who hadn't. Been a long time since a baby was rocked here, Caleb thought. He wasn't sure he was going to see that happen again.

Seemed no point in leaving it to Mack; his one chance at happiness had been killed years ago. The thought of Mack's old girlfriend Lauren still made Caleb angry. She and Mack had grown up together, thick as thieves. She had been so good for Mack; she made him happy, and Caleb wasn't sure that was a place his eldest was ever going to get back to. She kept him in line, too, kept him guessing. Man needed that. Nothing killed it faster than being too sure of a woman. But Mack couldn't stop tomcatting around when he was drinking, a bad habit in a small town. Blackouts, Mack said. Not his fault. He'd claimed not to remember what he'd done while drunk, but there were enough fallen debutantes around to gossip so that excuse didn't hold water for long.

Caleb should have been disgusted by the sight of Mack crying on his porch after Lauren broke his heart, throwing his ring in the dirt at his feet and walking away for the last time. McKinsey men didn't cry. Mack wailed with great heaving sobs that wouldn't stop, tears soaking his hair, his mouth twisted into an ugly mask of pain and despair. But Caleb understood. That kind of love came so rarely to a man, and sure as shit only once. The kind where you need her like you need to breathe. Where the world is dull ever after, a gray fog hanging over your future. Especially on those days that maybe, one day, years later, you might find something to laugh about. The tinkling memory of *her* laugh will fill your head then, and slap that laughter right the hell out of you. How dare you get to laugh. What've you got to laugh about.

So it was Mack likely wouldn't be rocking any of his babies in this chair. He was just shy of thirty. Not that old. There could be someone else to come along and make him a daddy, but Caleb thought Mack might be done. There was a deadness to his eyes now, and it grew every year.

Caleb had tried to toughen up Kieran and look where that got him. Kieran was always that big-hearted kid who brought home the strays; a mangy black dog missing a leg, a raccoon without a tail, once a litter of baby rabbits that Caleb had to take out back and drown since they were going to die anyway. Kieran had skipped college and jumped right into working for Bourbon Sweet Tea, charming customers, suppliers, and distributors with his gregarious demeanor. His manner was a little too trusting, and Caleb had had to pull back on a few questionable deals. Caleb had also worried about Kieran being taken advantage of by women. They flocked around him, and while he dated, Caleb was scouting for the nice young thing who would straighten him out one day. But the piece of mountain filth he finally dragged home was worse than anyone could have expected.

The second time Kieran had brought Roseanna Ortiz to his house, Caleb checked her out. He found out that she and her ma, along with a gaggle of little ones, had recently shown up at a cousin's house, itself not much better than a rusty tin lean-to. Poverty wasn't nothing to be ashamed of, but she had a cagey look in her eyes, this Roseanna Ortiz, and Caleb had seen that on too many crooked smugglers in the past who wound up dead after trying to cross an honest man. The first time he'd seen her steal, she'd slipped a fork in her pocket after Kieran had made her lunch. Next it was an antique paperweight. Caleb kept quiet until one Sunday as she and Kieran were about to leave the house and Caleb stopped them at the door.

"I think you maybe left the oven on, son," he said.

"I'll check." Kieran trotted back to the kitchen.

"What you got in your pocket there?" Caleb asked Roseanna quietly. Without breaking his gaze, she pulled out a salt shaker and held it out. As he reached for it she tipped her hand and it fell to the floor.

"Oven's off. Let's ... how did this get out here?" Kieran bent over and picked up the shaker, taking it back to the kitchen. Caleb stared Roseanna down, which usually made people look away, but she stared straight back before leading Kieran out the door by the hand.

So she thought she could challenge him, Caleb mused. She wasn't from around here originally, and that was unfortunate. For her. She didn't know who not to mess with. Nobody'd miss Roseanna. Just one more useless pet no one wanted.

As for Brigit, well, she was still young. Shooter Jackson kept panting after her although she had him on a string that she swung in and out at will. He was a fine boy, but his skin was a few shades too dark for Caleb's taste. He did not know why his younger kids thought they needed to date at the brown buffet, but he did not like it. At first, he'd thought Brigit was dating Shooter to get back at him. Hell, he knew the world was changing, but there were limits. Beside, he knew what Brigit really loved. He could see the gleam in her eyes, and he knew what it felt like to see Bourbon Sweet Tea just out of reach. But she was just a girl, and he needed to shut her down fast or get her brothers to do it. Caleb also knew she chased a drink like it was a bucket of ice water and she was on fire. He'd seen her stumbling around town, laughing her fool head off like there was nothing in the world to care about. A few weeks ago he'd wandered into the middle of a rousing conversation in the feed store featuring his daughter so far down in a bottle last night she'd need an excavator and a tub of butter to get her out. On the way out people watched Caleb carve a nice long scrape in Burt Pearson's truck in the parking lot with his keys, though no one stopped him.

Caleb had a sudden bout of coughing that lifted him right out of the rocking chair. He stood at the porch railing, bent over and barking up long wet strings of mucus. He spat into the bushes again and again. There was a burning in his chest now and he tried to slow his breathing, which was like trying to lower a flame without putting it out. Goddamn doctors. He stumbled back to the rocker and sat hard. He needed to stop pissing around thinking about who might rock what in his chair one day and figure out who the hell was going to run his goddamn business. Caleb put his head down but still couldn't catch his breath. The coughing was grating his throat raw. Finally a break came, and he gasped as he sucked in long drafts of air. As soon as he put his head back, it started again. The coughing went on, wet and full, with no space in between to breathe. He tried to stand and the chair tumbled over on its side, taking Caleb with it down onto the porch.

From the floor, Caleb saw Lonny thump up the steps, then take off at a run to bring the truck into the yard. Lonny leaped up the steps and grabbed Caleb under both arms, lifting him gently.

"No," Caleb whispered.

"Going to the hospital," Lonny said.

"No."

"Yes."

Caleb winced as Lonny carried him out to the truck, leaving his hat lying on the porch next to the fallen rocker. Something was squeezing his ribs together. He could not breathe. He heard the wheezing sounds coming out of himself like a pig being gutted. He kept his eyes closed and thumped his feet on the floor of the truck, trying to get some air. Each breath felt like a sledgehammer to his heart.

"Need some help out here! He can't breathe!" Lonny yelled as they pulled up to the emergency room. Caleb thought he'd never heard Lonny yell before, not even when the fence posts collapsed on his arms, crushing his hands. Doctors rushed out and got him out of the truck, and onto a gurney. They slapped his back hard, and put an oxygen mask over his face. He sucked in that sweet, cool gas as if it were his first drink of bourbon ever. He had to pull the mask off to cough, but the doctor forced it back on his face. Caleb panicked, clawing at the plastic mask, drowning under it. Then it was too much, and he let go.

CHAPTER 6

The last rays of sun were tickling the butterfly bush in Maeve's Garden. A large Monarch clung to the flower petals which were bowing under the weight, the magnificent wings spread so the sun shone through them like stained glass. Mack always took this as a sign from Kieran, and today he needed one.

He and his brother had always looked out for each other. Maeve told them that was the lot of Irish twins, born so close together. Mack missed Kieran desperately. As angry as he felt for his brother disappearing, he harbored the guilt of not being able to keep him from going in the first place. Kieran told him everything—except this.

Mack had heard Kieran's arguments with Caleb for a week before he left. The fights were never loud enough to hear any details, but the fact that Kieran raised his voice at all to his father was enough. Kieran was the great peacemaker, he never yelled. Roseanna's name was thrown about, and Mack guessed she had broken up with Kieran the same way Lauren had dumped him. He was prepared to help his brother with his broken heart, but instead Kieran had sought out Caleb.

What Caleb had to do with this was completely beyond Mack's understanding. Caleb was not the sort of dad you went to for advice on anything. It hurt Mack a little, and maybe, he had to admit, he'd backed away, waiting for Kieran to come to him. Mack was also three weeks into his latest sobriety mode, and he'd been determined to keep this one going for good. Arguments made him want to drink, so he avoided them at all costs.

It wasn't fair for Kieran to have a secret from Mack, and it was especially unfair for him to have one with Caleb. Mack and Kieran had many secrets as children, and sometimes delighted in the stories hidden from their parents. The McKinsey farmhouse where they grew up was built on secrets. Built in 1903, there were small closets within closets, built-in drawers with deep spaces underneath, cabinets with false backs that led into narrow corridors to other rooms. The grand center staircase had an intricately carved oak bench on the landing that was hollow, and could only be accessed by knowing which piece of wood to move. This made the house paradise for hide and seek, which Mack and Kieran could play for hours. Mack delighted in hiding quietly in a dark linen closet and bursting out with a yell when he heard Kieran padding by, scaring his little brother into a girlish shriek every single time.

The best room was the library, but it was off-limits to the boys. Caleb said it was a room for adults, though no one ever saw him reading in there. He usually used it to test his new run of shine. Kieran would peek in when no one was around and skitter away at the slightest noise, but Mack would saunter right in and set up camp when Caleb was gone. Though Mack and Kieran were almost always together, Caleb took Kieran with him to the distillery whenever the government inspectors came, to show this was a good family operation.

One day when Mack was eight years old and left behind again he snuck into the library. It was lined with heavy oak shelves built into the walls that reached to the ceiling. Everything was polished dark wood, with a heavy table in the center of the room surrounded by oak chairs with dark green leather seats. The windows were kept shuttered to protect the books, some of them priceless with age. Mack was not interested in the books, but the floor. The hardwood was smooth and flat and perfect for marbles. He held his blood red aggie crooked in his finger and flicked it with his thumb to the most satisfying rumble as it traveled over the floorboards. He was destroying all his cats' eyes with his aggie, when he overshot and the aggie got stuck at the wall. He went over to investigate and found a small indentation in the floor, into which he had to stick his finger. There was a small space under this bookshelf.

Mack sat back, puzzled, and looked around. All the shelves were built into the walls, there was no room underneath them, except here. He ran his finger around the inside of the shelf and felt a slight lip in the wood. Mack stood back and looked at the bookshelf. It looked identical to all the others. But it was not, he knew. This one was different.

He spent half an hour pulling out various books, running his hands along the top and the sides before he found it—a small metal button that released a latch. He caught a faint click and pushed carefully. The shelf slowly rotated inward to a dark landing with cement steps leading down.

Mack backed away and stared. This was better than *The Hardy Boys*. A real hidden passage in his own house. He closed it carefully and gathered his marbles, leaving the room as he found it. Caleb would be home soon, and this would get him in trouble. Mack didn't know what it was, or where it went; he only knew he wasn't supposed to know.

Mack was itching to investigate the secret door on his own. He knew Kieran could never keep this big of a secret. A few days later his father took Kieran into Kentucky to visit some distributors, and Mack saw his opportunity. Slipping down onto the floor, he flicked his aggie toward the same spot, and again, it stuck at the wall. He hadn't dreamed it.

Mack scrambled up and found the latch, pushing the bookcase inward. Armed with a flashlight, he made his way down the steps, the temperature dropping as he descended into a musty room with a cement floor. A ghost-white centipede scurried under a door in the farthest wall.

This led to a long passageway. Mack went through and found bare rooms with empty metal shelves off to the sides of a corridor. He continued down the dank passage, swatting away cobwebs as he went. He could tell the tunnel was turning and he had a sudden panic of being caught down here forever. His flashlight batteries would die, he'd be in pitch black with nothing to eat and they'd find his bones one day, if he was lucky.

The damp made him shiver. He started to worry that Caleb would come home while he was down here. Caleb would be furious—if his father wanted you to know something, he told you; otherwise you were to keep your mouth shut and your nose clean. Mack imagined the beating Caleb would whale on him for discovering his secret door.

He stopped suddenly; had he closed the secret door behind him? He wasn't sure anymore. Now he didn't know whether to go on or go back. Maybe this would lead to somewhere worse. Maybe he'd been tricked and it would lead straight to Caleb. Mack scratched at the sweat running down into the back of his collar. He began to run forward. The unknown was always better than facing the certain wrath of Caleb.

Mack almost stumbled on steps leading up. He clambered against them and up to a door at the top. He pushed on the door but it did not open. He pushed harder, throwing his small body against it again and again until he was exhausted.

He sat a moment on the top step and wondered if his mother knew about the passage. Surely she would come and look for him. A tear was threatening to spill out of his eye and he angrily swiped it away. He remembered opening the door from the library. Suddenly he got up and pulled inward, and the door swung quietly open.

He smelled hay, the familiar sweet scent of dry bales. Dust motes drifted, stirred up with the opening of the door. He was in an old feed bin in the hay barn.

He walked smack into a black 1940 Ford V8 coupe he had never seen, kept behind a partition in the back. Mack loved old cars, and he forgot to be scared now as he inspected the antique beauty. It was a two-door coupe, long and low and black, with a flat hood that narrowed to a point between the headlights.

Mack climbed inside. There wasn't much head room, and the windshield was missing. He got out and creaked open the massive trunk. It had a false bottom, and he resisted the urge to climb in it, though he knew he'd fit, and probably Kieran along with him.

He slammed the trunk and stepped back. You could fit a lot of gallon jugs in that trunk. He knew what it was for, he'd read about these cars, and here was one in his own barn. Caleb would never talk about the past, but Mack had heard rumors.

This was a rumrunner's car. His father must have driven this over the mountain at midnight, delivering moonshine. Mack stepped back. Besides the small bits of rust on the side panels, the car was in great shape, except for the small holes in the driver's side door. He stuck his finger in one before he realized they were bullet holes and yanked his hand away.

Something whined faraway down the road. Mack climbed over the partition that hid the car from the hayloft. Caleb's truck was coming up the road. He had to get out of here. If Caleb found him with this car, that would be the end of him. Mack snuck out the side door of the barn, then took off running, bent over and hugging the white rail fence along the path until he got to the road. Then he walked out to the road casually, wiping stray cobwebs from his pants and combing back his hair with his fingers. He forced himself to act unconcerned, but in his mind was the panic of Caleb finding the secret door open and then furiously thrusting him into the bullet-ridden car's enormous trunk.

He walked in the house, past the library and found his mother in the kitchen.

"Look at the state of you! You're white as a ghost. Where've you been, boy?" she exclaimed in her Irish lilt, coming over to put a hand on his forehead.

"Nowhere."

"You most certainly have been somewhere. What's scared you so?"

"Is Dad home?"

"He's in the library." She paused, eyes narrowing. "Did you have a fight?"

"No."

"And why are you asking after your father?"

"I don't know." Mack tried to squirm away from her, but Maeve wouldn't release him.

"What did you do, Mack?" she whispered.

"Nothing."

"Tell me," she said.

Mack could see a tiny flicker of fear in her eyes. He knew she would stick up for him against Caleb no matter what, but it was worse when she did.

"I have to go," Mack said and sprinted up the steps to the bench on the landing. He sat down to think. He had a secret. That part thrilled him. He and Kieran could have the best war games down there together if he could swear his brother to secrecy. But did Caleb know? Had Mack left the secret door open? That part terrified him.

A bang exploded beneath him as Kieran jumped from the cupboard under the bench with a load roar. Mack screamed, desperate like a rabbit suddenly caught in a trap. As he clawed against the wall to escape his bladder let go. Kieran was on the floor laughing when Mack stood and looked down. The warm wetness flowed down his legs and dark patches spread on his jeans. Kieran gasped when he saw Mack's pants and ran away up the steps. Mack stood alone, wet and in shock.

Kieran ran back down with a towel and put it on the bench, then pushed Mack quickly up the stairs toward the bathroom. Mack stood there in his wet pants, which were now growing cold against his legs. Kieran came back into the bathroom with a fresh pair of jeans, and began to peel the soaked pants from Mack. Mack suddenly realized

Kieran was pulling off his underwear and pushed him away roughly, out the door of the bathroom, and slammed it shut. He furiously tore off his pants and underwear and flung them away. Kieran had not brought him dry underwear but that didn't matter. He fell against the wall with a thump in his haste to get the dry pants on.

"What the devil are you boys getting into up there?" Maeve yelled from the kitchen.

"We're just playing, Mom," Kieran yelled back.

"Don't be tearing the house down."

Mack flew out of the bathroom, stopped to wrap his soiled clothes in the towel from the bench and sprinted out the front door. He ran across the road and deep into the woods until he was hidden from the house and threw the offending bundle down in the dirt. He dropped to his knees and began to dig with his hands. When the hole was big enough, he kicked the piss-stained pants and ruined towel in and covered them, piling rocks on top.

He sat back and looked around, panting. At least Caleb hadn't seen him screw up this time. He would have thrashed Mack for sure. He wiped his forehead and stood up, a flicker of defiance rising for the first time. It would be better if Caleb punched him in the face than to be this scared of him.

Mack marched back into the house and stood in the library door. Caleb was sitting at the library table with a jar of moonshine.

"What do you want?" Caleb asked him. The secret door was closed, but Mack could see his marble still wedged in the far corner of the floor.

"Dinner's on the table, boys," Maeve called out. Caleb stood, keeping his hand on the table and taking a swallow from the jar. His eyes narrowed, black pinpoints burning into Mack's head.

"Ain't you got the look of the cat who swallowed the canary. Where've you been, Mack McKinsey?" Caleb stared him down, then walked past him.

Mack did not say a word at dinner, and Maeve, afraid he was

coming down with something, sent him straight off to bed after he'd finished a few bites.

Later that night, Mack woke to a movement in his room. Someone was in here, coming over to the bed. This was it, then. Caleb was coming for him. He'd done this before, stumbled into their bedrooms in the middle of the night and smacked the boys around when he'd dipped too far down into a jar of liquor. Mack sat up, ready for the blows. He formed his small hands into fists. He would fight back tonight. His body quivered, muscles tensed as something plopped next to him on the bed and he jumped. He could just make out the outline of his brother Kieran padding silently out of his room. Mack ran his hand over the blankets and gathered a small lump. He'd carefully opened his fist to find his aggie.

As soon as the sun began to set in Maeve's Garden, Mack headed for the Alaskan cedar he had planted for his father. He kneeled down and felt for the moss-covered rock he used as a marker. Digging underneath he uncovered his treasure; the last jar of moonshine Mack had ever sipped. He unscrewed the lid and stuck his nose in the jar, inhaling just the fumes that promised a fiery escape from all of this. It was unfair how much he still wanted to drink after three years sober. He looked through the clear liquor for the answer on the other side.

What would stop him from drinking this time? He'd been moving so steadily toward the future, and that had been enough for a while. For three years, Mack had put his head down and worked, but every time he looked up, the finish line had moved farther out of reach. Commanding his own landscaping company had been his goal for so long he'd forgotten the possibility it might not work out. Even as a university grad, Mack had swallowed down the nasty jobs that Pete, sullen nephew of the owner of Sunshine Landscaping, always gave to him, "the college boy." Pete would make him wade out through a once decorative but now algae-covered stagnant pond buzzing with flies to remove a drowned raccoon, while hiring state-funded former convicts who'd once read a gardening catalog to draft designs of gardens that would die within a year. Mack felt the frustration, but kept his goal in mind, not the least of which would be the satisfaction of driving Pete out of business when he started McKinsey Landscape Designs.

But plans, like secrets, have a way of collapsing in upon themselves. After Maeve died, Caleb found out about the Ireland trip. He threw the ripped plane tickets at Mack's feet one night, well into a jar of shine, and cursed his son with a viciousness that made Mack tremble when he admitted that he'd known about the trip. Mack apologized and Caleb slapped his face hard enough to leave a perfect handprint. He knew his father blamed him only a little bit less for Maeve's death than he did himself. He and his father had spent the intervening years tormenting each other, and he saw no fix for this damage. He didn't know how to break this curse.

Now there was nothing to keep him going. The bank had turned him down. Brigit was fine without him and didn't seem to miss him, though he had tried to make amends several times. Kieran was in the wind, a loss that never stopped hurting. He missed his sister and brother deeply, feeling again the irresponsibility he shouldered at being unable to keep his family together after their mother's death. He and Caleb were better off without each other, that much was clear, but it also left him completely alone. No one would care if he slipped down into this last jar of moonshine. He could stay right here in Maeve's Garden, drink it all, and be done.

Mack clung to the jar, craving the drink. Just one. One drink, one shot, one beer. *Winners do what they have to do, and losers do what they want to do.* He focused on the last part of the saying. Mack regretfully replaced the lid on the jar of moonshine and buried it again, deep in the earth. He could no more pour it out than he could have when he'd first buried it. Maybe tomorrow he'd be back, but just for today, he would not drink.

He got up quickly and stumbled back down the side of the mountain as disoriented as if he had drunk from the jar. His mind was a tangle of thoughts. He had to keep moving, for if he stopped, he was likely to turn right back around. He jumped in his truck and drove down the road. His cell phone beeped at him insistently. He picked it up and saw an unfamiliar number, with several missed calls. Maybe it was Anthony calling him back. Maybe this was the sign that he needed. A new job in a new state could give him the focus he needed.

"Hello?" he said.

"Is this Mack McKinsey?"

"Yes."

"This is Doctor Hall at the University of Virginia Medical Center. We have a Caleb McKinsey here. Are you his son?"

Mack let his truck drift to a stop in the middle of the dark country road. He listened to the words, he heard what they were saying, but suddenly he noticed there was a long silence.

"Yes. That's me. I'm, uh, yes, I'm his son."

"Mr. McKinsey is in the emergency room."

"What?"

"You are listed as his emergency contact."

"Me?"

"When can you be here?"

"I … I'm on my way."

CHAPTER 7

Lonny hightailed it out of the barn after milking. He'd sat at the hospital all afternoon, but unless the world was on fire, cows had a schedule. He couldn't even call Seamus O'Hearn to milk them as a favor. Usually, Lonny's focus was sharp, but today doubts were crowding his head. Things were out of his control, and that was not a good feeling. Lonny liked routines. Not being able to help Caleb was making him jittery, and those nerves needed to be tamed. Fiddle-farting around with bourbon is what gets a cooker killed, Caleb had said more than once. Lonny didn't worry much, but when he did, it helped him to make up a nice life for his mother. Sometimes he still wondered where she might have got to.

Right after his seventh birthday, Lonny had known his ma wasn't coming back. He'd eaten the last can of creamed corn all by himself, then waited for the whupping Ma was sure to give him. She got mad if any of the kids touched her creamed corn. She hid it, behind the cans of grayish-green peas, because it was her favorite. She always saved it for a special dinner, a birthday or a holiday. On Lonny's birthday they'd had succotash instead. But she wasn't there to give him the beating he deserved for eating her corn. He guessed there wasn't going to be one of those dinners again for a while.

Three days before, Lonny had fallen asleep in Caleb McKinsey's cow barn. He had been out collecting firewood, but he had wandered too far, maybe on purpose, and had seen his cows. Course, they weren't *his* but Caleb's, but he could pretend. There were rumors, whispers, and most people kept an uneasy distance from Caleb McKinsey. Lonny had been born in these mountains, he knew Caleb made moonshine; he also knew McKinsey was good to his cows. Lonny had watched them lumbering up to the barn at milking time, slow and even, heads bobbing up and down to their own rhythm. He'd climbed up into the hayloft and looked down through a crack as they were fed, the warm scent of fresh silage wafting up. When Lonny had woken, moonlight was streaming down. He'd snuck quietly out of the barn and run home up the side of the mountain, forgetting the firewood.

His family's small house had been too dark, and too still. Lonny had stopped outside, knowing something was wrong. The dark was not new, they hadn't had the electricity on for a month now, but he felt the emptiness. He crept in quietly and sat alone in a corner of the empty two-room house.

His family had peeled away layer by layer, like an onion. His father had gone off to work in another state over a year ago, sending cash-filled envelopes for a few months. His oldest sister LaDonna had snuck off to get married at fourteen. His ten-year-old brother Leroy was wild, hunting and trapping anything they could eat; but he had been spending more and more nights away from home. The rest were younger, including his brother with the bad leg, who was four, and his three-year-old sister with the twitchy brain that caused her to fall on the floor and roll around. The triplets had just turned two and ran in all different directions, wearing Ma out. Even Lonny knew eight kids were a lot. He was stuck smack-dab in the middle. The younger kids all needed Ma. He knew she would have taken him along, if she could.

When Caleb found him that night, Lonny wasn't eating the dog food out of the dish, just the pieces of leftover ham Caleb had set out earlier. Caleb took a look at the layers of dirt on Lonny's face and the worn patches on his knees.

"You hungry?" Caleb asked.

Lonny nodded.

"Where's your folks?"

Lonny shrugged.

"Got a name?"

"Lonny."

"You the one been sleeping in my cow barn, Lonny?"

Lonny's head drooped.

"Cows must like you."

Lonny looked up slowly.

"Might's well come in the house, then," Caleb held the front door open.

Lonny shoved the last rind of ham into his mouth and chewed quickly.

Caleb brought Lonny in and fed him dinner at a table. He showed him to the bathroom, which was inside the house; Lonny didn't know how a shower worked, so he took a bath as instructed before falling asleep on a bed he didn't have to share. In the morning, Caleb let Lonny watch him milk the cows. He hung around the barn that day, peering into the dark oat bin, disturbing a mouse who dove deep into the oats. He found the metal ladder inside the silo and climbed to the top and jumped, lofting down to land on his back in the soft, springy fodder as the sweet-tangy smell of the silage wrapped him up.

Caleb found him back in the hayloft at dinner time, and invited him in again. After a week of this, Caleb had a proposition for him.

"How would you like to help me take care of these cows, Lonny?"

"Yes, sir."

"You might as well stay here until your folks get back."

"Yes, sir."

"I can pay you a little, but you got to do one thing; you been to school yet?"

"No."

Caleb pulled strings to get him into a first grade class, although Lonny could neither read nor write. School taught him arithmetic, and that was good, but he had little use for the rest of it. He went, because then he could come back to Caleb and the cows. After school each day, he headed into the woods to see if his ma had come back yet. When the ground froze for the first time that year, which was 93 days later according to the marks he'd made on the cinderblock wall, Lonny stopped his daily vigil. He was finally able to leave his ma a note, telling her where he was, but he wasn't entirely sure she'd be able to read it, even if she came back.

When Maeve arrived from Ireland three years later, Lonny was puzzled by her accent; words like "knackered" made him think he'd broken something. She was kind, too, wanting to bake Lonny his favorite pie. This was a form of pressure as he didn't know anything about pie and just said peach because there were peaches growing everywhere. Lonny had vague memories of his ma, but there hadn't been anything like all this so he asked Caleb what to do.

"Just say thank you, Lonny. She's doing her best," Caleb told him.

One morning Lonny overheard his name as he came down the hallway.

"Lonny doesn't seem to enjoy things much," Maeve said.

"What makes you think that?"

"I have never seen him smile, not once."

Lonny wished they would stop. People only talked about you when you were a problem.

"Maeve, leave him be," Caleb said with a slight warning note in his voice.

"I will not."

"You don't know about mountain people, Maeve."

"Oh, don't I?"

"His mother took off and left him. Even I can't find her."

"Where are his relatives?"

"People know he's here."

"But you can't just keep him, Caleb, like a stray dog that's wandered in."

"Maeve, he was sleeping in my barn. No one wants him."

Lonny had never thought of being wanted. He had begun to notice, in school, where Caleb still insisted he go every day, that some of the other kids had an ease to them, as if nothing bad could ever happen. Like puppies, Lonny thought. They didn't know yet they were going to get kicked. When he looked at Caleb, though, there was a mirror of understanding. He'd been kicked, too.

When their son Mack was born that winter, Lonny felt he was on the outside looking in. This was a proper family now. He wasn't blood, so he figured he'd have to move on. He'd miss Caleb, and he'd miss the cows. He wanted to say good-bye and thank you, too, but he wasn't sure how.

That afternoon, he rolled his clothes up and tied them with baling twine, so they'd be easier to carry. Maybe he could get work at the sawmill; he wasn't that big, but he was strong. Boys could get taken on if they just hung around long enough, working for food to prove they could.

Lonny stepped quietly into Caleb's library, his bundle hanging off one shoulder.

Caleb sat at the long table with a jar of clear moonshine. He took a sip and shook his head slightly. "Lonny! Come in here and celebrate with me." Lonny moved into the room, up to the edge of the table. "Sit, boy, sit. You're ... what, now, ten?"

"Yes, sir," Lonny said, still standing.

"That's how old I was when my daddy gave me my first sip," Caleb pushed the half-gallon jar across the table. "There, my boy, is the finest liquor you'll ever lay hands on. It's my private stock, strong, first jar out of the pot. I don't sell this, though I could, I could. And for a lot, too. But this is my celebration stock. Take a sip," and he nodded toward the jar.

Lonny picked up the jar. It was heavier than he thought it would be. He brought it to his face and recoiled, holding the liquor away. The smell was sharp and metallic, like a scalpel slicing through the nerves behind his eyes. His eyes watered, and Caleb laughed.

"Ah, you gotta learn, Lonny. You breathe out, then take a sip so's you don't inhale it at the same time. And you gotta hang onto something. Better yet, you should sit down before you drink. Gotta respect it; it's strong and alive."

Lonny sat down, breathed out, and took a drink. The moonshine burned down his throat and splashed into his stomach like liquid fire. He coughed, choking, and set the jar down hard. He shook his head. This was terrible. Why would anyone drink this if he didn't have to? It rolled around his insides, looking for a way back out. The room started spinning. He jumped clumsily to his feet, knocking over his chair. He ran for the door, knocking into the doorway and slamming his shoulder hard. He bolted out the front door and ran across the yard, into the woods. He fell to his knees and let the moonshine come flooding back out onto the ground. He had no control as he put his hands down in the dirt and retched, over and over again.

Finally he sank back on his knees and breathed in through his nose. Leaves crunched; Caleb, walking up behind him.

"It's okay, there, Lonny. Just breathe a bit," Caleb said.

"I'm sorry," he mumbled.

"Nothing to be sorry for, boy. It hits everyone different the first time. You just have to learn your limits."

"I can't drink it." Lonny couldn't meet Caleb's gaze. Many times he'd been with him out to a still site, watching him solder the copper for the pots. Caleb had not let him touch it, but he had gathered rocks to shore it up. He'd hoped one day Caleb would teach him more, but he'd failed. He couldn't make moonshine if he couldn't drink it.

Caleb held out the bundle of clothes Lonny had dropped.

"Going somewhere?"

"I was coming to say good-bye."

"How come?" Caleb reached down and took Lonny's arm, helping him stand. "I'm gonna need you even more now there's a baby here. Boy needs a brother to look out for him." Caleb turned Lonny's his tear-streaked face up to him. "This here's your home."

Lonny couldn't help Caleb now, but he did know where to go. He scouted the horizon through the sunset for any signs of movement, then headed quickly into the woods. He hiked between the pines, marking his way. He used a direct route today, unlike his usual trek of winding around to make sure he didn't beat down a path that could be followed. After nearly an hour of stepping over fallen trees and avoiding fox dens, he found the moss-covered boulder. He got down and shouldered it aside carefully and climbed into the small cave behind. He crawled forward on his hands and knees until he felt a piece of iron. He swung his legs around and climbed down the ladder into a tunnel. Now he could walk upright, and continued slowly through the tunnel, hands out to both sides to find his way in the dark. He could sense his path rising, and put one hand up to touch rough wood over his head.

Lonny pushed up ever so slightly, until a wan light shone. He froze for a full minute, listening. He could hear a chair moving, but no voices. He painstakingly inched the trapdoor aside and pulled himself up. He stood in semi-darkness, moving carefully across a room to a doorway. He peered around the corner to a lone figure.

Seamus O'Hearn sat alone at a table, a gallon jug of moonshine in front of him.

"Seamus," Lonny whispered.

Seamus's head moved imperceptibly.

"How many? Where?" Lonny whispered.

Seamus rose and stretched his left arm out with two fingers out, keeping his back to Lonny. He crossed to the front door, opened it and leaned out.

"I'm going off to bed now," he said into the quiet outside.

"Leave the door unlocked and the light on," a voice replied from his yard.

Seamus turned and walked slowly down the hall. It was the first time Lonny had ever seen him as an old man. He crossed into his bedroom as Lonny hovered behind the door.

"What the hell are you doing here, Lonny?" Seamus asked quietly.

"Seamus. We didn't know—"

"If I was dead? Just wishing it, right now. Thought about it. They took my guns."

"They wouldn't tell us anything, Seamus, even when we asked."

"I had to do it, Lonny. Caleb knows that."

"I woulda helped you."

"We was trying to keep alla you kids out of it." Seamus sat heavily down on his bed, talking softly into the floor. "Don't know why they suddenly started buzzing us with the surveillance again. Thought we might have fooled 'em, but they saw the smoke."

"Why didn't you tell us?"

"Caleb knew. I told him I'd blow it all up before they came in here with their axes and sledgehammers to bust it to hell and then photograph me in a pair of steel bracelets for the newspapers. Think that's what I want my grandkids out West to see? I ain't no criminal."

"No, sir."

"Hated to see it go. Lifetime of work. Think I lost a few chickens, too."

"Sorry about that."

"We got a plan, Caleb and I. Soon's I get this piece of jewelry off." Seamus lifted his right pants leg to show the monitor clasped around his ankle. He snorted. "House arrest. Guess I won't be doing any fancy dancing anytime soon."

"Caleb's in the hospital, Seamus." Lonny never had been good at easing into conversation. "He had a heart attack."

"Caleb? Jesus H. Christ. How is he?"

"He'll be okay."

"Damn, son. I can't believe it. They sure are trying to rid the world of all us old moonshiners. Ain't gonna be as easy as all that, though."

"No, sir."

"Caleb." Seamus chuckled quietly. "Guess this'll put to rest the rumors of him not having a heart."

"I should go." Lonny walked back to the closet where Seamus's escape hatch was hidden.

"You tell him, Lonny, you tell him I'll be there to see him just as soon as I can. You tell him to hang on, there. I mighta lost my business, but I ain't about to lose my best friend."

Lonny lowered himself back down into the tunnel. He heard Seamus put the trapdoor back in place. He scurried now, out the old escape tunnel built back during Prohibition. There were warrens of tunnels under the big bourbon cookers on Bucks Elbow Mountain, and almost no one knew they were there.

CHAPTER 8

Caleb's three older brothers bent over him, yelling in his face and poking him in the chest with savage scowls of revenge etched into their rough features. Jeb pushed forward, face twisted in rage, hands covered in blood. *They've come*, Caleb thought. He struck out at them, trying to escape, fighting with his last bit of strength. *They've come to pay me back.*

Before Caleb had even been born, the Moonshine McKinsey boys were feared. Their father was a grim disciplinarian with very little patience. Jeb was the oldest and the biggest, even towering over their father, who was not small. Jeb's massive strength made up for his simple-minded ways. He was fiercely loyal to their father and would do anything he asked, as long as there was a jar of shine for him at the end of the day. Tim and Frank were twins, thrill-seekers a year younger than Jeb and violently competitive to be first in their father's eyes. The twins took unnecessary risks building stills; once so sloppy with their soldering a cap burst, spilling mash over the sides to seep down into the ground. Their father grabbed them both by the hair and knocked their heads together, a punishment for which Frank declared himself the winner because, while he was stunned by the blow, he didn't pass out like Tim. The twins preferred making the runs, anyway, driving the car over rough mountain roads at speeds that had caused more than a few accidents. The last time they'd snapped the axle in a good Ford with a hollowed trunk specially made to hold moonshine. Their father took a hammer to each of their left thumbs, breaking them so they'd remember what it felt like.

Caleb was younger than Jeb by fifteen years. There had been four more babies before Caleb, all of them boys. They didn't last, succumbing to sad diseases where they just stopped breathing. This wasn't uncommon in the mountains, but it still struck his mother hard every time. When the fourth baby went silent, she ran to his crib as eight-year-old Jeb was leaving the baby's room with a somber face.

"That baby ain't gonna cry no more, Ma," Jeb said as he stood at the top of the stairs, watching her clamber up. "Pa don't like it when they cry."

Ma tried not to have any more, but that wasn't up to her. When Caleb was born, she favored him greatly. She fashioned an old pair of overalls that couldn't be mended any longer into a sling and carried him everywhere. When she was cooking or cleaning, she wrapped him in a blanket and nestled him in an old apple-picking basket she vigilantly kept by her side.

That winter was bad in the Blue Ridge, bringing deep snows and slicing winds. There was no money for new coats and boots, much less medicine when a bad flu started making the rounds. The sickness got hold of Ma and ate at her. She hung on as best she could, but just as the sun brought in a little spring, she stayed in bed one morning for good. Caleb was three, and he wished he remembered her.

His father made sure Caleb had enough to eat, most of the time, and that was the extent of their bonding. Caleb's brothers treated him as the runt of the litter he was. He was too small to help in the family business, so they shoved him out of chairs they wanted to sit in, took food off his plate if they were hungry, and kicked him out of the way if he didn't move fast enough.

Times were tough, especially out in the country. People were starving, begging, but they'd still trade what they had for moonshine.

Moonshine was the holy grail for the McKinseys and had been for generations. It was a treacherous business. Stills would blow up and take out an entire year's stock, desperate mountain men could raid a stash and steal the shine, deliveries could be ambushed by tipped-off renegades. It was this 'blockading' Tim and Frank loved best. They lived for the adrenaline rush of speeding over rough two-lane mountain roads in the dead of night, evading police roadblocks and, more than once, opening the throttle to race away from cops with tight hairpin turns that almost sent them over the cliffs. They hooted and hollered with glee when they made it home, slapping each other on the back to celebrate their victory.

After a successful run, the McKinsey boys pulled out their secret stash. The first drips out of the still were the foreshots, containing methanol and blindness for those too impatient to wait. Foreshots could be lethal, and a sip was every McKinsey man's initiation into moonshine. Tradition demanded starting with danger. The heads came next with a wicked chemical smell and a bitter taste, and were usually tossed away, but the boys kept a jar for themselves. It was a badge of honor to sip it, and although the peaches helped somewhat with the harsh kick and pungent aroma, distressing hangovers were guaranteed. The hearts flowed next, the sweet spot of moonshine, the best of the batch, where the money was made. The tails were at the end of the cook, and were usually slick and oily from the water and proteins, with the least amount of ethanol. These they saved for the hill people without much money.

Caleb had taken over his mother's duties by default; tending the vegetable garden, milking and feeding the cows, and cleaning the messes four men steeped in moonshine could make. He expected no thanks for this, but he was still surprised when the wedge between himself and his father and brothers grew deeper. With no one to teach him, he studied the maps over the mountain into Franklin County, and learned all the possible routes. When he was eleven, his brothers brought him along. He was old enough to see the risk, they insisted. During the drive over the mountain, Jeb, Tim, and Frank traded stories about other shiners who'd ended up dead, killed by rivals and double-crossers, and the grisly condition of their bodies when they were found—heads stove in flat with tree limbs, crushed under the wheels of their own cars, tied up in trunks with plastic bags over their heads. When they arrived at the drop-off, Caleb huddled in the footwell in the back seat, shivering, refusing to lift his head or even get out of the car to help unload the shine.

They crowed with malicious laughter when they made it home. Pa was waiting in the front yard, a fresh jar of clear shine in his hand. Caleb was caught in the middle of a circle of brothers, passing the jar to celebrate their run.

"Ya see that little pissant, squallin' in the backseat?" Tim laughed.

"Didn't do nothin' but take up space, wailin' like a baby," Frank agreed.

Caleb started toward the house, head down.

"Where ya think yer goin'?" Tim asked, grabbing Caleb by the back of his overalls, smacking him hard in the back of his head. Caleb tried not to raise his hand to the welt rising on his skull, but he failed, once again, to be strong enough.

"We was talking to ya, 'n yer gonna listen," Frank said. He slapped Caleb across the face, making his nose bleed. Caleb knew this looked worse than it felt. He stood still, hoping they were done. *Please let Jeb be too tired*, he prayed silently to himself. Jeb hit hardest of them all.

"Best part a' you done run down Pa's leg," Frank said. "Git on outta here." Caleb moved slowly, almost to the steps of the house now.

"You pansy-asses ain't gonna toughen 'im up like that," Pa groused, snatching the jar from Jeb. Jeb quickly flung a knee hard in Caleb's back.

Caleb saw the stoop coming up toward him without enough time to put his hands out. He landed face first on the edge of a step, and his left cheekbone cracked with a burst of pain like a firecracker under his eye. He let out a sob before shoving a fist in his mouth, as his father passed the jar on to Tim. Caleb crawled up the rest of the steps to the cawing laughter of his brothers and father and ran inside to his room.

He carried his swollen eye to school the next day, hoping a teacher would stop him and get the truth. But the truth was well known; he was a moonshiner's son.

Caleb kept his head down, his mouth shut, and learned about the business. It didn't take much longer for their father to finally smoke himself into the grave. His brothers then began to either ignore their little brother completely or beat him worse. They'd wing a lead pipe at his feet when he walked by and laugh when he fell, clutching his ankle. They locked him out of the house at night from time to time, making him sleep in the barn. Caleb continued to wash their clothes and bake their cornbread as they sat on the porch, drinking and laughing.

There was just Babe to keep Caleb company, but she was all he needed. One of the blue tick coonhounds they kept for hunting had a big litter of puppies, and Caleb was told to take the runt down to the river and drown it so it wouldn't take milk from the strong pups. Instead, he kept her hidden in the barn, in a nest behind some bales. She only peeked out of the hayloft when she heard the special whistle Caleb taught her. He'd come out at night with a pocketful of scraps, and lift one long, soft ear and whisper his day into it. He saw a little pink collar at the feed store one day after school and snuck it in his pocket when no one was looking. Babe stuck by him, pushing her cool nose against him when he was too silent. She would lick one of Caleb's new bruises or cuts, before settling her head between her paws with a sigh.

When Babe disappeared one day Caleb felt his heart begin to thump too hard, too loudly. Her nest was empty. He searched the woods, calling and waving a piece of bacon. There were bears in the mountains, he knew. Bears and coyotes, too. Two days later, he found her collar hanging from the rearview mirror of Jeb's truck. Jeb looked over at him and grinned.

"Keeping secrets is dangerous," he said. "That was one fast bitch. But not quite fast enough."

At eighteen, Caleb considered himself old enough to make a move. His brothers had never welcomed him into the business like he'd hoped, had never included him or passed a jar his way. All they trusted him with was loading the car. Tonight they had a big run for Franklin County, and Caleb loaded the gallon jugs carefully into the trunk of the 1940 Ford coupe, fitted with a false bottom to carry more. Tim, Frank, and Jeb sat on the porch drinking and tossing rocks at Caleb, threatening him with a beating if he dropped any product.

For weeks, Caleb had carefully plotted with half a dozen men who would ambush the car, steal the shine, and deliver it to another distributor Caleb had set up. They'd keep the profit, as it was not a small feat to double-cross the McKinsey boys. He'd already started circulating a fabricated story of Joe France Jr., rogue bootlegger from Kentucky, looking to branch out and take over existing operations in Virginia. Caleb had also planted rumors of increased police activity, so his brothers would have only their pistols, which were easier to hide in the car than rifles or shotguns and wouldn't be an invitation to a police shootout. His brothers would come back furious and ready to fight anyone, and finally realize they needed him too. He considered this a flawless plan, as there was no Joe France Jr., there could be no revenge, and no one would get hurt. But he'd be waiting with the rifle in hand, just in case.

Caleb had spent a lot of his solitary time at target practice in the woods. He was quick, had sharp eyes, and he didn't drink. Tonight, if his brothers came out shooting, Caleb would take out the tires on the car first. If he really had to, he'd aim for a foot or hand on Tim or Frank, enough to give them pause to take him seriously. He'd never attack Jeb, who, along with his hulking size and strength, had proven single-minded and cruel in his demand for revenge.

One thing his brothers had grudgingly begun to understand was that Caleb was smart. He'd made improvements to the stills to increase the output, and concocted ghost stills; old, barely running sites close to roads to throw off the sheriff when he brought in a crew to gleefully axe them down, not knowing the motherlode was much farther back into the woods. Caleb had also made adjustments to the cars to improve their speed and handling, and most of all, had bought more cows as a plausible farming cover to the Feds. None of his brothers acknowledged these improvements, though Jeb had finally asked his opinion on a new submarine still.

This was Caleb's moment. He'd proven his worth, and he would join the game now. They would realize he was valuable.

Well after midnight, Caleb crouched with his rifle aimed out the front window of the house toward the road. His hands shook only when he lowered the gun to rest. This was the biggest decision he'd ever made, and there was no turning back now. He sat at the window for hours past the time they should have returned, twice jumping as he thought he heard a noise behind him.

Finally headlights flickered up the road. An unfamiliar car was flying up it like a demon, back end fishtailing on the gravel in the turns. Caleb took unwavering, deliberate aim, but lowered the rifle when he saw it was young Hank Kennedy, who skidded to a halt and ran up to Caleb's front door.

"You gotta come, quick, Caleb. Something's happened with your brothers."

"What?"

"Oh, Lord, Caleb, they's been all shot up," Hank said.

"What? Where are they?"

"Not too far down. We got to hurry before the deputies get there."

They ran to Hank's car and peeled around in the grass to rumble back down the road. Caleb had grabbed a shotgun and carried it along with his rifle. Having two guns in his hands brought him calm. His brothers were probably already disabled, so he'd take them home and call in a doctor to patch them up.

There was the Ford, by the side of the road. Hank pulled up behind it, and Caleb slowly opened his door. He raised the stock of his rifle to his shoulder.

"Ya ain't gonna need that, Caleb," Hank said. He walked slowly over to the Ford, head down.

Tim and Frank hadn't even made it out. Blood oozed from their faces from the bullets that had come through the shattered windshield. Jeb had been driving, and now lay face down in the road next to the trunk, with several wounds in his back and a darkening puddle beneath him. The trunk had been popped. The moonshine was gone. Caleb had not counted on the desperation of the men he'd hired to ambush his brothers. None of them had even had the chance to draw a gun. He walked around the car and looked at Tim and Frank, nestled beside each other on the front seat, still upright. The strong smell of iron wafted from the car. Caleb carefully put his gun in the back seat and walked back to Jeb, staring down at his brother.

"Help me get him up," he called to Hank.

"Where ya gonna put him?"

"In the trunk, I guess." Caleb bent over to grab Jeb's arms.

"Can't ya put him in the backseat?" Hank asked.

"Jus' … just grab his feet."

They lifted him, slowly. He felt much heavier now that life had left him. Caleb folded Jeb's hands over his chest and closed the trunk. He was going to have to drive his dead brothers home.

"I'd appreciate it if you could not have seen nothing out here tonight, Hank," Caleb said.

"Wish to Christ that were true," Hank said, looking down, shaking his head.

"I'll owe ya one," Caleb said, straight on.

Hank looked up at him and nodded. He got back in his car, turned around and headed up the road.

Caleb could let his legs shake now, and he did. This was not what he had counted on, not at all. When he could stop the trembling, he opened the driver's door and slid in next to his dead twin brothers. Though he'd asked Hank to keep it to himself, Caleb knew the thieves would talk. It was too big of a score not to; someone had taken out the Moonshine McKinseys.

Caleb parked carefully in the driveway. He would leave them where they were and call the coroner, telling him he'd walked down the road and found them. It seemed disrespectful to leave his brother shut up in the trunk, and he popped it open.

Jeb opened his eyes and reached a hand out.

"Caleb," Jeb moaned.

"Jeb?" Caleb jumped back. He watched in shock as his oldest brother tried to raise himself from the dead.

"Help me."

"Jeb, I...."

"Where's Tim and Frank?"

"They're ... they didn't make it."

"You," his brother pointed a shaky hand at him. "*You* did this."

"No," Caleb stammered.

"Get me out of here," Jeb said. He twisted over to his side, but couldn't seem to get his feet to work.

Caleb backed a few steps away.

"I ... I wasn't even there, Jeb."

"They told us. You set us up."

"I didn't, I swear."

"You killed your own brothers." Jeb managed to push himself up on one elbow. "There ain't nowhere far enough away for you to hide now, boy." He clutched at the trunk lid, trying to pull himself out.

Caleb knew Jeb would hunt him down for the rest of his life. Loyalty was valued far above the law, and he would never outrun this betrayal. Jeb pulled himself weakly up to the edge of the trunk but fell back. Caleb rushed forward and slammed the trunk closed.

He made it to the porch and found the jar of shine hidden in a bush nearby. For the first but not the last time, he sat on the steps drinking until he could barely see.

As the sun rose Caleb watched blood drip slowly from underneath the bumper and collect in the soft dirt. When it stopped, he checked the trunk while holding his loaded rifle. He poked Jeb tentatively in the head with the barrel before calling the sheriff.

He sat on the back porch and watched his brothers make their last run down the mountain in the back of the coroner's black van.

The local deputies made a cursory inquiry but didn't dig deep enough to start a war. An I.R.S. revenuer came down from D.C. and poked around a bit, before finding his car without any wheels one morning and high-tailing it back to the city. Caleb hadn't lifted a finger, but moonshiners protected their own from the law, guilty and innocent alike.

No one else came near the McKinsey place for two days after that, but Caleb knew the operation was considered ripe for plunder. If he didn't act soon he might as well walk away, for other shiners would not leave him alive on all this prime land. After filling the trunk with premium gallon jugs from Jeb's private stash, Caleb grabbed his rifle and climbed back into the car his brothers had been driving, pocked with bullet holes and shattered windshield. He was not at all sure he'd make it home again. He did another run, alone, straight to the original distributor. To make good, he told the retailer. For his brothers. He got home whole, though still shaking, and sat on the porch with a jar of shine, alone.

Rumors and theories flew around the mountain and into the town in frenzied whispers. Some swore the killing had been a government job to shut down moonshine in the Blue Ridge Mountains. Others knew rival bootleggers from Tennessee were moving North and killing everyone in their way. A few were convinced that descendants of Bill McCoy, who'd always hankered after the finest shine, wanted to take over the McKinsey operation. Caleb remained silent as the stories grew and whirled around him. Caleb was lucky to be alive; Caleb had narrowly escaped; Caleb himself had killed them all.

At the end of the month, Caleb drove himself into town and walked into the Briar's Pub, his brothers' hangout. He needed to hire workers now that he was alone. Every head turned to watch as he strolled to the bar. Still not a drinker, Caleb ordered a shot of Jameson and a beer, which he knew was a mistake as soon as he swallowed the shot with a grimace. There were a few chuckles, and the chatter soon returned to normal.

He looked around the bar. He knew most of the faces in here, but wouldn't call them friends. Seamus O'Hearn gave him a nod from the far end of the bar. He and Seamus had been through school together, and Seamus had come out to the farm most summers to help bring in corn. Right next to Seamus sat Wayne Joe Biggins, whose scowl deepened as he stared at Caleb. He'd been Jeb's arm wrestling partner, both men more biceps than brain. Caleb felt hot under Wayne Joe's steady gaze; it was the first time he'd experienced such naked blame. If he expected outsiders to accuse him, that was one thing. But he'd thought folks from Touraine would understand.

He grabbed his beer and walked down to sit next to Seamus. "Seamus, how ya doing?" Caleb asked.

"Hey, Caleb," Seamus said.

"Looking for some men to work with me. Know any?"

"Ain't nobody in this town gonna work with you," Wayne Joe said with a snort.

"Mind your manners now, Wayne Joe," Seamus cautioned.

"And why is that?" Caleb asked.

"What you did was flat-out wrong."

"What did I do?"

Wayne Joe stood and crossed over to Caleb, leaning too far over him. "You killed your own damn brothers."

Caleb whipped around and delivered a solid punch to Wayne Joe's neck. Down Wayne Joe went with a splat like a sack of wet flour. Seamus jumped up and shoved Caleb toward the door as chairs squeaked back and boots hit the floor.

"Caleb, you gotta go or there's gonna be a hell of a fight, and I don't think you got many friends in there right now," Seamus said as they hustled across the parking lot. "There's a lot of talk in town, and there's some that agree with Wayne Joe."

"Do you? You think I killed my brothers?" Caleb asked him.

"Honestly, Caleb, I wouldn't blame you if you had." Growing up, Seamus had seen the bruises, broken teeth, and once helped Caleb patch up a knife wound near his ribs.

"Jesus, Seamus, they know me. Why would they think that?"

"Maybe because I let it slip that you did."

"What?" Caleb spun on his friend.

"I did you a favor. They're afraid of you now."

"I was trying to set things right," Caleb said.

"I'll help out as much as I can. But you can't talk about your brothers. Not at all."

That was the advice Caleb stuck to through the years. Though he had tried to be different from his brothers, he watched his liquor business flourish; not with friendship, but with fear.

CHAPTER 9

From the outside, the emergency entrance at the University of Virginia Medical Center was aggressive with activity; piercing red lights and warning sirens blaring, ambulances belching out gurneys loaded with the sick and the damned. Paramedics with grim faces and purpose to their determined stride paid no attention to Mack as he made his way carefully, almost apologetically, toward the front desk. After several minutes, a nurse in daisy-patterned scrubs finally looked up to tell him Caleb McKinsey had been moved to the clinical cancer center, and pointed Mack down the connecting glass hallway.

Mack peered around the doorway to his father's room. After three years, he expected to see a wasted old man, ruined by a lifetime of guzzling his own whiskey. But the grizzled bootlegger still cut an imposing figure, even in a hospital bed. His eyes were too blue, his lips too red; nothing on him had paled. He still had that way of making people fall silent with just a glance. Until he launched into a coughing fit that traveled through his entire body, shaking it violently. Mack had imagined the alcohol would kill him, but it appeared the smoking would win.

"Come in, son," Caleb growled when the coughing subsided.

"Dad." Mack stepped just inside the door.

"Got a bit of a tickle," Caleb said.

"You should see someone about that."

"Still a smart ass." Caleb's eyes narrowed. "Appears I might be outta your hair for good soon."

Mack stayed silent. Though he'd sometimes wished for this day, there was no satisfaction in it now.

"Well, thanks for not pretendin' to be concerned. Just had one last favor."

"What?"

"Wanted to see my kids," Caleb said.

Mack shrugged.

"Like to see your sister too."

"Call her."

"Don't have her number."

Mack was sorely tempted to ask when Caleb had last seen her, but stopped himself. Brigit no longer spoke to Mack either; he had no right to pass judgement. Even though he checked up on her from a distance, sometimes slipping money into her mailbox, he could lay no claim.

"Want me to track her down for you?"

"Just bring her to see me."

"Should I wring her out first?"

"Ain't a nice way to talk about your sister."

"How'd she get that way? You have anything to do with it?"

"She's an adult now. Ain't on me," Caleb bristled.

"Caleb McKinsey, famous moonshiner, whose children are all drunks," Mack said.

"Thought you quit drinking," Caleb said.

"I did. I haven't ... we aren't talking about me," Mack replied, almost quickly enough.

Caleb collapsed into himself with another heavy, phlegmy coughing attack. A nurse rushed in with a dixie cup of pills for him and a sour look for Mack.

"Visiting hours are over," she said, stopping in front of Mack until he backed into the hall.

"Bring your sister," Caleb yelled after him.

Mack did all he could to stop himself from running down the hallway to get away from his father. He'd come out of a sense of family obligation, though he only grudgingly included Caleb in that group.

"Mack McKinsey?"

Just outside the door, Mack whirled to a forceful voice. "Yeah?"

"We have some questions for you." Two men stood together, holding out badges. One said, "Did you set the explosives to blow up Seamus O'Hearn's stills?"

"*What?*" Mack felt like there was a spotlight on him.

"Sorry, Mr. McKinsey," the tall blond agent stepped forward. "I'm Mark Peterson, and this is my partner, Julian Miller." He shot a disapproving look at the other, who was yanking on the tight suit coat straining over his stomach. "ATF. My partner was wondering if you knew what happened to O'Hearn. There's some talk that the fire may have been set purposely."

"Why would Seamus do that? Why would he burn his own bourbon?"

"So you had knowledge he was illegally cooking liquor?" Miller asked, edging forward.

"No, I didn't mean that...."

"It's okay, we know. He's lucky no one died. That happens sometimes, doesn't it? Your father would know about that." Miller smiled at him.

"I don't ... I don't know what you are talking about. I don't work for Bourbon Sweet Tea. I'm a landscaper," Mack said.

"Landscaper, right." Miller snorted. "How did things go at the bank?"

"What?" Mack felt ice running through his veins. Caleb had told him to never, ever talk to anyone representing the government. Walk away, he said, just walk away. Mack turned abruptly and sprinted to his truck. He jumped in and took off.

"Nice job, Miller. Very subtle," Peterson said.

"What, are you planning to charm the truth out of them?"

"You know, this hunch of yours is wearing thin. There's no evidence Caleb McKinsey has a secret still hidden in the mountains. He's a rich old redneck with a big legal operation. Why risk that?"

"He started in moonshine, and these old bastards never change. I told you, my great uncle William swore to me Bourbon Sweet Tea was a cover, and he would know. He was one of the first revenuers to shut this shit down during Prohibition."

"And he left not one ounce of proof. The Bureau won't even let us interrogate the employees at the distillery, after that false arrest and lawsuit in Tennessee. 'Just question the family' is going to get us nowhere, Miller."

"We need to find the rest of the kids. We know Brigit's here, but Kieran skipped town a few years ago. They don't seem to be close, so one of them's bound to snap. With a little help."

Peterson pulled a pack of Marlboros out of his jacket pocket and lit a cigarette, inhaling deeply.

"That's a filthy habit," Miller said. "It's killing Caleb even as we speak."

"Even as we speak. Well, we got a win with O'Hearn," Peterson said through an exhale of smoke. "Maybe it wasn't what you were looking for, but let's take it. Division wants us back by the end of the week."

"You're my partner. You know I have good instincts. Trust me."

Peterson sighed.

"And give me a cigarette."

Mack stopped at a Lucky 7 convenience store and sat in the parking lot. This was good, it was well lit and there were lots of people. Rules Caleb had taught him he never thought he'd need to use, but here he was. He really didn't know anything, but now he felt that somehow he'd betrayed Seamus anyway. This is what they did.

He pulled out his phone and called Brigit. She wasn't picking up, which surprised him not at all. He was not doing his father's bidding by calling her, but he did think she should know how sick Caleb was. He also wanted to warn her about the ATF. He could only imagine the malevolence with which she would answer their questions.

His phone buzzed with another unfamiliar number.

"Mack McKinsey," he said. He listened silently. "I've been looking for … she's in jail? I'll be right there."

Brigit, in jail. He'd not asked for what, but he could guess. It was a hazard of the moonshine business. Should he call back? Because why, Mack? If there isn't a good enough reason you'll just leave her there? He looked down at himself. He was still wearing a mud-streaked work t-shirt, jeans and steel-toes. He jumped out of the truck and began to pace in the parking lot. Could he wear this to bail his little sister out? Would it show disrespect? He should go home and change. He was still trying to process the words "Brigit McKinsey" and "jail" and fit them together. Although, if he dug deep in his brain, it shouldn't be this much of a shock. He paced faster. The alarm was building in his head, shutting out everything else. Yeah. He needed to go home and change. Because you couldn't screw around with the law. Look who he'd just run from. They were everywhere. And you couldn't post bail wearing a dirty t-shirt.

Mack lifted his left arm straight up over his head, grasped his left wrist in his right hand, and pulled. The pain was still sharp, but the grinding pop was a release. A car accident a few years ago, where he'd been three times over the legal limit, had shattered his arm and shoulder, and the snap of his joint into place brought him back to reality. The accident had happened on his way to pick up Lauren, who would have been dead if she'd been in the car, the sheriff had told him. He climbed back into his truck, calmer now. No one cares what you're wearing, Mack, he told himself.

When he arrived at the Touraine police station, he stood by his truck for a moment before going in. What a nice, polite small-town building; clean, no trash, no graffiti. The red globe was lit. This meant the doors were locked. He'd have to be buzzed in. He considered the irony of having lockdown security on a police precinct, then hit the button. The door buzzed way too loudly, and he pulled it open.

"Hi, Mack," Donald Bartholomew came striding down the hall with his hand out. Don had been the funniest guy in his high school class, always drawing these great cartoons of teachers that just bordered on inappropriate. No one would have pegged him to grow up and become a sheriff. Funny how things turned out.

"Don, I guess, uh, Brigit's here? Is she okay?"

"EMTs at the site checked her out. She's got some nasty cuts and bruises, which she'll feel once she sobers up. Here's her dress," he said, handing Mack a paper bag with the top rolled down. "Not much left to it, looks like it was nice. We never did find her shoes." Donald turned and motioned down the hall.

Mack followed him down the cinderblock hallway, clean and freshly painted a calming blue. Mack's steel toed boots thunked down the recently waxed hallway.

"Was it … is it a DUI?" What else would it be?

"She was lucky. Most of 'em are. Alcohol seems to provide some sort of protective effect from trauma; we see it a lot, unfortunately."

"How bad?"

"Her blood alcohol's twice the limit. She didn't hit anyone with the car, but there's a possible assault charge pending from earlier in the evening, where she apparently started a fight at a bar."

"Jesus," was all Mack could say.

"Her car was not so lucky. She hit the Lickinghole Creek bridge, Mack." Donald stopped and turned back, clearing his throat. "I'd like to think it was an accident."

Around the corner were two holding cells across from each other. Fluorescent lights behind little metal cages blazed in both cells, showing them to be clean, but they were not quite fresh-smelling. There were shiny metal toilets, no lids, bolted to the walls. And a drain in the center of each floor. In case, Mack surmised, you missed the toilet. Which someone clearly had, from the odor. One cell held a man, neatly laid out on his back and covered with a blanket, but underneath the cement bunk instead of on top of it. Mack knew from his drinking days that this was the only place to escape the jail's glaring light.

The other cell showed more action. In one corner, two smearily made-up ladies lounged on the floor as if waiting to give their drink orders. Probably their hair and clothing had been impeccable at the beginning of the night, before they'd met their various "dates." Trying to look sixteen but pushing closer to forty, the unnaturally red-haired one had rips in her stockings and a torn spaghetti strap to her cropped top. The other, sporting an old, bleary shamrock tattoo next to her right eye, still wore five-inch stilettos, though one heel had been mended with duct tape.

The other corner held what looked to be a bundle of snarled hair. Dried blood made a line down a scraped arm, which trailed past two dirty bare feet. The smell of alcohol was overwhelming.

"Brigit McKinsey. Time to go," announced Donald. He unlocked the cell and turned to Mack. "Sorry, Mack," He stepped back, but not away.

"Brigit?" Mack asked tentatively, stepping forward.

The hair monster stirred, and Brigit came into view. She turned her head to Mack and blinked several times.

"Hey!" she slurred with delight. "Is my brother! Lookit 'at!"

The two hookers took this news with some interest. They both rose slowly and started forward.

"You wanna be my brother too?" purred the Tattooed Lady.

"Is not a ver' good one," pronounced Brigit, wobbling to her feet.

"He looks pretty good to me," said the Redhead, lewdly adjusting her breasts toward Mack behind her ripped shirt.

"Tell ya secret. He doesn' love me," whispered Brigit, wiping the dried spittle from her mouth with the back of her hand, which she then wiped on her county jail-issued sweatpants. She looked down at herself in astonishment. "What th' fuck am I wearing?"

"Your dress did not survive," Donald said.

"Let's go, Brigit." Mack suppressed the urge to cover his nose with his hand as his sister came closer.

"Tell me you love me! I'm not goin' till you tell me you love me!"

"Aw, he loves you," said Tattooed Lady. "He's here ain't he?"

"Oh, yeah, he's here. Hey, why're you here?"

"Let's take this outside, folks," Donald stepped closer, key in hand.

"No! I ain't going 'til he says he loves me," Brigit attempted to cross her arms over her chest in defiance, but missed.

"Brigit, for God's sake," said Mack.

"Just tell her you love her. Why's that so hard?" Redhead was snaking her way to Mack.

"See? I told ya. Shitty brother."

"Hey, I remember you." Redhead blurted, smiling at Mack.

"Figures," snorted Brigit, "he only pretens' t'be good."

"Brigit, we have to go." Mack felt his patience slipping.

"Little late, aren't ya, big brother? What's so damn important now?"

"Dad's in the hospital. He's dying," Mack said coldly. He turned and walked away.

CHAPTER 10

Lonny had nearly turned the key to start his truck when he saw Mack's rust-bucket Ford turn into the hospital parking. He should talk to Mack about what had happened with Caleb. But before he could open the door to get out, an auburn mess of tangled hair rose up in the passenger seat. Mack was with Brigit. Lonny had not seen them together in three years.

Lonny had spent Brigit's last three birthdays with her, although she didn't know it. He would drive into town early evenings and follow her carefully, just to make sure she was all right. He stayed hidden; he would step in only if she were in trouble, but her girlfriends always seemed to have the same idea and surrounded her on her birthday. After seeing her laughing, knowing she was having a good time, Lonny would drive back to her house and tuck a gift in her mailbox before heading home. Something small, like those fancy sea-salt-and-pepper Virginia peanuts she liked.

He knew it was tearing Caleb up inside not to have his daughter around. He also knew Caleb would never admit this. Growing up, Lonny had genuinely delighted in Brigit, with her fiery spirit and idealistic nature. She would be the McKinsey to triumph, although he could not tell you how he knew. It was the same quiet assurance that had let him know, so long ago, that Caleb was fundamentally a good man.

He'd wrapped his present, a carved oak keychain shaped like a bottle of bourbon. He'd found it on the internet. Caleb hated the computer, convinced it was another government spy tool. But he realized the value of keeping tabs on other people and had enlisted Lonny to take over as his computer whiz He had gotten his gift engraved with BST on one side, and her initials on the other. Attached was a house key, to replace the one she'd thrown at Caleb when she moved out after graduation. Lonny thought it was time to heal the family, and a little push from him wouldn't hurt. He'd tremulously floated the idea of a party to Caleb the week before, and Caleb had uncharacteristically snarled back that he was "thinkin' on it already." Caleb was still waiting for Brigit to come to him.

This year, Lonny had missed her birthday. Instead of peeking around corners to watch her celebrate with her friends, he'd been racing her wheezing father to the hospital. He wanted to see her now, both she and Mack together. There had only been a handful of times in his life that Lonny had truly felt a need for his family, and this was one. But when a bedraggled Brigit jumped out of Mack's truck followed by an angry exchange of words with her brother, Lonny shrank down in his seat. Anyone besides Mack grabbing Brigit's arm like that would have earned a swift smack from Lonny. But they needed to work this out on their own.

After tripping and nearly falling down the steps outside the station, Brigit stumbled to Mack's truck and he folded her inside. Ten minutes later he stopped for coffee on the way back to the hospital, but she'd passed out again by then. Mack was grateful for this. Now they were back at the hospital. The morning sun beat savagely through the windshield. Mack sat staring straight ahead through his dark sunglasses. He reached for his takeout cup, already knowing it was cold. And empty. He didn't normally drink coffee; it was part of AA culture, and he wanted to cast off all his crutches. But having survived this night, one that was still ongoing, he needed to be awake. It was just one cup of coffee. But this is how it always started. Just one. If he was going to go for just one, he should have started with just one sip of bourbon last night.

He sighed. If he'd had a sip, he'd have drunk the whole jar. If he'd known where he was going to end up today, maybe it would have been better.

Brigit stirred and sat up all at once. She worked a hand under her mass of snarled hair and battled it back from her face, wincing. Mack handed her the other cup of coffee without looking at her.

She took a sip and grimaced.

"It's cold," she muttered.

"You're welcome."

"Look, last night was—" she started.

"I don't care."

"I was just going to tell you—"

"No, I really don't care. I've heard all the excuses. I've *made* all the excuses. It just doesn't matter." He still stared straight ahead.

"Well, aren't you just a little ray of sunshine. So what do I owe you for the ride?"

Mack slammed out of the truck. He paced back and forth in front of the hood. He shot his left arm up and popped his shoulder. Brigit flung herself out and started down the street, barefoot and bloodied.

Mack went after her, grabbed her arm and twisted her back around, a little harder than he'd intended.

"Do you remember last night at all?"

"I'm going home."

"Caleb's in the hospital. He wants to see you."

"Isn't that nice," she snapped.

"Do you remember me—"

"Yesterday was my twenty-first birthday! Did you remember that? Did anyone?"

"You're not the star of the show right now, Brigit."

"I am *never* the star of the show, Mack!"

"Brigit," Mack said gently, "I think he's dying."

"Shit," she muttered.

"It's a disease, Brigit," Mack said.

"*Dad's* the fucking disease!"

"We need some closure with him."

"I hate it when you throw your ten-cent recovery words around," she said.

"I hate it when I have to."

"What does he expect me to say to him? 'You did a hell of a job there, Dad. Thanks for being such a fantastic role model?' "

"Thanks for running over my new bike in the driveway, Dad," Mack blurted.

"Thanks for smashing the dishes when I tried to cook for you," she replied.

"Thanks for pissing in the window of my car."

"Thanks for the broken arm!" Brigit began to giggle.

"Thanks for the concussion!" Mack laughed. They both gasped between intakes of laughter. Mack felt the hot tears coming to the corners of his eyes from laughing so hard he could barely breathe. He whooped the unstoppable howls that only start to subside when you look away from the fool who's laughing with you. Then you start to catch your breath until you glance at them and you're uncontrollable all over again. Yet he knew there was really nothing funny about this at all.

"Let's go, then," he said, finally settling down.

"You can't be serious."

"Brigit, you hit the bridge last night. The Lickinghole Creek bridge. Where Mom died," He waited. "Was it ... did you ..."

"It was an accident."

"Well, if there's a better reason to tell the old bastard what we think of him, I don't know what it is." She slipped the county jail-issued slides back on her feet. Mack lifted his left arm and began to grasp it with his right. Before he could achieve the satisfying pop, Brigit firmly took his left hand and brought it down. She held it, and led him toward the hospital.

When they'd been kids, the humiliation of Caleb's drunk-in-public behavior was often worse than the beatings he gave them later. Though he didn't forbid their activities, he rarely showed up. Mack had been a promising pitcher. He secretly wanted Caleb to see him play, so he posted his schedule of games on the refrigerator as he'd seen friends do.

Caleb showed up half-way through a game, pushing people out of his way and yelling loudly that he'd come "to see the little shit play baseball." Mack was focused with two strikes on power hitter Jimmy Schmidt when he heard his coach tell Caleb to watch his language. Mack looked out at his father, who was swaying in the stands, brown paper bag in his hand. People moved away from him, and most of the parents were scowling. He looked toward the dugout; his teammates were not pressed up against the chain link in excitement, fingers entwined, cheering him on and chanting his name. Instead they sat quietly, looking up in pity. Mack raised his arm back and fired the ball toward the batter, barely watching as it belted Jimmy in the shoulder and he went down with a cry. Mack had thrown down his glove and left the field for good.

Caleb also made an unexpected appearance at six-year-old Brigit's last ballet recital. Though Brigit was happily bouncing around backstage like a Mexican jumping bean, Mack and Kieran had to leave when a security officer hustled them out to the parking lot, where Caleb was hurling vulgarities at an older woman before leaning over and vomiting on her shoes. They missed Brigit's dance, but lied and told her she was the best one on stage. Mack watched her eyes light up with pride, even as she looked around for Caleb in childish hope.

The next morning Mack woke to shrieks. Another dancer had told Brigit the truth, and she was yelling at her father, who was collapsed on the sofa. Mack ran for them, but Caleb swiftly smacked her hard across the face before he could get there. Mack had scooped up a wailing Brigit and held her, longing for the day when she'd stop wishing their father would become a Dad.

Turning the corner now toward the cancer center, Mack heard Caleb before he saw him. Wet, crunching coughs snapping like thin ice under a heavy boot came rolling out of his room. Mack couldn't believe anyone could cough that long without taking a breath. When they reached his room, a nurse stood by his father's side, holding a bloodied tissue to his mouth. She adjusted his oxygen as he sucked in a long, ragged breath.

She stopped at the door on her way out.

"He's had a rough night," she said.

Caleb had paled since Mack saw him last night. His eyes were sunken now, barely open. The vibrant red had drained from his lips, leaving them ashen and cracked. He'd dissolved into a gray semblance of his former self, fighting for each breath.

"You both look ... like hell," Caleb wheezed.

"Dad?" Brigit exclaimed.

"Just wanted ... to tell you ..." Caleb began.

"No, you rest. We'll tell *you*," Brigit said, looking to Mack.

Caleb was rocked by another violent coughing fit. Mack watched him struggle to sit upright with no strength left. With his eyes squeezed shut, he reached a shaking hand out. Brigit took a small step, then rushed to his side. She put her arm around his back and helped him sit upright. His coughing settled into a mucus rattle.

"I see...." he gasped, "so much of your mother ... in you two. Tell me ... that's enough." He collapsed back.

Mack looked at Brigit, who was staring in horror at Caleb's face. He walked slowly over and took Caleb's hand.

"It's enough," he said.

"Need ... you here," Caleb rasped the words out.

"We're here," Brigit said.

"Kieran."

At his name, Brigit jumped up and backed slowly away from her father. Mack sank down a little into himself.

"Bring ... Kieran," Caleb whispered.

"It's been a long time," Mack said quietly.

"New ... York."

"Well yeah, once upon a time, he was. He could be anywhere now." Mack felt like Alice, tumbling down a rabbit hole full of sharp pointed objects.

"There's ... money."

"Bullshit," Mack said.

"Inheritance ..."

"Like the last time? We're not stupid, old man." Caleb had always tempered his stinginess with the promise they'd each have a hefty inheritance if they managed to make it to age twenty-five before getting married and settling down. Mack had depended on this, he and Lauren waiting patiently for his birthday, only to be informed that evening by a fully-soused Caleb that he, Mack, still wasn't ready. Mack had been furious. He'd threatened to sell his shares of Bourbon Sweet Tea to a competitor, but Caleb just laughed. Family had right of first refusal and he'd be glad to take them off Mack's hands at pennies on the dollar. There was no money for Mack; there never had been, and he'd finally realized there never would be.

"Bourbon Sweet Tea," Caleb gasped. "You boys ... take over." He drew in a raggedy breath. "While I'm here." He paused and closed his eyes. "There's ... more money."

"Goddamn it! Why don't you just keep your fucking money?" Brigit spat.

"Wasn't talking ... to you," he said.

She glared down at her father, red points rising on her cheeks where the humiliation always burned on her face. She whipped around and stomped out, fists clenched.

"Bring ... Kieran ... home!" Caleb demanded. He groped for the oxygen mask and clasped it over his face, breathing heavily. Mack was stunned; even now, the old man could still bully his children.

He studied Caleb as if from a distance. He was removing himself from the situation now; this was why people thought he was cold, when he was really screaming on the inside.

Caleb narrowed his own eyes and stared at Mack. They were both silent, except for the faint hiss of the oxygen.

"It was always Kieran, wasn't it?" Mack asked.

Caleb stared him down, his eyes never leaving Mack's face.

Mack turned slowly and walked out.

CHAPTER 11

Caleb listened to his children walk out, wondering if he'd ever see either of them again. He hadn't meant to be so forceful, but he was having a hard time getting the words out. His mind was going dark again, twisting into little corners he'd kept boarded up for years. Kieran was around the bend of many of those corners. Once Caleb had hung all his hopes and dreams upon his middle son. Now he never mentioned his name. Kieran might as well be dead. For all Caleb knew, he was.

Kieran was the place where love lived, Maeve used to say. Caleb would have snorted at this nonsense, except he agreed. Privately. He would never admit it out loud. Where Mack was strong and protective, and Brigit tough and feisty, Kieran was, well, he was just happy. He was the happiest goddamn kid Caleb had ever seen, and a few times he wondered if Kieran was really his. Though he knew better, if only because Kieran looked just like him. Both were black Irish, straight black hair and dark blue eyes with rings of black; eyes you could not lie to.

When the kids were young, if Mack fell off his bike he'd jump up in concern to check and see if he'd damaged it. If Brigit fell, she'd kick the bike in anger, before climbing back on and riding away fast. But if Kieran fell, he'd laugh at himself. He'd call himself a clumsy boy and tell the bike he was sorry, with a smile. He did this even when a pedal ripped through his jeans and cut his ankle so it bled. Caleb didn't know why his son was always in such a good mood; he'd given the kid no reason to be.

Once, and he had to admit there'd been a jar of Bourbon Sweet Tea involved, he'd come home to find Kieran's Lego pyramid in the middle of the living room, not put away like he'd told him to do earlier. It was a hell of a building, and Kieran had been working on it for days. It was red, with jutting ledges of blue and small windows of yellow (in case the mummies need to breathe, Kieran had explained), and a tall white spire coming out of the top. Kieran had asked if Caleb wanted to work on it with him, but Caleb didn't have time for toys. Seeing the pyramid had triggered something in him. He drew back one of his steel-toed boots and slammed his foot into the side of the plaything. With satisfaction, he watched as tiny plastic bricks flew everywhere about the room.

Kieran ran in just in time to witness the destruction of his master-piece. There was a moment of silence before he smiled. "Wow! It looks like it was hit by a giant sand worm!"

"I told ya to pick it up, goddamn it," Caleb growled.

"All the mummies are released now, Daddy! They can rule the earth again."

"Mummies are dead, don'tcha know that?"

Caleb stalked around the room, smashing as many of the Legos as he could find with his boots. They shattered with a crunch under his feet. He watched Kieran's face carefully, waiting for the shock and tears, but the smile just grew.

"Well, I guess *now* they're all dead, Daddy."

"What's wrong with you? I just ruined yer damn toys." Caleb stared at him.

Kieran looked up at his father. "It's okay. I know it was an accident," he said.

Every once in a while, some other kid would try to cheat Kieran out of his marbles or his lunch money, and Mack would swoop in and avenge his little brother. Mack was much bigger than Kieran, and a lot less patient. But the truth was, eveyone liked Kieran. He was hard not to like. Hell, if you just asked him for his marbles, he'd give them to you.

Mack could be devilish with his brother. The two were just ten months apart in age, and one didn't seem to be able to exist without the other. Kieran would follow Mack anywhere, and never minded playing second fiddle in Mack's schemes. Mack would set up a bike ramp, some useless piece of plywood over an old aging barrel, and have Kieran try it out. The barrel would go rolling away as soon as the weight of the bike hit the wood, and he'd tumble to the ground. Then they would try it again. The next time, Mack was almost clobbered by the bike when it went one way and Kieran went another. At Mack's urging, Kieran again pedaled hell-bound for leather up the ramp only to be catapulted over the handlebars of his bike. He crashed down into a pipe and sliced his thumb on the rusty metal. This made Maeve hysterical and they were off for a tetanus shot.

They came out of the doctor's office, a bandage over Kieran's thumb and a band-aid on his arm for the painful shot. As Maeve was cooing over her boy, Caleb clubbed Kieran in the back of the head.

"Jay-sus, Mary and Joseph, what is wrong with you?" Maeve spat at him.

"Don't you ever pull a stupid stunt like that again," Caleb said to Kieran.

Kieran nodded. Mack let out a snicker. Caleb whacked him in the back of the head, too.

"What? What did I do?" Mack asked, in all innocence.

"You should'a stopped him."

But Caleb learned why Mack sent his brother into danger, time and again. He wasn't jealous, or spiteful, or mean. Mack watched Kieran's face light up with pure exultation at the feeling of flying and his absolute assurance that this time it would work. Kieran's happiness was infectious; it spread out from him like a rainbow after a storm. Even Caleb could feel it.

Kieran was also the natural peacekeeper in the family. Brigit's temper was quick and flared up at the smallest provocation—she was most like her father in that. Caleb had tried to teach her it was okay, preferable, in fact, to let the anger rise but not to let it out. She wouldn't hear that, though. She would stomp her feet if he told her to get on to bed. Kieran could soothe her down every time. Mack, when angry, would give Caleb the hard stare of silence, just as Maeve had done. Sometimes Mack and Caleb didn't speak to each other for days. Kieran, though, could swing in and defuse the situation in no time.

There was something shameful about fighting in front of Kieran, like battling in front of a priest. Kieran would walk into a fight with Caleb and ask him what was wrong, and if he could help. Truth be told, Caleb sometimes hit him just for being so calm about things. Kieran would always apologize when Caleb hit him, which made him want to smack him even harder. He wanted Kieran to fight back, just once.

Caleb needed to toughen his son up, because Kieran was the one he'd quietly chosen to take over Bourbon Sweet Tea. Kieran was doing well working at the distillery. Caleb could see the way people warmed up to the kid like they'd never done with him. People feared Caleb and did as he ordered, but Kieran put them at ease and they'd do what he wanted just because he wanted it. His trusting demeanor, however, put him at a disadvantage to get double-crossed, a concern of Caleb's and a sure way to end up dead as a moonshiner.

Caleb knew Mack would be there for his brother, whether he wanted to or not. Though he was running about as far away from the distilling game as he could get now, mowing lawns for Christ's sake, he'd never let his brother get in serious trouble. Mack had drunk enough moonshine, but he had no interest in making it, and he'd made that clear to Caleb. He didn't have the personality, anyway. But the business had to be a tight circle; you never knew who you could really trust outside of family. Even then, Caleb knew, sometimes choices had to be made.

And no goddamn gold-digger was going to ruin Caleb's plan. That

Roseanna Ortiz, Kieran's trashy girlfriend, had refused to accept her place at the bottom of the pile. Caleb didn't know what in the hell drove her to think so highly of herself, and he supposed it was her unbounded confidence that attracted Kieran. Caleb had hoped he'd grow tired of her; instead, Kieran began to spend all his free time with Roseanna. Caleb made a point of overhearing many of their conversations.

"I think I'm going to start a bakery someday," he'd heard her tell Kieran.

"Why a bakery?"

"Because people are always happy at a bakery," Roseanna said. "Nobody really needs a cake, it just tastes good."

"That's true," Kieran said.

"But I won't have it here, not in Touraine."

"Why not?"

"People here don't want to be happy."

Entwined in a family doomed to another generation of hunger and need, Roseanna was determined to break out. She was going somewhere. That was fine with Caleb, but she was going alone. He wasn't going to let her drag Kieran along. Bourbon was his legacy, his birthright, and that was where he belonged, to carry on the McKinsey tradition.

Caleb was the only one who knew why Kieran had left. He had fully expected his son to come back in a few weeks so he could explain, but after so long, it seemed unlikely. Now there might not be much time left. Caleb was the one who had finally broken Kieran, and he believed he could fix his son, if he still had a son to fix.

CHAPTER 12

As Mack walked away from Caleb's hospital room, his head grew more crowded, not less. He needed to get away from here, but the farther he went, the louder his thoughts. His father was gravely ill; he was probably dying. There was so much anger between them, and it still simmered. He'd thought maybe time and space apart would lessen the feelings, but he'd walked into Caleb's room last night and they were right back at each other. He had to accept that it was never going to get better.

He felt bad that he didn't feel worse. Caleb had tried his best, he supposed. He'd bailed Mack out of jail a few times without even a lecture. Had sat by Mack's bedside in the hospital after his drunken car accident and afterward stood up for his son in court. After Lauren had left, Caleb had scooped Mack up out of the Trickle Inn a few times when he was too drunk to stand. He never asked him what the hell his problem was; he seemed to expect this behavior from his son. Maybe Mack needed to try a little harder, now that Caleb was down. Maybe he needed to man up and take the reins.

He leaned back against the wall. He wished Caleb hadn't flaunted his money in their faces. They always knew he had plenty, but it was his and his alone. Growing up, they'd always had whatever he decided they needed and no more. Anything extra was their problem. At ten,

Mack had saved up money he'd earned mowing lawns and bought all his own baseball gear. When Kieran was twelve he spent a year collecting bottles to buy himself a secondhand bike. Brigit had begged for a horse for her fifth birthday, and they certainly had the land for it, but Caleb wouldn't hear of it. Mack was the one who'd paid for Brigit's ballet costumes and shoes, since he was already working for Sunshine Landscaping then. It was torture to think about what Caleb was worth, and there was no point. If anyone could figure out how to take it with him, it would be Caleb.

But ... if he truly meant to give them an inheritance, maybe Mack could stay here and start his landscaping company after all. He let his mind wander. He pictured himself leasing land, buying equipment, even maybe hiring a pretty office assistant. Local estate owners might still be leery of him, but he had a plan. A large colonial house with a four-bay garage and a stable stood on Route 250 between Touraine and Charlottesville. It had once been a showplace, but the owner had died and the grounds were covered in weeds. Distant relatives were having a hard time selling it with that air of abandonment. Mack would strike a deal with them. He'd take over the landscaping and renovate the gardens. Plant an abundance of summer flowers to continue into fall and even winter. A couple of blue spruces would set the buildings off nicely and provide a windbreak, with charcoal-gray paving stones connecting stables, house, and garage. He was ready to do all this for free. He'd hire a photographer for glossy brochures, and tell potential clients to drive by and take a look, since it was visible from the road. It would be an investment in his future, but one that would take thousands of dollars he did not have. His needs were simple, but all his extra money went into Maeve's Garden.

Mack suddenly smacked his head back against the wall with a loud thump. What was wrong with him? His father was probably dying, and he was fantasizing about his own future. A nurse walking by looked at him sharply.

"Sorry," he murmured. She walked on briskly, but glanced back before turning into a patient's room.

This was the dangerous path. This is what always got him into trouble. He let himself hope. Hope was not a thing with wings, lifting you up and gliding you through clouds struck with rays of sunshine. Hope was the demon that slowly sank in barbed fangs and would not let go, an endless torture of possibilities just out of reach. Mack pushed himself away from the wall. Caleb had gotten to him again. He'd planted these poisonous seeds, to see them fester in Mack and then die, like a sweet pea he'd once tried to grow in a closet, as a science experiment. Devoid of sunlight, it still struggled to live, a sickly albino stalk. Mack had felt terrible for the plant and tried to save it, but it in the end it had starved to death.

Caleb would starve Mack. He'd give him just enough hope to kill him.

Mack stalked toward the exit. He stopped when he saw Brigit outside. On the hood of his truck was a parking ticket, for leaving it in an emergency spot. Mack watched as Brigit lifted the ticket carefully off. She looked at both sides, and slowly ripped it into many small pieces, scattering the ground like ashes.

He walked over to his sister. Her eyes were red-rimmed, but dry. Mack wanted to hug her. He was afraid to try.

"Let's go," he said.

They climbed into the truck, and he sat with his hands on his knees. He turned to Brigit. "So, do you, uh, want to get some pancakes?"

Brigit looked at him as if she didn't quite recognize him. "What?"

"Mom used to make us pancakes, when we were kids. To make us feel better."

She stared at him, her forehead wrinkling up. "I don't remember that."

He couldn't look at her. He stared, instead, at the dirt on the knees of his pants. "I knew it was your birthday," he said softly, finally looking over at her. She stared back. He sighed and started the truck.

He drove them to a college diner. They probably wouldn't know anyone here in Charlottesville. They walked in and sat down at a cracked yellow Formica booth with a slim metal edge. They picked up the plastic-coated menus, the kind printed on both sides, hiding behind them from each other. His still had a sticky coffee stain on it.

"Have whatever you want," Mack offered.

"No shit."

"Let's call it a late birthday breakfast."

"Don't."

"I am sorry. I wish—"

"And yet, he's still talking about it."

"If I could have—"

"Could have what? Shown up? Acknowledged it in any way at all? Thrown me a surprise party like you were supposed to?"

"What?"

"Never mind." Brigit glared at her menu. "I'm twenty-one now, in case you were wondering."

"Happy—"

"Shut up. It's over! You missed it." She was deep into the pictures of breakfast food. "Things are going to change now, Mack. Now that I have voting rights with my stock."

"Brigit, think carefully." Now there was fire in her eyes, a tremor of excitement in her voice. This was the sister he knew. There was also hope blooming, which scared him.

"I've got it all mapped out. My plan is to start with an expansion of the distillery. Instead of the public reception area at Bourbon Sweet Tea right now, which, as you know, is a boring box of why-bother, we turn it into a classy tasting room. We build a nice bar, oak, of course, and set up tall pub tables. We put in custom shelves, oak again, that feature Bourbon Sweet Tea and proper glasses for sale, Glencairn snifters and solid square rocks glasses with the BST monogram. For the purists who look down on ice, we'll have whiskey stones, silicon molds with ice inside, and even chilling whiskey bullets. We'll have local artisan salty snacks like jumbo Virginia peanuts and gourmet pretzels to keep people drinking, and we can also sell those.

She leaned forward. "See? We keep it local and exclusive, because tourists like to take treasures home and brag that they went to the very distillery that makes Bourbon Sweet Tea and look at what they found. We bring in local musicians, for happy hour specials, and have local artists hang their paintings, which will also be for sale. Soon we're hosting private parties right at the distillery. People eat that shit up.

"Of course all of this will need major work on the outside, too, get rid of that fucking black paint, which is where you come in to create landscapes that people will marvel over, I mean wonderful sculpture-thingies with boxwoods—"

"Topiary," Mack supplied.

"Yeah, and flower arches that will make people stop for pictures. Then we get to the big plans; we build a really sweet hotel, a luxury spot with a spa, a golf course, stables. And a restaurant, fine dining, with high-end recipes featuring bourbon. We make this town a destination; someplace people plan to visit, not like an afterthought. More fancy boutiques will open in Touraine as a result of all that fat tourist money, and Charlottesville's not so far away they can justify their drinking with a historical tour. Let me get a pen, I'll draw it out for you." She grabbed a napkin and waved to the waitress.

He rubbed his mouth. "Brigit, this is interesting, but it'd be a lot of work. I'm not trying to be mean, but Caleb will never let you change Bourbon Sweet Tea."

"He doesn't have to. We can take over now."

Mack sat back, speechless.

"When they incorporated, you know, Mom insisted on making all of us stock holders. Caleb generously gifted those whopping twelve shares each to Mom and us, which didn't matter since he'd always be in control with his forty-four shares. What he didn't count on was Mom dying and splitting her shares between the three of us. I'm sure he thought he'd get them back, but even then, she was looking out for us."

"Caleb has the right of first refusal if anyone wants to sell their stock."

"So why haven't you sold him yours?" She looked up at her brother. "You say you don't want anything to do with Bourbon Sweet Tea. It brings no income, since all the proceeds are reinvested in the company. So why don't you just get rid of it?"

"It's a little early in the morning for a stockholder's meeting, don't you think?" He was trying to lighten the mood, but Brigit had her claws in now.

"But I've been to a stockholder's meeting. All of them, since I was eighteen." Brigit leaned into her brother. "You don't sell it because then Caleb would have even more power."

"Why do I feel like I'm on the end of a justice department investigation? You haven't spoken to me in three years, Brigit. Ever since…."

"Graduation. I should have just let you beat him to death then."

"I was *not* trying to beat him to death. You know what it is like to try to say a step ahead of Caleb. He just steps sideways."

"Well you should have—"

"What? What should I have done? Please, tell me."

"How did my party turn into a horror movie?"

"You had the bad luck to have Caleb for a father. He's an alcoholic, you know."

"Yes, Mack, I know, and any day now he's going to admit he's 'powerless over his addiction.' Christ. We're *McKinseys*. We're *all* alcoholics." She waved her menu in the air.

"I just think you need some help, before it's too late."

"Stop it, Mack. This is where you always, always go. Just because you can't drink, doesn't mean the rest of the world is going to memorize all twelve steps right along with you."

"I wasn't asking you to—"

"You can be so self-righteous. Perfect Mack, with his shit firmly together. How will I *ever* live up to his shining example? Will you draw me a map so I can have the great life you have? Because you are so, so happy, aren't you?"

The waitress appeared, polyester uniform not quite clean, her attention not quite focused. Her hair was pulled so tightly back into a ponytail you could see the lines from the comb, as if it were molded back from her tired face. "What can I get you?" she asked, pen poised over her pad.

"Could I have a stack of pancakes?" Mack asked. She scribbled on her pad and turned to Brigit.

"I'll have the strawberry pancakes, with whipped cream, and could you add bananas too? Also an order of bacon, hash browns, and a blueberry muffin. Oh, and a large orange juice. And coffee too, please," Brigit said.

"Coffee for you?" she asked, half turning to Mack.

He hesitated. Until last night, he hadn't had coffee in years. The alluring smell masked the taste of burnt toast, hot and sour and bitter. Just like Bourbon Sweet Tea: the aroma drew you in and the taste knocked you down. He had learned to improve the coffee by adding one large dollop of milk and five sugars, stirred three times. That was good, until he began to experience the same shaky hands he'd seen on his mother. Then he'd worked to get rid of the caffeine fix too. Last night, though, he'd had to stay awake. And he hadn't slept yet.

Mack looked up. Both the waitress and Brigit were staring at him. "Yes, coffee please."

She ambled away, calling out the order as she went.

"Guess you got your appetite back," Mack said.

"Oh, so sorry, was that too much?"

"No, no, it's fine."

"Is it?" She snorted derision. "Jesus, Mack, stand up for yourself for once! Say what you think. You walk around like you're afraid of stepping on your own goddamn shadow."

"I don't know what to say to you, Brigit. Everything I say is wrong and I'd like to do one thing right today." Their coffee arrived; Mack stuck his nose in the cup but felt no better.

"Why should today be any different?"

"Because I know you had a shitty birthday. I want to do something nice."

Brigit sighed and put her head down. "Just be you. Whoever that is now."

Mack turned away quickly as he realized they really didn't know each other at all anymore.

"Tell me something about Mom," Brigit said.

"What do you want to know?"

"Tell me something funny she said."

Mack had thought most of what Maeve had said was funny. But then again, he was filtering it through an eleven-year-old's ears. "Well, restaurants were always fun, because there are some different words for things in Ireland."

"Like?"

"Like she'd go out to eat and order a hamburger and chips, which to her were fries, but in America are potato chips. So they'd bring her potato chips. She'd get this sour look, and she'd say, 'Why the bloody hell can't they understand when I say chips and give me chips and not crisps?' And I would tell her, 'Crisps are chips here, Mom.' And she'd say, 'But I wanted chips.' And I'd tell her, 'Then you have to ask for fries.' And she would say the same thing, every time; 'What a backward country is America where you have to ask for one thing to get another.' And then she'd laugh, and eat the potato chips anyway."

"She never learned to ask for fries?"

"She learned. She just wouldn't ask. It was the stubbornness in her."

Their breakfast arrived. Mack looked down at the plate of three light brown circles stacked on top of each other, still steaming from the griddle, a melting square of butter in the exact center. Brigit sat back and watched with a smile as the waitress unloaded her arms of her breakfast. A plate of pancakes loaded with strawberries swimming in a dark pink sauce, with a circle of sliced bananas in the center, the whole thing topped with wavy whipped cream from a can. There was also a plate of bacon strips gleaming with fat, another plate loaded with crispy hash browns, and still another small plate with a muffin, blueberries bursting out of the top.

"I thought the stubbornness came from Caleb."

"Oh, it does. It's the Irish," Mack watched as she carefully removed the banana slices from her pancakes with a fork and placed each one around the muffin, forming a circle. "You can't help it."

"Me? You should talk."

This as Mack added one plastic creamer to his coffee, shook five sugar packets, ripped them open at the same time, and poured them all in, followed by the three stirs. "This is just an old habit," he said.

"But if there were only four sugars, you wouldn't drink it, would you? It has to be five, doesn't it?"

"Fine talk coming from you, banana girl."

"I like the bananas, but I don't want them on my pancakes."

"So order a banana."

"No, because when they come on pancakes, they're nice and warm. You order a banana, you just get a cold banana."

Mack watched Brigit eat. She mashed up all the strawberries and the whipped cream and took a large bite of pancake. She gobbled down a strip of bacon in three bites, using her hands. Her face relaxed as she ate, completely uninhibited and free. God, how he envied that. Mack could only think of the obligations piling up that had to be dealt with. Caleb in the hospital, which meant finding special doctors, oncologists, and treatment, he guessed. He'd have to find Caleb's insurance and call them. He'd have to go out to the house and talk to Lonny, to make sure he understood the situation—as soon as Mack himself understood it. Someone would have to see to the distillery, and the board of directors would have to be informed. All of which meant he was going to have to spend time with Caleb. And Caleb wasn't going to just tell him these things, Mack would have to drag it out of him.

He looked down at the pancakes on his plate. He had not taken one bite, and now they mocked him, growing cold and soggy with congealing butter. What the hell was he doing sitting here eating, when there was so much he had to do? He pushed the plate away.

"He's not going to die if you eat a damn pancake, Mack," Brigit said, her mouth full. She was almost finished with her food. Mack felt a little disgusted at her ability to shovel in all of this breakfast, when the looming problems grew by the minute. She focused on this one thing as if it were the only thing in her world. Did she care how much trouble she was in?

Then he flashed back to the jail cell, and her sad pronouncement that he didn't love her. Her ruined birthday. The accident. She could have died. He put his head down. How could he deny her her meal? He took a bite, chewing through the now cold and slightly rubbery pancakes.

"Jesus, Mack. They're not poisoned. If you don't like them, don't eat them." She took the last gulp of her coffee. "You giving me a ride home?" Without waiting for an answer, she slid to the end of the booth. "Hey, make sure you tip her good, okay?"

Brigit fell asleep again in the truck almost immediately as they drove from Charlottesville back to Touraine. Mack was jealous of her ability to relax so completely, though she did have a large amount of food in her stomach. He wasn't sure where to go as he approached town. For the first time in a long time, he had no plan. He wasn't sure dropping her off at her house was a good idea. When she woke up and reality slapped her in the face, she might go on another bender. She'd been signed out to his custody last night. He was responsible for her, another job for him. He could take her to his house, but he didn't like having people there.

He decided to drive out to Caleb's and talk to Lonny. As he pulled in the driveway, Lonny was sitting on the top step. The old rocking chair sat on the porch, but Mack knew Lonny wouldn't sit in it. No one but Caleb sat there. He wondered if Caleb would ever rock in it again. Only his misshapen old felt hat, mostly stains and tears now, sat in the chair alone. Lonny stood as Mack got out of the truck.

"Lonny. How are you doing?"

"How is he?" Lonny looked like he'd had no sleep either. Mack thought briefly of offering to make him coffee. Then he realized that Lonny lived here, and should probably be making the offer to Mack.

"He's not good, Lonny," Mack said.

"Gonna go back over and see him, if that's okay," Lonny said. After all these years, Lonny would still ask Mack if what he did was okay. Mack was under no illusions of hierarchy, nor did he question Lonny's devotion; he was pretty sure Lonny would run over him to protect Caleb.

"It's okay with me. Can you tell me what happened last night?"

"Came out, he was on the porch. Must have fell outta his chair. Couldn't breathe. Took him straightaway to the hospital."

"Why didn't you call me?"

Lonny shrugged, uncharacteristically staring back at Mack. That was fair, Mack thought. Lonny was always here for Caleb. He made a better son, though he didn't share in all the beatings. As far as Mack knew, Caleb had never touched Lonny.

"He's dying, Lonny," Mack hadn't meant to blurt it out. He'd meant to build up to it, let the guy come to that conclusion on his own, though Mack felt Lonny frequently had to be told things outright.

"S'pose so," Lonny said, standing. "Can I go?"

"Yeah. You can go."

Lonny reached for Caleb's hat and headed to his truck. Mack wished that Caleb would ever be as happy to see him as he would be to see Lonny.

Mack looked at his childhood home. His last visit had ended in the brawl at Brigit's graduation party. He hadn't lived here since he'd moved to Blacksburg to start at Virginia Tech. He was surprised Caleb had paid his tuition—until he found out that Mack was majoring in landscape architecture, then Mack was on his own. Like too many college students, he'd scrambled to make ends meet with multiple jobs and student loans. Desperation drove him to get that degree, even if it sometimes meant sleeping in the back of his truck. Now that he was back, Mack couldn't seem to walk up the steps. He didn't want to deal with doctors, insurance, or Bourbon Sweet Tea. He didn't even know where to start.

Before he could put a foot on the lowest step, Brigit rolled out of the truck, stretched her entire self out like a starfish, shook it off and regrouped. She trundled straightaway up the steps and swung open the front door with no hesitation. Brigit had moved out just a few days after the cursed party. He'd offered to help, but she'd told him point blank that he and Caleb were both to blame, and she didn't need either one in her life. Now he worried she wasn't smart enough to show caution. Or maybe she was just getting it done.

She turned back to look at him. "You coming, or what?" The door swung closed behind her.

Mack had to open it again for himself. As he walked in, he almost ran smack into Brigit. She stood frozen in the entry, nose wrinkled.

"That smell ..."

"Yeah," Mack sniffed; old whiskey, sweated out and sickeningly sweet, layered with stale Camel smoke.

"I forgot," she said, covering her nose.

Mack didn't have the heart to tell her the smell was in her, too. "We ought to see if he has any insurance," he said.

"I guess," Brigit said, not moving.

Brigit took a deep breath and headed for Caleb's office. The door was locked. That was a new one. She struggled but it wouldn't give.

Mack stepped up and yanked; the handle was new, a heavy gold switch plate attached to a deadbolt.

"What the fuck?" she said, pounding it with the flat of her hand. "Why's he locking the door all of a sudden?"

"I don't know."

"There's really no reason to be here, Mack. We should probably just go."

"Probably."

Brigit turned and ran up the stairs. Mack followed as she barreled into their parents' bedroom, but stayed in the doorway as she went to Maeve's dressing table. Though Caleb had shed all other signs of his dead wife from the house, he refused to touch her dressing table. One thing was missing, as Brigit had suspected.

"It's gone. Her Donegal jewelry box is gone," Brigit said. "It was the one thing of Mom's I wanted when I left, and he tore it out of my hands. Said it didn't belong to me, I could only take what was mine. But she was mine, too." She pushed past him and trudged back downstairs.

Mack slowly followed his sister through the empty house where neither of them belonged any longer. He stepped outside to the porch and watched Brigit propelling herself in Caleb's rocking chair with an urgency that belied the complete lack of expression on her face.

"What happened last night?" he asked her as he sat on the top step, facing away.

"Rumors and bullshit."

"Brigit," he said.

"There was supposed to be a surprise party. You and Caleb were supposed to be giving it. Turns out there was no party. I had some drinks and I crashed my car and I went to jail."

"Well Christ, could you be any more vague? What *happened*?"

"What do you want to know, Mack? How excited I was, looking for my secret party? The one you and Dad had made peace over and now maybe we'd be a family again? How small and humiliated I felt when it finally, finally occurred to me that I was looking for something that didn't exist? Would you like me to *share* my *feelings* with you?"

A million questions ran through Mack's mind. He asked none of them. Just, "Where were you going?"

"Nowhere, Mack," she sighed. "Nowhere at all."

"You hit the same bridge as Mom did when she died."

She stopped rocking.

"When you were a baby she carried you all the time. We used to joke to her that you'd never learn to walk since your feet never touched the ground. She needed to hold you close, she said. She shouldn't have worried. Once you did walk, you followed her everywhere."

"I don't remember." Totally flat affect. No expression at all.

"She made the best of a bad situation, Brigit. Don't let that all be for nothing."

"I was two years old, Mack."

"I know," he replied.

"She might as well not have existed."

"But she did, Brigit. There's a place…" He took a deep breath. He had not planned this, and once out, he could not take it back. "Come with me," he said, standing. "I've got something to show you."

"What?" Brigit said.

"A garden."

CHAPTER 13

Resentment oozed out of Brigit's alcohol-soaked pores as she pulled her sweat-stained shirt away from her back with one hand, swiping at a cloud of gnats with the other. It was muggy, clambering up the side of the mountain after her brother. The hangover had finally arrived, her head pounded, and her cuts and scrapes were stinging. Yet he pressed on in front of her, urging her on, and she followed grudgingly, silently cursing the back of his head.

"Almost there," Mack said, pausing to hold back a tree branch. "It'll be worth it, I promise."

"I doubt that very much," Brigit muttered under her breath.

She tripped over a tree root and stumbled out of the shady woods into a clearing. Painfully bright sunlight exposed a mad scientist's jungle of vegetation rising out of the backwoods. The greedy mouths of blue lobelias burst toward her from their stalks like starving orphans. Hibiscus the size of dinner plates swayed, their white petals flat open with bleeding red centers. Yellow coneflowers obscenely thrust up their phallic seed pods, spent petals drooping down. Despite the heat, Brigit shivered when a passionflower brushed against her neck. She mistook the stamen for a praying mantis and flicking it away from her goose-bumped skin.

"What the hell's this?" she asked Mack.

"This is Maeve's Garden." Backlit by the sun, Mack stood straight and tall and proud; not a look Brigit was used to from her brother.

"Where … I mean, where did it come from?"

"I planted it."

"You made this?"

"It's for Mom. You're the first person ever to see it," Mack said. He turned his head, and through shadow, she could see the naked expectation in his face.

"It's a medicine wheel," he said. "This is Kieran's section, the South. It's summer and warmth with the butterfly bushes. The Alaskan cedar is for Dad, showing strength in the North. Right here is the West, that's me with blue hydrangeas, and, well, I put in lily of the valley for Lauren." His voice dipped slightly, then rose again. "The East is you. Spring, and hope, with the pink turtleheads you love." He walked quickly to the center. "This is Mom. She's the gardenia in the center." He put his hand on one of the many tiny white flowers that trembled under his touch.

"Jesus, Mack," Brigit said.

"What?"

Everybody had to hide their crazy somewhere, Brigit thought. Mack had always, always been the strong, cynical, rational brother—except for reconstructing his entire damaged family out of plants on the side of a mountain. She counted on Mack to be responsible, not delusional. Even if she hadn't spoken to him in three years, she always knew he was there. Except he'd just revealed his preference for a tangle of ravenous plants who couldn't talk back, bowing in eternal supplication to their dead mother.

"This is really something," she muttered, looking away from Mack.

"The gardenia was first," he said. "I stole it from that estate with the iron gates that's on the way to Charlottesville."

"You *stole* it?" She looked at him.

"I left money for it."

"Why didn't you just buy one?"

"I was eleven."

"You were *eleven*? You made this when you were a kid?" She stared at him now.

"Started it, yeah. I've drawn plans, too, if you want to see them. Whatever I make from working at Sunshine Landscaping goes to Maeve's Garden. Right now, I'm saving for these stone benches. Yours is pink and white quartz, speckled and—"

"Wait—you've been doing this for *nineteen years*?"

"It's a tribute," he said.

"It's creepy, Mack. It's—it's like seeing yourself in a wax museum with Vincent Price hovering around the corner." She knew she'd said too much when she saw the sting in his eyes. She'd always said whatever was on her mind to Mack, that was the way things worked with them. He expected it, she knew that. Here, though, he was like a little boy again; he loved something, and she had just crushed it.

"We should go," he said, turning away and walking back toward the woods.

They should leave, she thought. Just leave and forget the whole thing. Pretend it never happened. They'd pretended that nothing was wrong their whole lives with Caleb. Like going to school in sneakers with holes and pretending they were intentional. Never asking for new shoes, already knowing the answer was no, though they could afford them. Then scoffing at the other kids that anyone could buy new shoes, but hers had character. Survival meant twisting her mind around to make whatever was wrong into a positive.

"Did you bring Kieran here?" That stopped him.

"No," Mack said.

"But you guys were so close."

"I've never brought anyone here. Even Lauren." Mack shrugged. He held his hand out to a swallowtail butterfly, which briefly hovered before flitting away to a bright coral bloom.

"But you brought me," Brigit said.

"Yeah, well, looks like that was a mistake."

"So why did you?"

"I thought it would make you happy." Mack wouldn't look at her.

"Really? Is there a lot to be happy about right now?"

"I thought if you could see ... I thought you might like to be around Mom. All we had keeping us together was her memory."

"But I don't have that. You had her a whole ten years longer than I did. What do I have?"

"You have me, goddamn it," he whirled on her. "You have *me*."

Brigit sat down hard in the dirt. She looked at the dried blood crusted under her fingernails and dug her hands into the earth.

"We have to go," she said.

"So let's go," Mack said.

"No," she said slowly. "I mean we have to *go*. We have to go and find Kieran."

He tucked his chin, staring at her. "That's . . . insane, Brigit. What makes you think I'm going to take you on a wild goose chase to find a brother who clearly does not want to be found?"

"First of all, I don't need you to take me anywhere."

"Well good, because I'm not."

"And second, how do you know he doesn't want to be found?"

"Because we're a fixed point, Brigit. He knows where we are."

"Maybe," she said. This had occurred to her many times since Kieran had left. "Maybe he needs our help."

"Is this about the money?" he asked. "Caleb and his 'inheritance' promises. Because you know that's all bullshit, right? You know he's just dangling it over our heads. Make the puppets dance again. It's never going to happen. He'll never give us a cent."

"It's not about that."

"Then what, you feel sorry for Caleb? Now he's dying, you want to be the good daughter he always wished for?"

Brigit dug her hands further into the soothing cool dirt. Mack was hitting back hard. Brigit knew she'd hurt him, and now he would lash out at her. Then she would get mad at him and yell until she was out of breath.

Not this time.

"Believe it or not, it has nothing to do with Caleb," she said calmly.

"Then what brings you to this divine Hallmark moment of family bonding?"

"You. Because you were right, Mack. I do have you." Her head was screeching for aspirin and her throat was dry and scratchy. Her body hurt, out here in the sun, sweat gliding down the back of her neck. "I don't know how it all got so out of hand, but I'm sorry. Mack, I don't remember Mom making us pancakes. I really wish I did. But I do remember you teaching me to ride my bike. I remember Kieran and the tickle fights. I remember us and the rope swing in the barn, and Kieran making us bangers and mash. That's our family. And I have plans for the future."

"Your big plans are a pipe dream, Brigit."

"But they're not. If the three of us combine our holdings, Mack, we have the majority."

"Caleb will fight us."

"Then we'll fight back."

"You make it sound so easy."

"I know it won't be easy. I've been thinking about this for years, just like you and this garden. It's family."

"Our family is broken."

Brigit stood and wiped the dirt from her hands, watching it tumble back down to the earth where it belonged. She walked over to Mack and stood in front of him.

"We need to do this for us. It's not about Caleb. We were a family, we can be one again. We have to go and find Kieran. For us."

CHAPTER 14

Mack awoke in a panic on his scratchy living room couch. He jumped up and checked the front door. The cans he'd stacked in front of it were still there. He walked quickly through his kitchen and checked the back door as well; still secure with his makeshift alarm system. He peeked into his bedroom and breathed a sigh of relief at the shape of his sister tangled up in the blankets on his bed, still sleeping.

They'd needed this sleep, both of them. A few hours would give them both clear heads to figure out how to proceed with their father. When he flipped open his phone to find three missed work calls from his boss Pete, he punched the work number into his phone.

"Sunshine." Naomi, Pete's secretary, growled into the phone.

"It's Mack. Can I talk to Pete?"

"Oh, Mack, he's really pissed you didn't show up today."

"My father had a ... he's in the hospital."

"Geez, Mack, I'm sorry about that. Listen, I hate to ... Pete said you need to get over to the Henderson's and start clearing out those weeds around the pond. He—"

"I need a couple days off."

"Oh, shit. You know what he's gonna say," she sighed. "I'm awful sorry 'bout your dad. Good luck." She clicked off the phone.

Mack stuffed the phone back in his pocket. Another soul-crushing humiliation for him to find Pete later and beg for his crappy job back. What if he didn't, though? He wished Anthony would call back.

He walked back into the kitchen and checked the freezer. There were several square boxes of frozen peas. The front one contained peas, but the rest were stuffed with hundred-dollar bills. His savings account for the garden. Caleb had taught him years ago: you put some in the bank to knock off suspicion, but you keep most of it safe where you could get to it quickly. Mack suddenly realized how foolish this was. He had nothing to hide, he wasn't making moonshine and hadn't for years. He shut the freezer door. He had a lot of money saved up, but it was earmarked for the Garden.

He had another call to make, and punched the numbers into his phone.

"Albemarle County Sheriff's office," Bartholomew answered.

"Hi, Don. It's Mack McKinsey."

"Mack. What can I do for you?"

"I, uh, need to know where things stand with Brigit."

"She's in your custody as of now. She appears for a hearing in ten days."

"How serious is it?"

"Between you and me, it's not good." Donald sighed. "Her BAC was point-two-four, which puts her in the third category. Automatic loss of license for a year and possibly six months in jail. She's been brought in before for underage drinking, so that doesn't help. There's some hefty flatbed charges for hauling away what's left of her car, which is totaled. I don't know how in the hell she made it out okay."

"Jesus," Mack said.

"There's assault charges from in the bar. If your dad can make any phone calls, now would be the time."

"Thanks, Don."

"Mack?"

"Yeah?"

"There's ..." Donald paused, his voice lowered. "There's a couple of ATF agents sniffing around down here. You know about Seamus O'Hearn's place going up in flames?"

"I heard."

"It was an accident, except it wasn't," Bartholomew said. "And they weren't here looking for Seamus. You and I know there are people living back there. We could have lost the whole mountain. You need to talk to your father."

"But Bourbon Sweet Tea is legal."

"Sure."

"Wait ..." Mack's head felt as thick as concrete as he searched for the answer he knew was there but couldn't, or wouldn't, acknowledge.

"I didn't tell you any of this."

"Okay."

"And Mack? Brigit is not to leave the county."

He no sooner closed his phone than it rang with an unfamiliar number.

"Hello?"

"Mack, it's Shooter Jackson. How's Brigit? Is she okay? She's with you, right?" Questions tumbled out, one on top of the other.

"She's okay, Shooter."

"Jesus, I tried to stop her, man, I really did. I ran after her car but she just flew out of there. I'm sorry, Mack. I should have stopped her."

"It's all right, Shooter."

"Can I see her? Can I talk to her?"

"She's sleeping right now. I'll tell her you called."

Mack closed his phone again and turned to face his sister, who lumbered slowly into the kitchen. A putrid cloud of alcohol-tinged sweat preceded her. He'd given her one of his t-shirts to sleep in. Now he could see both her knees were swollen and purple, with scabs of dried blood clinging to cuts on her legs. Long scrapes ran down both her forearms. Her mass of tangled hair had come free from her ponytail and covered most of her face, but he could see a cut on her forehead. He hadn't been thinking straight last night; they'd been at the hospital, but he hadn't thought of getting her seen by a doctor.

"Oh, Brigit. Your head, you might need stitches," he said.

"It's okay. There was an ambulance there last night. I'm fine," she said crossly. "But I could use some coffee."

"Brigit, you are not fine. Let's go." He scrambled around for his keys.

"What, you want to find me a room next to Dad's? That'll take care of everything, won't it? Gee, maybe we can have lunch together. Play checkers," she snorted.

"Stop it. I'm trying to help you."

"Then make me some damn coffee. I need to call work." She sat carefully down in a kitchen chair and winced. "Can I use your phone? I don't know where mine is. I don't even know where my wallet is."

"Call work? And tell them what?" He held out his phone to her. She hesitated.

"Who were you just talking to?"

"Sheriff's office."

"That must have been a cheerful call."

"I did it for you."

"That's so thoughtful of you, Mack. Let me bake you a cake." She got up and started to rummage in his cabinets. Cans of soup were lined up alphabetically, labels out, by type. Chicken noodle next to chili next to tomato. "Christ, we a little OCD here, Mack? Everything in its place, perfectly lined up. Expecting the Queen?"

"I don't think you understand how much trouble you're in here, Brigit."

"I don't think *you* understand how much trouble *you're* gonna be in if I don't find some effing caffeine in me real soon." She opened another cabinet door, pushed the contents around, left it open and moved on to the next one.

Mack rose, lined the cans back up and shut the doors behind her. "I don't have coffee."

She looked at him as if he'd announced he drank arsenic instead. "I thought all alkies drank coffee. Isn't that, like, your thing?"

"Caffeine's just another drug. And stop deflecting, Brigit. We're talking about you."

"While that is usually my favorite subject, right now I'd actually rather not. Let's just get going. We can grab a Doubleshot when we gas up."

Mack stared hard at Brigit. He could tell she was in pain by the way she flinched sitting down. He could almost admire her strength, if it wasn't so wrapped up in her stubbornness.

"Where, exactly, is it you think we're going?" he asked her.

"To find Kieran."

"Brigit, we are not going anywhere."

"We talked about it this morning."

"No, *you* talked about it."

"Don't you want to see Kieran?" She stared at her brother.

"Let's not make this about what I want. What I want is to go back to yesterday and have none of this shit staring me in the face."

"But it is. Sorry my messy life intruded on the perfect existence you have carved out here. Sorry Dad collapsed on your sweet plan to have nothing ever, ever happen to you. Shall I re-alphabetize your soup cans for you? Would that make you feel better?"

"Shut up."

"No. No, I won't shut up!" She stood and faced him, face twisted with anger. "You have a choice to make, Mack. Fix this goddamn family or forget about it!"

"Sit down. Don't get all excited!"

"You know what, Mack? Fuck you! Nothing's changed. You were a different person out there, in your precious little garden of death. I liked that Mack much better." Brigit stormed out of the kitchen. She kicked the cans away from the front door, flung it open and walked out.

Mack raced after her.

"You can't leave!" he shouted. "I'm responsible for you!"

"No one's responsible for me anymore!"

"You're not allowed to leave town!"

"I'm going to New York!" she yelled back over her shoulder. "I'll find him myself."

Mack watched her thundering down the street in her bare feet, t-shirt flapping behind her, into the setting sun. He waited, but she didn't even turn around to look at him. She would go to New York, he knew this suddenly. He'd lose her, too. For a moment, he pictured the peace in his life without Brigit to worry about. Without Caleb. Without anyone.

When she turned the corner, he jumped in his truck and barreled after her. He slowed and rolled down his window as he caught up to her.

"Get in the truck!" he yelled.

"No!" she yelled back without looking.

"Brigit, get in the damn truck."

"I'll hitchhike. Someone'll pick me up."

"Look at you. You look like someone already picked you up and flung you back out."

"I'm going!" Cars were honking as they steered around the two of them.

"Could we please not do this on the street?"

This finally halted her.

"Why? What possible difference could it make? You think people don't know about us? You think people don't know all about the McKinseys? This is who we are!" She waved her arms over her head, jumping up and down frantically and yelling. "Hey! I got really drunk last night and crashed my car! I should have died! I should have died!" She sank down to the pavement suddenly, sobbing. "I should have died."

Mack pulled to the curb, turned off the truck, and got out. He walked over and sat next to Brigit. She put her head in his lap and cried as he stroked her hair.

"We'll go, Brigit. We'll go."

"I don't need you," she sobbed at him.

"I know."

Mack helped her into the truck and let her cry. By the time he'd driven past his house and parked in front of her apartment, she was quiet. She trudged through her front door and he stepped in after her. He stopped, taken aback. Someone had ransacked her place. Books were tossed open upon their spines, desk drawers were pulled awry, couch cushions littered the floor and tangled clothes were thrown everywhere.

"Stop!" Mack grabbed Brigit's arm. "Someone's broken in. They might still be here."

"No one's here, Mack," Brigit pulled her arm away. "Welcome to my house."

A dirty gray tabby, licking out an empty tuna can balanced on top of a pile of unopened mail, looked up, hissed at Mack, and scurried out.

Brigit waded through a pile of clothes on her way into the bathroom. He heard her start the shower. He didn't remember her being such a slob, but that was something Caleb wouldn't have allowed. Everything had to be up off their bedroom floors or he'd take it. Mack had lost a valuable baseball card collection that way. This was Brigit's freedom. Suddenly he wished Caleb could see it.

She came out of the bathroom wrapped in a towel. Some of the blood had been washed off, and her hair was clean now. She grabbed a pair of jeans and a shirt off the floor and retreated back into the bathroom. Mack pushed a bra and a Rolling Stone magazine from a chair and sat down. She came out with a canvas bag and proceeded to stuff clothes in it. Then she stood in front of Mack.

"I'm ready."

"What about your cat?"

"Not my cat. Just hangs out sometimes. Let's go. Let's go right now."

The sun was fading behind the mountains. What they needed,

Mack thought, was a good dinner and a solid night's sleep. A map. A plan. Something. Anything.

"Mack, if we don't go right now we never will. Please, can we go?"

He took out his phone and called the hospital.

"This is Mack McKinsey. I'm calling to check in on my father, Caleb McKinsey."

"Mr. McKinsey, I'm afraid your father had a stroke last night. It was right after you left, we tried to get hold of you."

"Did she say, a stroke?" Brigit set down her bag and looked at her brother. "How is he?"

"He's stable now. Your brother is with him."

"My brother?" Mack felt an electric charge to the back of his neck.

"Lonny? Isn't Lonny your brother? He's been sitting with him all day."

"Right. Good." Mack should have known. "Would you just tell Lonny that I have to go out of town for a couple of days?"

"Do you understand how serious your father's illness is?"

"My father asked me to bring him something. There's no point in me coming back to the hospital without it."

Mack hung up. He turned to Brigit. "You still want to do this?" Brigit nodded. "Because before we leave, I have to make sure you know what's at stake. And don't give me any grief, Brigit. This is how I operate."

"Okay," she said.

"Don Bartholomew told me you are not allowed to leave town," Mack's voice was flat. "So that's number one. We're breaking the law. There might be criminal charges against you. Or maybe me too, I don't know. You have a hearing in ten days to decide if you're going to jail. Your car's totaled. And Caleb can't call in any favors to get you out of this one. Do you understand?"

"You would have made a good cop, Mack."

"Number two is you can't tell anyone we're leaving. Not even Annamae. I will call the restaurant and tell them you had an accident and won't be back for a while."

"Okay."

"And you can't drink. That's number three."

She looked up at him.

"You *cannot* drink."

"Okay, Mack."

"You promise?"

"I promise."

"You *promise?*"

She nodded.

"All right." Mack bent over and picked up her bag. "Then we'll go."

CHAPTER 15

Lonny sat in the lot of the University of Virginia Medical Center and thought how very much he didn't want to go into this hospital. He watched the sparkling glass doors slide quietly open and shut as people walked in and out. They didn't even having to pull a handle. When the doors opened, each whoosh of escaping air carried the faint scent of artificial lavender air freshener that didn't quite cover the smell of diarrhea and decay.

There was nothing good in there. Nothing except Caleb, and he didn't belong here. But Lonny himself had delivered him here, panicked when he thought Caleb might die.

Lonny thumped his palms rhythmically against the steering wheel, beating the feeling back into them. They'd been clasped around the wheel for the half-hour drive from Touraine, and too long in any one position froze them up. His hands functioned okay, though he couldn't feel much there. Now that he'd hit forty, it was harder in the morning to get them limbered up. He flexed each finger, forcing it to bend.

His teenage accident was his own damn fault, he knew that. He'd let his mind wander. A heifer had just freshened and was not mixing in with the rest of the herd; she'd charged the fence, splitting a rail. Caleb was fixing the post with new timber, Lonny using both hands to hold up the middle rail. Mack and Kieran had been climbing a tree nearby, getting higher and higher out onto skinny little branches that surely wouldn't hold them up. Lonny did not think they should be so far up in the air. But the boys were laughing and teasing each other to go higher. Mack disappeared behind some leaves and Lonny turned his head to look for him. One of them was going to fall, he was sure of it.

"Lonny!" Too late he heard Caleb yell.

The heavy top rail slipped the notch and crashed down on his hands with a crunch of bones. He fell to his knees and gasped as he tried to move his hands, but they were trapped between the logs. Crushing, solid pain rose in clouds when he closed his eyes. Crows fled the telephone line with a warning cry. Caleb ran over and hoisted the rails up.

"Pull 'em out, boy," Caleb said.

Lonny opened his eyes. Caleb was straining to lift the logs, but Lonny's hands wouldn't move. They lay against the unyielding wood, all ten fingers bent too far back in the wrong direction.

"Lonny! Pull yer damn hands out!" Caleb yelled. He was shaking now with the effort of holding up both rails.

"I can't," he said, looking up in confusion.

"Jesus," Caleb bent over, slid his shoulders under the rails, and shrugged them away. They crashed onto the ground, taking down the posts on both ends. Lonny's ruined hands slipped off the bottom beam. He watched them pulse with blood, pumping up and down. He squealed like a mouse he'd found once, pinned across the middle in a trap, furiously scrabbling its feet uselessly as blood seeped out of its middle.

"It's okay, boy. It's okay." Caleb was right there.

"Hurts," Lonny whispered.

"It does, I know it does. Shh, now. It's okay," Caleb rubbed Lonny on the back. Lonny let a couple of tears roll down, but he wasn't really crying if he didn't let it out on purpose.

"I'm gonna pick up your hands now, and that's gonna hurt worse," Caleb told him.

"No," Lonny said.

"We got to take a ride to the doc and get you a band-aid or two. Mack! Get down here and bring me my jacket."

It was Kieran, just seven years old, who skittered down the tree and grabbed his father's jacket, running it over to them. Caleb took it without looking and slid it underneath Lonny's flattened, bleeding hands. They were swollen, split and covered with dirty wood chips. Lonny thought they looked like a slow animal by the side of a fast highway. Caleb wrapped his jacket tightly around Lonny's hands. He squealed again and could feel Caleb wince. Lonny wobbled on his feet. He wanted to close his eyes again and fly off with the crows.

"Lonny! Ya got to stay with me, here, boy," Caleb said sharply.

Lonny was strong, he knew this, everyone knew this. He figured it was what made him worth having around. He always wanted to do what Caleb told him, but he was shivering now and it wasn't even cold.

Caleb gathered Lonny up in his arms and carried him across the field. He placed him carefully across the seat of the truck, then jumped in and drove off. Kieran ran after him and straight into the house, yelling for Maeve. Mack had watched it all from the top of the tree.

Lonny did not like the medical people at the hospital. He was confused; too many faces came in too close to his, yelling at him. Someone slapped him, but he couldn't put his hands up when he tried. They asked questions that weren't really questions and they'd just do whatever they wanted no matter what he said. "We're just going to have a shot now, okay?" And it didn't matter if he said no, they didn't even give him time to say no, they just gave him the shot. They were not to be trusted. They wrapped his crushed fingers in huge white bandages, giving him glove-like Mickey Mouse hands and leaving him helpless. Caleb sat in the hallway and waited until Lonny finally came out, drugged and miserable, unsteady on his feet.

"Where are his parents?" The nurse asked Caleb, holding some kind of forms. Lonny leaned back against the wall and closed his eyes.

"God only knows," Caleb said.

"He's under eighteen, he needs a legal guardian."

"Give it here. I'll sign it."

"Are you his legal guardian?"

"I said I'll sign it."

"Legally, we cannot release him without a parent."

"I'm guessing this is about money." Caleb stood and stepped forward. "I'm Caleb McKinsey. You'll get paid." The nurse backed away.

Caleb had put his arm around Lonny. "Come on, son. I'm taking you home."

A flash of sun glinting off the windshield of a car pulling in the hospital lot jolted Lonny back to the present. He forced his stiff hands to unclench from the steering wheel. He grabbed the old fedora along with a bag containing the items Caleb had asked him to bring, including the manila envelope from his lawyer. He had not fulfilled Caleb's other request. He needed to hear it one more time, because there was no undoing something like that. He slid out of the truck, heading toward the doors.

"Mr. Allen?"

Lonny turned to see two men in sunglasses and suits standing behind him.

"I'm Mark Peterson from the ATF, and this is my partner, Julian Miller. I wonder if we could ask you a couple of questions?"

Lonny glanced up at Peterson and the shield he held out. He recognized their car right away; he'd seen it driving up and down the road to the farm a few times. The day before Seamus O'Hearn's life went up in flames, they had driven right up to the McKinsey house. Lonny had watched from the barn as they knocked, then walked around the entire place very slowly, looking at everything. The tall one had even tried a window, but gave up when he discovered it was locked. They'd started for the barn, and Lonny froze. A cellphone rang, and both stopped when the short one answered, then sprinted back to the car and sped away.

"Is there a place we can talk?" Peterson asked him.

" 'Bout what?"

"We're investigating the accident at Seamus O'Hearn's place. You know anything about that?"

"No," Lonny turned around and stepped toward the hospital doors. Peterson slid around fast to block him, towering over him; he had to be six foot six at least.

"Did you know O'Hearn was making illegal whiskey?" Miller asked abruptly from behind him.

"That right?" Lonny did not turn back.

"You know what that business is like, don't you? Dangerous."

"Don't know."

"Seamus O'Hearn is in serious trouble here, Lonny," Peterson said. "Those fires can get way out of control, and we don't want to see anyone get hurt."

Lonny knew the best thing he could do was keep quiet. They had him caged in, and he could feel the sweat blossoming, his shirt sticking to the small of his back as he stared at the sidewalk. Caleb was their prey, and he had to keep them away. He slid quickly to the left and inside the hospital doors.

"Tell Caleb McKinsey we're waiting for him," Miller yelled after him as the doors swooshed shut behind him.

"There's the guy we should be watching," Peterson said, staring after Lonny.

"Huh? He's not even family," Miller retorted. "Just a hired hand."

"Then why's he so terrified? When I looked in Mack McKinsey's eyes, I saw confusion. When I look at Lonny Allen, I see fear. He's spent more time with Caleb than any of his children. He's the Tom Hagen here, Miller. He knows more than anyone."

"Lonny Allen? He's not that smart." Miller headed back toward the car.

"Don't confuse quiet with stupid." Peterson turned to his partner. "It's time to call for a drone."

"You sure?" Miller's voice rose in excitement.

"That sloppy FBI surveillance flight spooked O'Hearn and made him blow up the whole operation himself. But an unmanned aircraft system will find McKinsey's still."

"You know how much those things cost, right? It's five figures plus the pilot," Miller said.

"I thought this was what you were hoping for all along."

"It is. I'm glad you're finally on my side." For the first time during this trip, Miller's entire face broke into the grin of a child at Christmas. "Have you seen the new ATF drones? They're white, just two thin blue stripes on the top, invisible against the sky. No one'll see it coming."

"You want one for your birthday? Make the call."

Lonny caught the eye of a nurse who'd seen him cornered by the agents, and quickly looked down as he made his way to Caleb's room. He tried to shake off the accusations, but they'd scared him. They'd dig in like stubborn gophers, until they were forced away, by any means necessary. Lonny knew how to keep vermin out of the fields. He'd plan for that later. Right now, though, he needed to see Caleb.

He'd known Caleb was sick before the old man had. He got a smell to him. Like an old cow drying up; a floury, powdery scent. It was as if you could stroke their hides and pieces of the soft skin would flake off in your hands like a worn-out leather jacket. It wasn't until the cow smelled it on herself and got the look in her eyes that meant she knew she was dying. But Lonny hadn't seen that look in Caleb's eyes. Yet, anyway.

He was sleeping, so Lonny sat on the hard plastic chair next to his bed. He put the bag with the items Caleb wanted under the chair, and held the envelope Caleb had asked him to bring. He was bound to ask if he'd taken care of the other task, and Lonny was not prepared to lie. He did not want to wire up explosives on Caleb's secret still, as Caleb had demanded during the furious ride to the emergency room. He understood the urgency, but the position of the still site was far off any road and so thickly covered with trees it was likely the entire mountain would be engulfed in flames. There would be no saving anything up there.

Lonny stopped anxiously twisting Caleb's hat in his hands. The old man never went out without the hat. He still had a full head of thick hair, silvered and swept back like a lion's mane. Lonny leaned over the diminished man in the bed and took a big sniff; the floury scent still lingered. He'd hoped maybe the doctors could give him a shot or something and fix it.

He supposed there were some things beyond fixing, though, and this might be one of them.

CHAPTER 16

Caleb braced himself before opening his eyes. He hated goddamn hospitals. He knew how to heal his own self. He cracked his lids and tried to push himself up on his elbows, but it felt like they'd set an anvil on his chest. He flopped back down; couldn't even sit up, wasn't that a damnable thing. Couldn't remember how he'd gotten here, either. On his front porch one minute, here the next. That was a little bit scary. He'd lived his life knowing what was going on all the time. Doctors kept stuff from you, though, he knew that. He'd be making his own decisions, by God, that was for sure.

He swiveled his head around, but he was alone. On the chair next to his bed was his hat, and under it, the envelope from his lawyers. He squeezed his eyes shut. Lonny. He'd asked Lonny to bring these things, along with … something else. What was it?

A memory was poking his brain, and he could see Brigit standing in the doorway, yelling at him. Now what the hell had she done? That girl was always on about something. He'd thought her mother had been stubborn and hard to please, but Brigit had it tenfold. Well, he'd soon teach her a thing or two. He tried again to rise, but again, he could barely move. Did something fall on me? he wondered. Am I paralyzed? He stared at his toes and willed them to move. They twitched. That was a relief. He'd rather to break his neck clear through than be pushed around in a wheelchair, and he didn't care who thought he was nuts about that.

An image of Mack flashed in his brain. Another memory. They'd been here together, he was sure of it. Brigit and Mack, the two of them standing side by side after all this time. His daughter and son talking. The picture brought a smile to his face. That was a start. And he'd told them … Christ, it was too damn sunny in here. Couldn't think with the sun in his eyes like that. He'd told them what? It slipped away.

He rolled his head from side to side, trying to clear his brain. There was a lump in his throat which he tried to swallow and couldn't. His air pipe seemed to've necked down to a pinprick. The gravel at the back of this throat rubbed him raw. He needed a drink of water. Caleb saw a plastic cup on a table next to his bed. He reached for it and watched it crash to the ground, water flowing away under his bed. He licked his lips, but even they were dry.

Kieran came to him suddenly, making his head hurt. He stood silently in the hospital room doorway. Caleb waved him into the room, but his youngest son didn't move. Just stood looking down on Caleb.

"Kieran?"

But he would not reply.

"Come on in here, boy. It's been a long time."

There was something wrong, though. Kieran wouldn't speak. Caleb shook his head. Now the doorway was empty. Shit.

Caleb needed them all together, in the same room, at the same time. He didn't give a crap what kind of shape their lives were in, he had something to say. He remembered telling Mack and Brigit there was money, and how that'd perked them up. All that money. He'd been chasing it his whole damn life. He knew his kids having money would probably make their lives worse, not better. Let them earn it, same as he did, had always been his motto.

He was so goddamn thirsty. He'd give them money for a drink of water right now, that was for sure. He tried to sit up again, but couldn't.

What the hell was going on? The sun was burning his eyes, and his throat was on fire. He wished he was back on his own porch.

Brigit was yelling at him again. Why wouldn't her mother tell her to hush up, now? Couldn't they see he wasn't feeling well? Stupid women. She was on about the jewelry box. Maeve's damn jewelry box, which Brigit had tried to take when she moved. It was the only thing she had of her mother's, she said. But....

The box. Caleb shook his head to clear it. Had to concentrate. That was the other thing he'd asked Lonny to bring. Only Caleb knew what was in there. He had to set things straight before it was too late. Another fall off the porch, or whatever the hell, and it might could be too late. He looked again. There was a bag under the chair, and the lawyer's envelope lay under his hat. He stopped; had he signed those papers? He clenched his eyes shut tight to remember, but it wouldn't come. He tried to reach the envelope to check, but his arm refused his command.

"Luuh," Caleb croaked. Maybe Lonny was in the hall.

A gray-haired nurse poked her head in, pasting on one of those fake smiles they kept in a jar for patients.

"Oh, you're awake, Mr. McKinsey."

"Luuh," He needed Lonny.

"Let's see how you're doing." She crossed to his bed.

"Luuh." Damn it, the words were in his head, but they were getting stuck in his throat. He needed her to bring him a drink of water.

"How are we feeling today?" She cooed at him like a baby, as she adjusted monitors and tubes and all that other nonsense they hooked you up to in hospitals.

"Wuuh ..."

"What can I get for you, Mr. McKinsey?"

"Luuh!" He had to get Lonny to bring him that jewelry box. Maybe he could write it down. He tried to shoo the nurse away with his right hand, but the arm just lay there.

"Calm down, Mr. McKinsey."

Caleb thought he could reach the tray table, but this damn claw that used to be his left hand tangled in a tube which disconnected his catheter and crashed to the floor, splattering the bed and Christ, nothing worse than the smell of a man's own piss.

"Oh, Mr. McKinsey," she chided. They both looked at the clinging yellow drops on her shoes.

"Luuh!"

"Do you remember what happened? You had a stroke in the middle of the night."

"Luuuuuh!" Where the hell was Lonny?

"Try to calm down. I know you're in pain, and I have your shot right here."

No, he couldn't go back to oblivion. He had things to do. She approached him warily, the hypodermic vertical in one hand, silver needle gleaming.

You stupid old cow, he thought as he twisted around on the bed, batting at her. She held his right arm down easily and the needle pierced his skin. Get away from me with that needle. You stupid woman....

... And then the scent of Maeve filled his head, all windblown grass and Virginia wildflowers. He relaxed and scanned the field for her. She was planting, spade stabbing into the dirt and loading tulip bulbs as the boys toddled after butterflies nearby. Kieran had been born right on top of Mack, a little over nine months later, and they were inseparable. Caleb thought Maeve would be overwhelmed by two infants, but she blossomed instead. She looked up and smiled at him, and his heart was complete. He'd never known how much he was missing until he had found her.

After the wedding and her coming to Virginia, it didn't take her long to learn of his criminal enterprises. The good life he could provide contented her to look the other way—for a while. She almost enjoyed the thrill, until she became a mother, when things changed. She wouldn't have her babies grow up outlaws. Maeve had given him an ultimatum: go legitimate with the moonshine or she'd leave, and take her sons back to Ireland.

Caleb's hackles rose at the thought of having government grunts crawling up his ass. He'd done so well, why couldn't she leave him be? But she was adamant. And there was no middle ground. He had to admit, she did the research, the endless paper filing, the meetings. The money he'd had to front for the license was obscene, and he never let her forget how much she cost him. But Maeve could, and did, charm the very pants off these guys from Alcoholic Beverage Control. It was all Caleb could do to shake their damn hands at first. He found it more than a little ironic being judged by assholes who never said no to a "product sample." Especially one served by Maeve, with her lilting accent and saucy smile.

When the lawyers suggested it was time for him to incorporate, Caleb was again resistant. But there were tax breaks that would save them a lot. Forming the board of directors was another headache Caleb didn't want, but Maeve was happy to attend meetings with him, and acted as a great soundboard whenever there was a conflict, which, with Caleb, was often. There were raised voices at one meeting over a safety issue at the distillery. Maeve had stepped in with a comment and gently steered them back to a compromise instead of accusations and finger-pointing. After the meeting, Fred Baldwin, a well-dressed young county commissioner and new board member, took Caleb aside.

"She's quite an asset to the company," Fred said.

"She is."

"Makes me want to go to Ireland."

"I hear Dublin's beautiful."

"I thought Maeve was from Galway."

Caleb winked at him without smiling, a subtle message.

"Don't ever lose her," Fred said.

"Don't intend to."

Caleb shook his hand before joining Maeve. By a unanimous vote,

Baldwin was voted off the board by the next meeting.

But she'd faded, somehow, or become smaller. Caleb could see the mane of russet curls in the distance; it was Brigit, not her mother, although the resemblance was strong. Brigit had just turned six, and was skipping down Touraine's Main Street, captured in a lively conversation with a leggy young blonde. Estelle, the librarian, Brigit's new friend, who looked to truly enjoy his daughter.

"Estelle says the Little House books set a good foundation for a serious reader," Brigit announced one evening at dinner.

"Is that so?"

"Yes, she says reading is a fundamental skill."

"Girl must be new here."

"She is. And she likes me because I am a fundamental reader."

Each night there was a new pronouncement.

"Estelle says good spelling is very important."

"Estelle says everyone needs to stay in school."

"Estelle says you must match your socks and brush your hair every day."

This was when Caleb decided to check out Estelle the librarian. He was cautious to have another adult, who wasn't even family, take such an interest. Turned out she was a graduate student pursuing her Ph.D. in library science at the University of Virginia, and doing an internship at the Touraine Public Library. Maybe a little too much education, Caleb thought, but he didn't see any ulterior motive. Brigit needed a female influence in her life, and Estelle seemed like a good fit. She made Brigit smile, chattering on about school.

Then one night Caleb saw two sloppy bandages covering both of Brigit's knees.

"What happened to your knees?" he'd asked.

"Estelle doesn't like me anymore." Brigit stared at her plate with a wet-eyed refusal to cry, but would say no more.

Caleb tromped out to his truck and drove away in the middle of dinner. Everyone knew he did not suffer fools, and if he was bored, he simply went on his way.

The next week Estelle was gone from the library, gone from Touraine, and gone from Virginia. A rare collection of first edition *Little House* books appeared under a brass plaque that meant someone had made a significant donation to the library. It read simply, "For my daughter, the reader." Caleb waited for a thank you or a hug, but it never came. He groused silently about the ingratitude of his children once more. Brigit never saw the rare books or the plaque; she was done with the library.

But Caleb knew something was wrong now. Maeve should have been reading those books to Brigit, but she couldn't. Maeve was gone. He didn't want to remember that. He hadn't done the right thing by his little girl, somehow. Now he reached out to comfort Brigit, but she, too, was gone.

CHAPTER 17

A white-hot sun beat down on the solid, sweltering block of cars at the entrance to the Holland Tunnel going into Manhattan. Mack sighed as he shifted the truck into neutral until the traffic started to inch forward again. They were driving entirely too slowly and his engine had the worrisome high-pitched whine which meant it was about to overheat. He wiped the sweat off the back of his neck. Too early for it to be this hot. The heat was scorching everything, visible waves of it rising off the hoods of vehicles floundering slowly onward, like toddlers learning to walk. There was no air moving at all, and a throbbing headache was taking over from the fumes of exhaust and hot engines. Cars and vans and trucks and even buses cut in front of him repeatedly. Mack kept slamming on his brakes as they forced their way into his lane, missing his front bumper by inches as they winnowed down from sixteen lanes into nine toll lanes and then into two, just *two*, lanes through the actual tunnel. Mack knew this because he had plenty of time to count them as he lurched and stopped repeatedly. If his truck overheated in the middle of this muddle of steaming, pulsing vehicles, he'd just get out and walk away.

He glanced over at Brigit to gauge her level of misery. Her bare feet on the dashboard were beating to the rhythm of the music in her headphones. Her head hung out the window, staring up with a stupid grin like a golden retriever. She acted like she was on vacation. He frowned in wonder at his sister. She was in so much trouble, and yet, she could just let it all go and enjoy herself. His head throbbed. Someone laid on the horn behind him, waking him from the momentary reverie to shift back into drive and move the six inches he'd been afforded. Brigit turned around and waved happily. Christ, he thought, they couldn't look more like hicks if Grampa Joad was sitting in the back of the truck playing a banjo in a rocking chair.

"Ooh! Take this!" Brigit yelled at him, too loudly because of the headphones.

"What?" Mack flinched.

"This part here! Over to the right. See? It says 'EZ Pass' so it must be easier."

"Well, shit, Brigit, if it was easier why wouldn't everyone take it?"

Mack decided he needed to grow a bigger set if he was going to make it through this trip. He veered sharply to the right, barely missing the long, sleek hood of a black Mercedes SUV. He gunned it again, gluing his front bumper to the rear of the car in front of him. Not giving an inch. This was how you did it, then. You forced your way into the city.

When his truck was finally spat out the other end of the tunnel, cars leapt forward like escaped piglets running from the barn. They zigged in front of one another, swerving wildly and speeding away. There were signs to uptown and downtown and Brooklyn and he knew he wanted downtown, but that was two lanes over to the left and he could not get over fast enough with all the squealing vehicles shooting out behind him like they'd been lubed up and released. Mack stayed in his lane, ignoring the sharp horns reminding him he did not belong here. Sweat continued to trickle down his neck. His shoulder was tight, he needed to pop it, and he desperately wanted to get out of this truck.

What with packing, locking up his house, and readying the pickup, they'd not gotten on the road until well after nine p.m., much to the consternation of Brigit, who sat and commented loudly on his careful planning. Finally, calls made to cover their absence and maps highlighted for their journey, they drove out of Touraine. They first got lost driving through D.C., caught in endless circles because Brigit wanted to see the Capitol at night, although not several times in a row, as she stated to Mack, in case somehow he'd missed that they were lost. They made it back to I-95 only to hit construction, two accidents, and a logjam around Philadelphia. Brigit had suggested they stop there too, to see the Liberty Bell, but one glance from Mack silenced her. What should have taken a little over six hours edged toward nine as they watched the sun rise over the Hudson River.

Mack found the downtown streets all twisted and dark, some of them going in diagonal directions and most of them one way. When he'd driven around the same block twice, dodging jaywalking pedestrians and car doors flying open suddenly on the narrow lanes, he was ready to explode. He glimpsed an opening next to the sidewalk and stomped on the gas, forcing the truck over to the left and narrowly missing a cab. He slammed on the brakes to furious honking and yelling in a language he did not understand. Mack violently flung his door open and jumped out. He was ready to bludgeon the cabdriver for this patch of curb. But Mack was not even a blip on the cabby's radar; the yellow taxi had already moved on.

"So where are we?" Brigit jumped out of the truck and came over to him.

"I don't know. We need to look at the map."

"Coffee!" she yelled suddenly. "Can I have some money?"

Mack pulled out his wallet and handed over a bill, and away she skipped into a deli with a big smile, hair swinging behind her. Mack pulled the map off the dashboard, trying to figure out where they were. The map lay on top of his stash of Kieran memorabilia, which he'd given to Brigit last night. It wasn't much. There was a postcard Kieran sent after his first week in the city, which showed a picture of

St. Mark's Place. He'd written *my new home* on it with an address on Avenue B. There were a couple of letters, one talking about how he played music at a bar called Blackie's and a phone number, which had been disconnected long ago. Two more postcards, the last asking Mack to please come soon.

I was only hours away, Mack thought. All these years, and Kieran had seemed so far. Kieran had asked him to come, begged him, in his letters. Mack had answered each one promptly, always telling his brother "Soon." Each had been returned stamped *not at this address*. One of the returned letters had a handwritten note. *Moved,* was all it said. Now he stared down at a map so crowded with miniature intersecting streets he expected them to start crawling off the paper like tiny ants.

Brigit came out with two cardboard cups and a brown paper bag. She rested their breakfast on the side of the truck bed, flipped down the tailgate, and jumped up. She held out a cup to Mack.

"This is tea, not coffee, since I saw you had tea in your cupboards. I did put a little sugar in it because you look like you need to wake up." She held it out, then rummaged in the bag. "And this is a chocolate cheese muffin which is about as big as your head. Or you can have the cranberry orange, also as big as your head. You look like a man in need of some comfort chocolate."

She held the muffin, nestled in a wax paper cover, out to him. Mack walked back to the tailgate, put down the tea, jumped up next to her and accepted it. She smiled and took a big bite right out of the top of her pastry.

"Oh, man, that's good," she mumbled through her chewing. "I was really hungry."

I don't have a plan, Mack wanted to tell her. He sat with tea in one hand, muffin in the other, staring at the cracked asphalt beneath his boots.

"Eat your muffin, Mack," Brigit said.

So he did.

They spread the map out when they were done eating. They would start at the last address Kieran had sent, then move on to the bar where he once played music. Looking at the addresses Mack could see that they were all in the same area, which made it a little easier. Maybe someone would remember him, or still knew him. He realized he was doing this all for Brigit now; it was the first time since her high school graduation party he'd seen her so full of hope.

"Youse gotta move the truck," a voice commanded.

"What?" Mack looked around.

A cop stood on the sidewalk, looking at them.

"Move the truck, buddy. This ain't no national park. Wrap up the picnic and move the truck."

"We were just—" Mack started.

"Hey, buddy, everybody's got a story and I heard plenty. I don't care if youse are bleeding to death here, *move the truck.*"

"Why?" Brigit asked.

"You kidding me, right? They don't teach you to read in the South, sweetheart?" The cop pointed up at the sign. *No standing, commercial trucks only, Sundays 7 a.m. to 7 p.m. only except alternate days, loading and unloading, 2 hour limit.* Mack wasn't sure if any of it applied to them, but the truth was, he hadn't even noticed it. Also, Brigit was talking back to a cop. Also, a rude cop. This would be it, the journey ended before it really began. He'd be bailing her out of a Manhattan jail this time, unless he occupied the cell next to her.

"What?" Brigit asked, her eyes narrowing.

"I got about five different tickets I can write you, and then I'm calling a tow truck." He pulled a fat ticket book out of his back pocket.

Brigit grabbed the map and jumped down, going over to the cop. Mack watched her paste a wide smile on her face and flip her hair back.

"Ah am just so glad to see a police officer!" Brigit said.

Mack was stunned at the sudden thickness of her accent, and the way she stood with her chest out, the map held out in front of her like an offering. "You can tell we are not from here! We drove all night long from Virginia, and now that we are here, well, we are just as lost as a pile of newborn puppies. See, we just have to find our brother. Our dad's real sick back home. If you could help me out a tiny bit, just take a quick little look at this map and tell us how to get to this address, we will scoot right on out of here."

The cop sighed. He looked at Brigit and shook his head. He leaned over the map and pointed.

"Youse take this street up three blocks, make a right on Houston, take that all the way down to Avenue A and make a left. Then you're a couple blocks from the park and it should be right around there."

"Thank you so much." Brigit gently touched his arm. "I don't know what we'd do without your help."

"Good luck. And pay attention to the street signs next time," he said, standing back with his arms crossed.

"Oh, we surely will! Thank you kindly, sir!" Brigit quickly climbed into the driver's seat. Mack wanted to object, but he jumped in the other side and off they drove, Brigit waving to her new-found friend in the New York City Police Department.

"Bye now! Thank you!" she yelled, smiling. As they joined the traffic up the street, she continued to wave as her smile turned to sneer. "Buh-bye, you condescending prick!" Her fingers fluttered merrily. "Choke on a doughnut!"

"What the *hell*, Brigit?"

"He can't hear us now, there's too much traffic."

"But how did you … ?"

"You learn all kinds of things as a waitress. Hey, did you notice? I'm driving your truck," she said gleefully.

"I did notice, and I didn't want to start an argument in front of a cop. But you knew that, didn't you?" Mack asked.

"Yup."

Brigit had no license anymore, so apparently barreling down the crowded streets of Manhattan was the logical choice. Mack stomped on the non-existent passenger side brake a few times before deciding that it was useless and just stared straight ahead out the windshield. Just roll with it, he decided. Brigit drove with confidence, not cowed by the traffic around her as he had been. It was impressive, he admitted to himself. After three years in exile there were things he did not know about his sister. He was both proud and sad at the same time.

What they hadn't counted on was parking in New York City.

"This is the address, I think," Brigit said, slowing the truck down. "Nice, he lives by a park." She ignored the honking behind her as she crawled around the block, looking for any opening big enough for the truck. There was nothing.

"Look at these signs, now. I don't want to have to suck up to another cop. Leaves a bad taste in my mouth."

They drove around several blocks, many times, hoping someone would leave. Mack cursed small cars he thought from a distance might be spaces. This was valuable real estate, and Mack began to wonder if these vehicles ever moved. Finally Brigit cut the wheels and dodged into a spot inches in front of a late model Honda, when she was rewarded with her first Bronx salute. They climbed out of the truck to look at the unyielding concrete city.

They were surrounded by tall buildings on all sides. Every half block a small, sad tree stood in a hard-packed square of dirt, struggling to reach any sunshine through the shade of the buildings. A rusted cage around the bottom served to catch the trash blowing down the sidewalk and thrust it up against the skinny trunk. A "Curb Your Dog" sign had been completely ignored as was evident by the hard piles of what Mack hoped was just dog poop. Why did they even bother, he wondered. This hostage tree was more depressing than the concrete.

Mack heaved both of their duffel bags into the back of the truck. He unlocked his aluminum toolbox, which ran the width of the bed behind the cab and was soldered to it. He stowed their bags in there, checking on the boxes of frozen peas as he did so. He'd hesitated on how many to bring; how much money would they need, really? It was New York; he packed them all. He was afraid to walk around with all that cash, but it would be safe here. No one was breaking into this steel-reinforced box. He secured the hidden built-in lock and jumped down. Brigit was already heading toward Kieran's last known address.

She was climbing the stoop to a building Mack could not imagine anyone wanting to call home. Pale gray cinderblocks poked through the chipped brown plaster of the exterior walls, which had been decorated by Paz, or so it read in large black, dripping letters of spray paint. Three dented metal trash cans overflowing with torn garbage bags spilling rancid food and cigarette butts were chained to a twisted fence in the front. Behind the fence was a tiny brown patch of empty garden, littered with sharp pieces of broken glass and used condoms. Not even a weed had attempted to root here. The windows directly above the dirt garden were secured by flaking metal bars on the outside, like a jail. Ripped vinyl shades, patched with duct tape, blocked their view of the inside.

Brigit was yanking on the thick steel front door, also painted courtesy of Paz. She turned back to him.

"What the hell, Mack? We came all this way and we can't get in?"

"You have to push the buttons." He climbed the steps and joined her. He pointed to the intercom, dented in several spots as if it had been punched; probably by Paz, he thought. Most of the tabs next to the buttons were empty, a few with barely decipherable names; none labeled McKinsey. "You push the button to his apartment, then he buzzes you in."

Brigit pushed a button and waited. When there was no reply, she jabbed at the other buttons like a carnival chicken waiting for a prize to pop out.

Mack thought this is where they became the most annoying of accidental tourists in New York.

"Wait a minute," he said. He pulled out Kieran's last letter. "Don't just randomly press people's call buttons. You trying to get us shot?"

"Okay, genius. Which one?"

"It's apartment 6R." There was a flicker of the shade at the garden window, then the studied stillness of someone who was watching them.

"Top floor, doesn't that figure," she said. She pushed that button and waited. There was no answer. She pressed it again. Same result.

"There's no one home," Mack said. He wondered if there was a way to leave a note.

"Mack, no offense to you buddy, but it's six-forty-five in the morning. *Someone's* home. They just don't want to answer," Brigit said, not looking at him. She pressed it again.

"So you're just going to keep buzzing until you wake someone up?"

"Yup."

"Brigit, we'll have to come back later. No one's going to answer."

"Excuse me, Miss Manners. Were we here on a social call?" She had a point, Mack thought. She kept pressing buttons.

"Yeah?" A crackly voice came through the intercom. Brigit let go and took a step back. Mack quickly leaned in and held the button.

"We're looking for Kieran McKinsey," he said into the box. There was a long pause.

"Not here," crackled the box.

"Does he *live* here?"

"Not here."

"Do you know him?"

"Not here."

"Can you tell me—" Mack started.

Brigit pushed him out of the way.

"Kieran's my brother. We drove all night long from Virginia looking for him. We really need some information," she said. "Can you just let us in to talk for a minute?"

Silence. Mack and Brigit looked at each other. Brigit jammed her thumb down on the buzzer and held it.

"Look, I got nowhere else to go. You might as well let me in and tell me what I want to know. I mean, I'm not going to leave, so if you are trying to sleep you might as well—"

The door buzzed and Mack grabbed it quickly open. He shoved Brigit inside and followed as the door slammed shut behind them. The smell inside made them both cover their noses. Not all the garbage was in the cans outside, and piles of sticky food containers were crunched into corners. Putrid cooking odors mixed with mildew almost masked the scent of dogs who had not made it outside to defile a tree. They felt their way to the back and up the stairs, holding a sticky railing to pull themselves through the gloom of the single unbroken light bulb on the second floor.

A thick waft of pot smoke drifted out from under a door on the fourth floor. Something glass crashed behind it, and peals of hysterical laughter followed. Mack pushed Brigit on until they reached the top floor. They rang the bell for 6R. There was no answer. She tried the knob, which was locked. She rang the bell again. Still no answer.

"Kieran? Are you in there? It's Brigit and Mack. Sorry it's so early. Sorry if we woke you up, but we really have to talk to you. Could you please open the door?" Mack heard a shuffling behind the door, then silence. "Hey, anybody in there? If Kieran's not here, could you please just open the door for a minute and talk to us?"

"Shut up!" A voice yelled from behind the closed door to an apartment down the hall. Brigit wheeled and kicked the bottom of the door, hard.

"Look!" she yelled. "Open the door! I don't know why you buzzed us in and made us climb through the seven circles of hell to get up here if you were just going to ignore us. We're trying to find our brother."

Mack's head was pounding now. Brigit leaned on the doorbell, and they could hear the buzzing inside. "Help us and we'll go away."

"Shut the fuck up out there!" Apartment 6A yelled.

"Why don't you come on out here and make us, you cockroach?" Mack yelled. He felt the explosion coming. "Someone here at some point knew Kieran McKinsey and they're going to tell us where he is or we'll call the police and report a burglary in progress. So unless you have a pretty big meth muscle on right now, *you* shut the fuck up!" Mack was red-faced and sweating now. Even Brigit backed away from him. But the door to 6R opened a crack.

"Tell Nick I don't have his money right now," a small voice whispered around the safety chain. "I can pay him next week."

Mack strode up and stuck his foot in the door. He leaned in close. "We don't know Nick, and we don't care about your money." He spoke just above a whisper. "We need some information about our brother Kieran. Let us in, it will take five minutes. Keep us out here and your neighbors are gonna beat the shit out of you because we will not stop." Mack slowly removed his boot from the door. The chain slowly rattled back, and the door swung slowly open.

Mack stepped inside, holding the door for Brigit. A scrawny teenage boy wrapped in a rough brown blanket stood down the hall. His hair was a mass of unwashed white boy dreads, flattened on one side and with a lock missing in the front where it looked like someone had snipped it off with scissors, as the remaining hair stuck straight out. He shifted from one foot to the other. Mack put his hand out, but the boy stepped even farther back.

"I'm Mack, this is my sister Brigit. We just drove up here from Virginia to find our brother," he said patiently.

"Yeah, Kieran, I know. I heard. Everybody in the whole damn building heard. Jesus." The boy turned and walked down the hall while scratching scab-covered arms. Mack glanced back at Brigit and they followed him.

"I didn't buzz you in, by the way. It was prob'ly the old lady on the first floor. She hates it when people use the intercom. She'll buzz anyone in just to shut them up. She never leaves her apartment, either. Used to have one of those little yappy dogs, and she'd let it out in the hallway to take a dump. I think it died, though. Probably someone she buzzed in killed it."

He dropped the blanket and stood clad only in a pair of boxer shorts so dingy they'd never see white again. He darted around the room, scratching at his elbows and searching under open books and newspapers. There were random piles of clothing in heaps everywhere as if dropping things where you stood was the order of the day. He found a half-smoked cigarette and lit it surreptitiously.

"I'm Ghi." He turned to Brigit. "You holding?" he asked with a hopeful arch to his eyebrows.

"No," Brigit stepped forward. "We're honestly just looking for Kieran. Does he still live here?"

"I don't know any Kierans. I know a Karen. But I don't think that's her real name." He scratched behind his ears.

"How long have you lived here?" Mack asked.

"Here? I don't really. I just crash here sometimes. That's what most people do. So, you know, maybe Kieran crashes here too. But I don't know him. Still, that doesn't mean he's not here. Except for right now. I know he's not here right now. You sure you don't have anything?" he asked Brigit again.

"Look, uh, Ghi, whose apartment is this?" Mack asked slowly. He'd seen this same unfocused look before. "Don't scare the wild donkey," Caleb had told him. "Damn fool's been in the jimson weed and you don't know what it'll do." The donkey had brayed suddenly, violently twitched its ears, then taken off at a dead run into a tree, breaking its neck.

"My cousin Tess lives here. I mean, I think it might actually be her apartment." He picked up a dingy, half-empty glass of a clear liquid and drank it.

"Do you know when she'll be back?" Mack asked.

Ghi stared at him, unmoving. Then he scuttered over to a pile of rags and kicked it with his foot. "Hey, Tess, when will you be back?" he asked, snorting through his laughter.

A pure white head of silky hair rose up out of the rags. Without looking up, a hand shot out and smacked the cigarette out of Ghi's mouth. It rolled across the floor as Ghi crumpled to the ground and grabbed his face.

"Told you not to smoke in here, Ghi," she growled in a low voice.

"Excuse me? My name is Mack and this—" Mack started.

"Your sister Brigit and you're looking for Kieran," she replied. "I heard."

Brigit watched the cigarette smolder against a newspaper; she stepped on it.

"Thank you for putting that out. Idiot's going to burn my place down," Tess said.

"Do you know Kieran?" Mack asked her.

"I haven't seen him in years. Of course, I haven't seen much of anything in years, really," she said.

Tess finally raised her head and parted the curtain of her alabaster hair so Mack could see the fine blue veins pumping blood down the sides of her face underneath paper-thin translucent skin. She turned her face to him, revealing blistering red irises couched beneath long snowy eyelashes, framed by feathery white eyebrows. Her oval face was startling and morbidly beautiful. Mack couldn't look away. Her eyes were intensely focused and unsettling, until he realized that was an illusion she must have perfected.

"Holy shit, are you ... can you see?" Brigit said.

"Brigit!"

Tess rolled out a low laugh. "S'okay, I'm used to it. I'd rather people were forward like that. My sight's been fading for a while now. I can see your shapes, that's about all."

"I'm really sorry," Mack said.

"Why? It's not your fault," Tess said. She laughed again. "Another nice Southern boy."

"Do you know where Kieran might be now?" Mack asked.

"I heard a lot about you both. I was a little jealous, actually. He always said you were coming soon," Tess said. She stretched her thin frame into a long column and sat up. "Glad you finally made it."

"But we can't find him," Brigit said.

"I don't know where he lives currently. He used to play at Blackie's, it's a bar on Avenue A between Seventh and Eighth. Maybe someone there knows where he is."

"Does he have, like, a band?" Brigit asked.

"He plays with different bands, they change names and members too frequently to keep track. Late nights, sometimes, he used to play these old Irish songs by himself on his acoustic. Kieran could really bring in women. The owner's name is James Killroy, another fine Irish lad."

"So you don't have any idea where he lives now? Maybe a phone number?" Mack asked.

"A phone?" Tess rolled out that deep laugh again. "Whenever Kieran had a phone we'd all take bets on how long it would last. You could just ask him for it and he'd flat out give it to you, no questions. I don't know if he was careless, or tenderhearted, or both." She stood slowly, the cocoon of a quilt dropping to the mattress on the floor. "Honestly, no one was ever really sure where he lived. He stayed here for quite a while, but we had a, falling out, let's call it, and he never came back. I'd know him, though, if he walked in today. He always smelled clean, like Ivory soap."

"Thanks," Mack said. He shifted uncomfortably on his feet. "I didn't know ..."

"What, Kieran didn't write you long letters about taking his albino girlfriend to work at the Coney Island Sideshow?" Tess laughed.

"We should go. Sorry we woke you up and made such a fuss," Brigit said.

"Where're you staying? If I hear from him, I'll tell him to call you," Tess said. Mack pulled out his wallet and extracted a Sunshine Landscaping card. He wrote his cell number on the back and placed it in Tess's long, cool, white fingers.

"This is my cell phone on the back of the card," Mack said. He paused. "Is there anything you need?"

"Oh, you are Kieran's brother," she said softly as she released his hand. "He wanted to save me, too. But I don't need to be saved."

"You need food, though," Ghi said suddenly, jumping up. "I'll go get you some."

"Sit down, Ghi. You just want to score," she said.

"Thanks again for your time," Mack said. "If you can think of anything else, please call me." He felt large and unwieldy, suddenly, as if he were about to back into something precious and break it.

"Listen, if you need a place to crash, you can come back here," Tess called to them.

"Thank you, Tess. We appreciate it," Mack said. He stole a glance back at Kieran's unknown life. Dingy walls with cracks in the plaster, piles of clutter, strange drawings tacked up on the walls, and still more lived-in than his own home.

Ghi scrambled out the door after Brigit. She turned quickly to him. "You need to cut this shit out," she said. "Take care of your cousin." Planting a palm on his chest, she pushed him back inside the apartment and shut the door.

Mack sat down heavily on the stoop outside. He put his face in his hands.

"Well, that was a learning experience," Brigit announced as she joined him on the stoop. "God, these New Yorkers are weird."

"And what do you think they're saying about us right now?" Mack asked.

"I guess we were a little aggressive," she admitted.

"I don't know what we're doing, Brigit. I'm making it up as we go along."

"Yup," she said as she stood. "We should get some food."

He looked up. "How can you be so okay with all of this?"

"What would you like me to do, Mack? You're clearly in charge of all the worrying. What good will that do me? You worry, and I'll have ideas. Right now, my idea is food," she said as she set off down the sidewalk.

"You're going the wrong way," Mack yelled after her.

"Really?" she yelled back without turning. "How do you know?"

CHAPTER 18

Brigit knew they'd find Kieran. She refused to let the possibility of failure enter her mind. Growing up, there hadn't ever been much she was certain of, but she would bet her life on her brothers. They never talked about it, but she knew both Mack and Kieran had saved her as a child from much more severe beatings by Caleb. There had been bruises and scrapes, people saw them, and so what? You minded your own business in the country. She'd never considered that maybe, one day, she'd be the strong one. That maybe she'd be saving Kieran. She wasn't sure from what, but she knew the three of them needed to be together now.

In addition to finding Kieran, Brigit was determined to get as much out of this New York trip as she could. Since she'd never had the money to travel, she wanted to try everything. She wondered if she would be able to talk her brothers into showing her Fifth Avenue and the sparkle of Tiffany's, or going all the way to the top of the Empire State Building to see all of the city at twilight. She'd heard horror stories, especially about downtown where they were now, but the East Village didn't seem that scary. When she'd told people in Virginia that Kieran had moved to New York they shuddered and swore you'd never get them up there. But she inhaled the vivid streets, so full, so damaged, and so alive. She found a restaurant on St. Mark's Place, basing her decision on the groan it brought out of Mack when she halted in front of it. There was a patio, so they could enjoy people television from the street. She loved to look at different passers-by and try to imagine their lives.

Little tin holders perched on wobbly Formica tables, spitting out the kind of thin white paper napkins you'd get at an ice cream stand. Photocopied menus littered the table. The server strolled up in what Brigit could see was a sort of New York uniform—black pants, black shirt, heavy laced black boots with thick rubber soles of neon yellow. The sides of—her?—head were shaved to better display rows of earrings climbing all the way around the shells of her ears. The tuft of hair along the crown of her scalp was a brilliant magenta, combed straight down her forehead. Brigit tried to imagine dressing like that working at the Southern Way Cafe and burped a snort of laughter. The waitress looked at her.

"I'll have fa-la-fel," Brigit declared, pronouncing each syllable carefully. She had no idea what it was and wasn't going to ask.

"One falafel."

"Oh, okay. Fa-*la*-fel."

"Tahini with that? Hot sauce?" the waitress asked.

"Of course," Brigit replied confidently.

"Which?" the waitress asked.

Brigit did not flinch. She would not be bested by a hairstyle. "Both."

The waitress scribbled in her pad and turned to Mack.

"I'll have a cheeseburger please," he said.

She went off to put in their orders and, Brigit hoped, not to spit in them. Food service was hard, and tourists could be idiots. She herself treated her customers like toddlers about to have tantrums; she was patient, smiled a lot, and, when need be, called them "sugar." It bothered her not in the least, and she made excellent tips. She could teach this hairflop a thing or two.

Mack was staring blankly into space, eyes glazed. Brigit felt sorry for him. She'd bullied him into coming here. She followed her impulses a lot, and they were not always successful, she had to admit. Mack, on the other hand, craved security. She'd appreciated that as a teenager, when she could rail at him for injustices done to her by Caleb, and he would sit and listen without speaking. Then he would tell her that she had a lot of life to live and her time was coming, if she could just be patient. He'd usually slip her some money and tell her that their mother would be proud of her.

A flicker of shame shot through her. Mack was still slipping her money. Now he was paying for everything. Her purse had disappeared; her wallet, bank card, driver's license, all gone. She'd left a pile of wreckage back in Touraine. Her car was totaled. And she might go to jail.

Stop it! she thought. She wasn't tumbling into that briar patch right now. They had a mission. To find Kieran. And she'd pay Mack back.

Right now, though, she had to pump him back up. The lines around his eyes were set in the fashion of regret he wore too often. Brigit remembered him happy with Lauren until she broke up with him for good. The irony was that Lauren's leaving had driven him into sobriety; that was what she'd wanted, but it was too late, and the damage he had inflicted was too deep. With his dry spell came almost complete isolation, as if he were in a holding pattern. The only time she'd seen him excited in years was when he showed her Maeve's Garden.

Brigit flinched. She'd crushed that happiness. She had tried to see the beauty in his garden and understand the purpose, but she was sad that the carefully hidden foliage circus had been Mack's entire life for nineteen years. He had made a monument out of the dead, and now he needed a reason for living.

"Do you want to get a tattoo?" she asked him. His head rotated slowly toward her, as if he'd forgotten her. "There's a place across the street. We could go after lunch."

"What?"

"Maybe you could get one of those Celtic knots on your shoulder, that'd be cool. You know, like an Irish warrior."

"Right."

"I might get a leopard, something fierce, but I don't know whether to put it across my back or somewhere I can see it. Seems a waste to have a tattoo you can't see on your own body, doesn't it?"

"Waste would be a good word," he noted.

"Annamae was going to get a Tweety Bird on her forearm once, big one, going all the way from her elbow down to her knuckles, to cheer her up. Luckily she sobered up in time."

"Surprised you didn't try to talk her into it."

"Well she is kind of a Tweety Bird, if you think about it. You know she still has a little crush on you, right?"

"What?"

"Yeah. 'Course she's also a little afraid of you."

"Okay."

"She's actually sweet, she just comes across as kinda foolish because she says what's on her mind before she filters it through her brain."

"So you two have a lot in common."

"Was that necessary? Seriously, though. Do you have a girlfriend? Do you date at all anymore? And I ask because you seem pretty much a hermit. Your house is like one of those generic rentals they show on the news where the serial killer lived. I don't even have to look to know there aren't any lacy red panties under your couch cushion."

He sighed. "Why are we talking about this?"

"Because it's what people do, when they go out to restaurants. They talk. When was the last time we had an actual conversation?"

"Asking me about panties under my couch is conversation?"

"How is your love life?"

"I don't want to talk about this." Mack turned his head away again.

"I know you really loved Lauren."

"She was right to leave me. I was a mess."

"But you're not anymore."

"Brigit, stop."

"Sooner or later you have to pick the scab off. Maybe it's healed." She'd pushed too far, she thought suddenly. He was going to strike back at her now. At least he'd be angry instead of worried for a little while.

"There could be someone else who would make you smile," she added gently.

"Like Shooter Jackson makes you smile?"

"Well, the thing is …"

"Is that off or on this week?"

"How do you—"

"I pay attention. I know you two flip like fast food burgers. Where's it going, though? Any future there?"

"Okay, Mack."

"And speaking of the future, what exactly is your plan?"

She frowned. Hadn't he been listening, in Charlottesville, at the diner? She'd told him: take Bourbon Sweet Tea big time. Renovations. Topiaries. Curated high-class tours. Fine dining, a luxury hotel, a golf course. Make Touraine a destination. She wriggled with excitement, remembering the new flavors. She was twenty-one now. They could all vote their stock. Oh, she had plans, all right.

"Because waitressing is a fine career goal."

Was that a sneer? He was baiting her; this was their self-protection game. She needed to back down, for now. He wasn't ready, and she knew better than to sell sand to a thirsty man. She looked away.

"I get it, Mack, I get it."

"I'll make you a deal; I'll leave your future alone if you stay out of my past."

Plates were set down unceremoniously with a clatter.

"Anything else?" the waitress asked as she snapped the bill down. Brigit shook her head but the girl was already walking away.

The mouth of a tan pita leered up at her with chopped cucumbers spilling out around hard brown patties dripping with a gray sauce that smelled like horse feed. This was not what she was expecting. She'd thought it would be some sort of sausage. She stared down at it, not even sure how to eat it. She glanced at Mack, who had the same look of confusion as he examined a hefty pile of pungent bean sprouts piled on the top of his organic goat cheese burger. Everything smelled like hot, sweaty livestock. Mack looked up at her at that moment, and they both burst into laughter, unable to stop and drawing attention from nearby tables. They pulled themselves together, only to fall back into more laughter as their lunch mocked them.

"At least a bite?" Brigit said, wiping her eyes.

"A bite," Mack conceded.

She picked up the unwieldy package and took a large munch, which was a mistake. The hard, raw vegetables and rough chickpea concoction scraped the roof of her mouth while her tongue immediately rejected the fiery sauce and her gag reflex threatened to send it right back down on the plate. She held it in her mouth, not sure what to do. She grabbed a handful of napkins out of the dispenser and put her head down to spit her falafel into the napkins. Trying to surreptitiously scrape the dried-brick texture off her tongue, Brigit deposited the soggy wad back on her plate as the waitress reappeared. She glanced over at Mack, who looked like one of Lonny's cows with a wad of drooping bean sprouts hanging out of his mouth.

"Everything okay here?" she asked.

Mack was already standing and putting money down on the table.

"No, um, yeah, it's all good," Brigit said as she too rose. What the hell, she'd never see this fashion victim again. "We're just going to get some actual food," she said as she followed Mack out to the street.

"What the hell was that?" he asked as she joined him outside. "I felt like I was grazing in the cow pasture."

"Well, no wonder they're all so skinny here," Brigit said. "I think I need my mouth vacuumed."

"At least I chewed and swallowed. You spit it out."

"That was far too nasty to swallow," Brigit said. "What we really need to get that taste out of our mouths is a shot of something. This is when Bourbon Fire Tea would be great."

"Bourbon what?"

"It's a new flavor I'm thinking of. Bourbon and jalapeño. Spicy, powerful bourbon."

"*New flavor?*"

"*Additional* flavor. Look around, Mack. Don't these people look like they could shake things up? We need to think bigger."

"I just never thought of, I mean, it's always been Bourbon Sweet Tea."

"Yeah." She watched her brother considering the idea, which was what she wanted. "Things are gonna change, Mack, you watch."

"Look," he said, pointing. There was the sign they needed; *PIZZA,* in large red neon letters. They headed immediately toward Stromboli's on the corner.

After devouring what they both admitted was the best pizza they'd ever had, grease and all, they headed up the street toward Blackie's. The expanding metal safety gates were open, but the doors were still locked and the bar dark beyond the windows. They walked down Avenue A, stopping into tiny music stores and vintage clothing shops while checking on band flyers hanging from bulletin boards. Brigit had a picture of Kieran that she showed to store clerks, asking if they'd seen him. She knew the photo was old, but it was all she had.

Guitar music beckoned from Tompkins Square Park. They began to circle around in the park to see if any of the buskers were Kieran. Brigit followed Mack, trying to ward off the defeat that was dropping on her shoulders. She was not going to give up, though she was sweating from the still air engulfing them, not even a breeze moving between the buildings. She'd forced her brother to take her here; she couldn't let him see her give up.

She stopped in front of one of the musicians, a nondescript Latino guy who looked like he would pump gas off the interstate except for the ratty top-hat he wore. When he sang, however, he transformed into a puppet with jerky body movements and facial contortions like he was being electrocuted.

"Do you know him?" she asked, shoving Kieran's picture in his face when he was done. He looked not at the photo but stared silently at her. Brigit nudged Mack, who put a dollar in the guitar case open at his feet. She thought a flicker of recognition crossed his face as he looked at Kieran.

"The question is, does he know you? Maybe I don't know him, but I don't know a lot of people, if you know what I mean," he said to Brigit. She didn't know but she nodded anyway. "Call this drummer, Marshall, he knows everybody." He rattled off a phone number and looked straight up at her.

Mack called, listened for a moment, then hung up. "Voicemail."

Brigit grabbed his phone away. "Jesus, Mack, what's wrong with you?" She hit redial. "Hi Marshall, my name's Brigit McKinsey and I'm looking for my brother Kieran." The Southern Belle took over. "He plays guitar and a guy in the park said you were a real good drummer and might know him. If you do, could you tell him to call this number? Ah've come all the way to New York from Virginia and Ah really need to talk to him. Tell him his little sister misses him," she said, and hung up.

"And you think that's going to work," Mack said. Brigit slumped down on a bench desperate for a paint job.

"No, Mack, not really. But I'm trying," she said.

By early evening the previous night's long drive north was starting to take its toll. They'd dutifully marched all the East Village sidewalks, in and out of shops and restaurants, holding photos of Kieran and asking "Have you seen him?" in each, but with no results. The ludicrousness of their search was becoming clear to Mack. He was tired and frustrated. They circled back around to Tompkins Square Park and sat on a flaking green bench eating a "dirty-water dog" from a cart. It was decidedly less satisfying than the pizza. Brigit hung over the fence to the dog run, watching Pomeranians chase huskies and then victoriously kick up dirt with their tiny back feet.

"We should find a hotel, I guess," Mack said.

"I saw a place up the street," she said, reaching to pet a mutt, but it snapped at her so viciously she snatched her hand back.

They made their way to the St. Mark's Hotel. The front door opened on a dimly lit, windowless staircase. They climbed to a lobby with a small, old-fashioned reception desk. Someone had attempted to apply an Art Deco theme, but they'd either given up or run out of money halfway through; a large gilded frame on the rear wall was blank. Mack couldn't decide if the painting had been stolen or forgotten. A large man in a resplendent brown fur Cossack hat sat behind the desk, leafing through a foreign newspaper.

"You want room?" he asked with a seductive Russian accent.

"Yes," Mack replied. He pulled out his wallet. He tried to push down the resentment he felt about shelling out another wad of cash he'd saved for the garden. It was always for the garden. Always. He held the money out to the clerk.

"You have no Visa?" He scowled.

"What is wrong with cash?"

"Is my insurance you take care of room." The clerk crossed his arms and stared Mack down. Mack looked around the tattered, neglected lobby.

"Can't you give him a credit card, Mack?" Brigit whispered.

Mack looked back at the clerk, who hadn't blinked. He dug into the secret pocket of his wallet, and there was the unused card. Years ago, in an effort to establish credit, Mack had faced the humiliation of begging Caleb to co-sign for him to get a credit card. There was a lecture about responsibility, and Caleb had made him sign a note promising he'd never use the card. Mack had kept that promise until now. He pulled out the plastic, which released from the leather pocket with the sticky rip of having lived there too long.

The clerk entered the numbers on his computer and handed over a key.

"Two flight up, second door on right. Bathroom down hall," he said, checking them out, noting their lack of luggage. "No visitors," he scowled.

"Wait, what? The bathroom's down the hall?" Brigit asked.

"Knock first. Is last room available."

The room was tiny, and that was being generous, Mack thought. A double bed was crammed up against one wall. A window on the other side looked out on the brick of the building next door and cast a gray shadow. A scuttle of insect feet met the glare of the single naked bulb when Mack flipped the switch.

"This looks like a good room to drink yourself to death in," Brigit commented. "We should go back to the truck and get our stuff."

"Let's go back to the bar first. Maybe someone'll know Kieran there and we won't have to sleep in Motel Hell," Mack said.

"Right, it's just going to be that easy."

"Hey, I'm trying to live in your fantasy world for a minute. If we strike out, we'll go get our clothes and come back. I was going to suggest we grab some sleep now, but this honestly looks like the kind of place you don't wake up in with any sort of hope."

Down the stairs they headed. He felt guilty walking by the reception desk; they had no bags, Brigit was much younger, he could guess how it looked. He was slightly sickened by the thought, and he hesitated, wanting to tell the clerk she was his sister and they were going for their suitcases. He was torn between honesty and privacy, and privacy won in the end.

Now that it was dark, the streets took on a carnival atmosphere. Bright lights of dive bars and cheap restaurants beckoned to starving artists, college kids, and brave uptown trust fund babies. Thumping bass music poured out of a head shop next door. Across the street on a stoop sat three teenagers whose clothing consisted primarily of safety pins and plaid remnants, pointed hair glued high and earlobes stretched open by black metal tunnels as they shared a styrofoam container of food that Mack hoped had not come out of the trash. Post-punk kids in ill-fitting Salvation Army suits, one even sporting a bowler hat, stomped down St. Mark's as if they were on the way to a random night of the old ultra-violence. Mack wondered if they were choosing to be bad to counteract the suburban good imposed upon them by mothers who still picked out their school sweaters at a New Jersey mall.

Back at Blackie's, Mack grudgingly paid the cover for Brigit and himself to get in. No amount of cajoling, begging, or veiled threats on Brigit's part could sway the bouncer into believing or caring that they were not here to enjoy the band, but just to take a quick look for their brother. On the stage at the other end of the room, a girl band was wailing for all they were worth. Lots of black leather and long hair whipped around as the women performed like they wanted to kill their instruments. The singer was growling into a microphone, but Mack could hear no words.

He headed for the bar while Brigit stood and watched the band. The place wasn't crowded, so he didn't think he was in danger of losing her.

"I'm looking for James Killroy," he told the bartender. His face was a mixture of ethnicities with a fresh parade of tattoo tears crying down the left side.

"He's not in yet, should be here around eleven," the bartender answered. Mack looked at his watch; nine-fifteen, early for New York.

"You here about the job?"

"No. I'm looking for my brother. Kieran McKinsey."

"Don't know him." He went back to polishing glasses. Well, now what, thought Mack. He could suddenly feel Brigit's presence behind him.

"Do you know Tess?" Southern Brigit came out to play again as she settled herself on a bar stool and leaned over to the bartender. "She sent us on over, said Kieran plays here sometimes. Our brother's a guitar player, Irish ballads usually. Tess said James could maybe help us find him. We drove all night long from Virginia because our dad is really sick." She looked down, then back up through thick eyelashes. "He's been asking for Kieran, only we can't find him."

"I'm sorry to hear that." He'd stopped polishing and was watching Brigit.

"My name's Brigit, I'm Kieran's little sister."

"I'm Hurley. You're from Virginia? Haven't heard a lot of Irish girls with Southern accents," he was leaning over the bar now.

"Y'all need to come on down South, then."

Mack was entranced by this Brigit and the lyrical accent, which danced as it had with the cop. She seemed to think anyone north of Virginia assumed living in the South meant accents out of *Gone With the Wind*, and she knew when to take advantage of that. He watched Brigit reel poor Hurley in.

"Got a picture of your brother?" he asked. Brigit pulled out the last photo she had, Kieran and one of his stray mutts on Caleb's front porch. Kieran was smiling like an apostle on Sunday.

"Ah, he must be the black Irish in the family," Hurley smiled.

"He is," Brigit replied. "The spitting image of Dad, with the black hair and blue eyes. And the smile."

Mack stood back at this. He'd never thought about it, not once; Kieran *did* look like Caleb. He was the only one of the kids who did, but Mack always thought Kieran just looked like Kieran.

"We need to take him home. Kieran's got to see Dad." Brigit looked down at the bar top, then solemnly up at Hurley.

"I get it. I got brothers too; pains in the ass, but wouldn't trade them. I wish I could help you. I'll ask around, talk to James when he comes in. Leave me your number."

Brigit nudged Mack, who held out a Sunshine Landscaping card with his cell number scribbled on the back.

"This is Mack. He's the oldest; you know, the smart one who takes care of us."

"I know what that's like," Hurley said. He locked eyes with Mack as he took the card.

"Can you think of anywhere else we might try? I mean, in Touraine, where we're from, there are all of three bars, but here—it's a little overwhelming," Brigit said.

"Try the Beauty Beat, it's down two blocks on the right. Or maybe Nightlight on Second Avenue, around the corner from that. And come back later, maybe James can help."

"Thanks, Hurley," Brigit said as she stood. "We'll be back."

"Good luck. If you were my sister, I'd want you to find me."

Mack felt like smacking him at the weak pick-up attempt. Big brother standing right here, buddy. But Brigit just smiled and they left.

They walked down the street, stopping at the corner. Mack couldn't even form words, he was so surprised by Brigit being so in control. Somewhere along the line she'd indeed grown up, and he had missed it. She had a whole set of skills that were foreign to him.

"Who are you, anyway?" he found himself asking. He hadn't meant to speak out loud. He meant to keep it in his head, but his head was so crowded with New York noise the thoughts sputtered out on their own.

"I have people skills, Mack. You don't," Brigit said.

"I'm not so bad," he answered defensively.

"Really? You ask for Kieran, he says he doesn't know him, you retreat. Where does that get us? You have to give him a reason, Mack. Everybody wants to help you, but they need to hear the story."

"I can't do that like you."

"You don't have to. That's why I'm here. C'mon, this is the next place," Brigit said, holding the door open for him.

Kieran wasn't at the Beauty Beat, but a cocktail waitress there sent them on to Dug's. He wasn't at Dug's, either, but one of the band members on a break suggested Flannagan's. Despite the sympathy there for a missing Irish brother, no one knew Kieran. There was a bar next door they decided to try called Ramrod, but there were no women in it at all. Mack did get a few invitations to the back room, which he politely declined. Brigit still made him ask the bartender about Kieran before she pulled him away, because you never really knew.

At Nightlight they had their first break. A woman at the bar there, one of the regulars, had actually seen Kieran; at least, she was pretty sure she had. Mack needed to buy her two drinks before she could remember any details, which, when pressed, were scant; he was cute, he had blue eyes, he played guitar. Maybe she'd seen him, Mack thought, or maybe she had seen any number of the earnest loners women loved. He left her his card just in case.

Mack was sure Kieran had left the city, and they were on a fool's errand. He didn't care if Caleb got his wish fulfilled, but he did not want to let Brigit down again. Mack allowed himself, for a moment, to picture seeing his brother again, and found he couldn't. Somewhere in the years, Mack had quietly accepted that people he loved left him.

They took a break from bars and sat on a bench in the park. There were only a few dogs in the dog run now, mostly pit bulls with choke collars, Mack noted. There was a lot of furtive activity, though. Single people walking quickly up to others who stood in semi-darkness, partially blocked by trees. They paused for only a moment, and then walked quickly on, heads down. Getting closer to midnight, he figured it probably wasn't the best time for them to be wandering around a park in New York.

Mack wanted a long, hot shower, followed by a night's uninterrupted sleep in clean sheets. And quiet. He bet it was quiet in Colorado at night. And cool. August on the East Coast was brutal, with humid, dirty air hovering between the buildings, clinging to skin already sticky with sweat. He'd labored for years for his family and his town. All the free work he'd done, behind the scenes, just to help out. No one had noticed or cared. Mack let self-pity submerge him for a moment, until it felt too comfortable and familiar. It was time. He needed to solve this last McKinsey family drama and get out.

Brigit was slumped over on the bench, still staring at the drug dogs. All the animation had left her face like a discarded mannequin, left on the street, ready for recycling. Mack forgot the shower. He could see Brigit had thought Kieran would be waiting for them in every new place they went into tonight. And every time she was deflated. Hope kept her going; he needed to feed that.

"Come on, let's go back to the truck. We'll get our bags and go back to our posh resort and sleep," he said.

"We can't give up," Brigit replied. But she did not move.

"We'll stop at Blackie's first."

"And then what?"

"Best case, he's there. Worst case, the owner showed up and can tell us something."

"What if neither of them is there?" An undercurrent of helplessness flowed through her words. Mack pinched his eyes shut. He knew this feeling. That's when the whiskey started to whisper. Bourbon would tell you that you did your best, it wasn't your fault, the world conspired against you. Her song was subtle, but strong. She'd been singing to him all night.

"Then there's tomorrow, which will be better because we'll have slept."

"Yeah," she snorted. "Really gonna sleep in that roach tent."

"We can try some music stores, they might know him. Maybe he even works in one. Hey, you know what else? We passed by this recording studio. We could start calling them tomorrow. After I find you some more pancakes."

This brought the shadow of a smile to Brigit's tired face. "Yeah, okay." She dragged herself off the bench. "Let's go."

CHAPTER 19

There was a whole new atmosphere to Blackie's now. It was packed, with people waiting outside. The bouncer they'd paid earlier was gone, and the new one didn't care they'd already been here—they'd still have to pay the door charge. Brigit was jumping up and down, trying to wave down Hurley. Mack gave up and paid; he was learning.

Once inside, Brigit began to snake her way toward the stage at the back. The music was loud, incoherent, but still infectious, the bass reverberating throughout the floor. Dark pulses of sound moved the crowd back and forth. People spoke to each other over the sound, but no one heard, they were just words released into the thick air. Mack hung back, scanning the crowd. There seemed to be so much riding on this, he was sure they would fail. He turned quickly back to the door, much to the irritation of the couple who'd entered right behind him.

"Make up your mind, buddy," snarled a sleeveless flannel shirt.

"Sorry," Mack mumbled. It was too crowded. He wanted to leave. He stepped to the side, almost on top of a buzzcut in Doc Martens. Straightening up, Mack was rewarded with an elbow in the back. There were too many damn people pressed so closely up against him. Suddenly the glaring, metallic hospital, the pungent odors of the jail, and the blistering trip to New York were all crashing together on his head with the exhaustion of no sleep. If he could just step outside, breathe some air … but he couldn't. Not this time. Whether or not they found Kieran, Brigit was here, she needed him, and this time, no one was going to drive him away in humiliation.

Mack started to slowly insert himself into the crowd. He looked around for Brigit, knowing she'd probably set herself directly in front of the band. "Excuse me, pardon me," he muttered over and over, putting a gentle hand on a back here and there to swim his way forward.

Beer sloshed on Mack's feet with no regard or apology by a man who had no idea he'd done so. He had the far away, murky look in his eyes; seeing what he wished for, instead of what was there in front of him. Pull him out of his fantasy and he would blame Mack for the spilled beer and demand he buy him another, though it was the drinking that had caused him to hold his glass almost horizontally. But it was never the beer, Mack knew. He shook the drops off his shoes and moved on.

"Mack!" A familiar voice as a hand reached out and grabbed him on the shoulder from behind. A shock ran down his arm, and he was frozen. He was afraid to look. He wanted so much for it to be Kieran. He turned to see the bartender, Hurley.

"Your sister might need a hand," Hurley leaned in to shout in Mack's ear. He pointed toward the side of the stage nearest the bar, where a cloud of auburn hair was dancing wildly, arms flailing and taking up space with no regard for anyone else. "I'm sorry for you both," Hurley said, and disappeared back behind the bar crowded three-deep with people desperate for drinks.

Mack began to plow through the crowd with less patience. He'd turned Brigit loose in a crowded New York City bar, while she was facing DUI charges back in Touraine. He might as well have handed her matches and a gas can. On the ledge next to his sister were four empty shot glasses.

"Mack! Dance with me!" For a moment, Brigit was luminous. Her face was bright and worry free. Her body undulated to the music, her arms over her head. There was nothing in the world to worry about, her whole body said. Mack knew that whiskey tease. It burned you at first, as a warning. But if you could proceed, it wrapped you up in warmth and euphoria, loosened your muscles, lifted your mouth into a smile. The world was a fine place and all the people in it were your friends. You were always welcome, and you could come back anytime. He would never have that alcohol assurance again. But why not, really—they were in New York, who would know? His father was sick, his brother was missing, his sister was facing jail—Mack could count off all the ways that would justify his first drink. He wanted to drink it all away like Brigit could. She would be fine, of course, because someone would always be there to pick up the pieces of her sodden nights. But tonight that someone was him. Spikes of resentment began to prickle.

"I can't believe you're *drinking*." He was simmering, trying to hold down his rage.

Guilt flashed in her eyes for a moment as she looked down. "It's just a couple of shots, Mack."

"You promised."

"Sorry," she muttered.

"Let's go, Brigit," he said, taking her arm.

"Go? We just got here." She turned away.

"This is how you look for Kieran?"

"Stop it," she said, pulling roughly away. She knocked into another girl waiting for a drink.

"Watch it!" the girl yelled.

"You watch it!" Brigit yelled back.

"Really? You want to do this?" This girl was whiskey-brave too, and she had friends behind her. Brigit either didn't notice, or didn't care.

Mack stepped between them.

"Ladies, I'm sorry. My sister's upset … please let me buy you a drink." He held bills out over the top of the crowd to Hurley.

"I have money, you know," Brigit said.

Mack put his arm around her shoulders and leaned in.

"We need to leave, now."

"You don't get to tell me what to do, Mack," she said, squirming away under his grip.

"According to the Albemarle County Sheriff, yes, I do."

The heat in the club was rising with the number of sweaty bodies pushing in through the door, crushing against one another. Mack clamped one hand on the back of Brigit's neck and shoved her forward. She stumbled, but he kept forcing her toward the door. They knocked into the crowd, and people pushed back. "Out of the way! Coming through!" he yelled. Brigit flailed her hands back, slapping at him. She caught him across the face once, but Mack did not loosen his grip. The bouncer at the door was watching their approach as Brigit kicked back at her brother, screeching unintelligibly. The bouncer pushed the crowd back as Mack drove Brigit through the door and released her on the sidewalk.

She turned on him immediately.

"What the fuck, Mack?"

"You promised me no drinking."

"It was just a couple of shots!"

"You promised!" He shoved his fists in his pockets to stop his hands from shaking, and spoke slowly through the fury. "We are going to the truck to get our bags. Then we are going to the hotel." He strode across Avenue A toward 7th Street. He did not hear footsteps behind him. He did not look back.

"Fine. Fine!" she yelled, running after but staying a step or two behind him.

When he made it to Avenue C he looked right and left for his truck. Most of the lamps in the streetlights had been smashed, darkening the street. There was only the thin light from a few shaded windows to guide him down a street he'd spent a few minutes on early this morning. Nothing looked familiar now. He walked up a block, then back down the other side.

"We already went this way," Brigit complained.

Mack was lost, but not willing to admit that to his sister. He'd walk until he found the truck. There were shadows of people in doorways, and he almost wished they'd come out and start something. He shoved his fists deeper into his pockets.

"We've been down this block three times, Mack."

"Then where's my truck, huh?"

"It's … I don't know."

"Well, there's a surprise, Brigit."

"It was right here, I know it. Right by this tree with the broken limb and the rusted bike lock on the fence."

Mack turned to look; the tree did look familiar, but there was a dented beige hatchback parked by it. He stepped out into the Avenue and looked up and down. There was no sign of his old green Ford.

"We must be on the wrong street. Let's walk over one more," he suggested. A curl of fear gripped his neck.

"It was here, Mack. I know it was," Brigit insisted. "Maybe it was towed?"

"There are no signs here, why would it be towed?"

"What if there are parking rules we don't know about?"

"Jesus, Brigit, that's helpful."

Metal shrieked above them as a window was forced open. "Hey, you the one with the green F150?" A dark man in a black wife-beater with a marijuana leaf outlined on it and a long beard leaned out.

"Yeah."

"Cool ride, bro. Vintage. Your mechanics took it, like, three, four hours ago."

"What?" Mack asked.

"Yeah, I asked them what they were doing, they wanted to know if it was mine. I wish. They said you broke down and called them to come fix it. Took them like, two, three minutes under the hood and it started up. Must be at their garage by now."

Mack felt all the noise rush out of his head.

"Holy shit, Mack, I think somebody stole your truck," Brigit said.

Mack walked around in a tight little circle on the sidewalk. He stopped and raised his left arm, yanking viciously with his right until the tendons popped but the snap offered no release right now.

"Mack? Did you hear me? I think somebody stole your truck."

"Yeah, Brigit. I got that."

"What're we going to do?"

"It was a couple of white guys, that's all I seen," offered the helpful neighbor in the window.

"We need to call the police, Mack." Brigit called up to the neighbor, "Could you come down and give us a description of the guys?"

"I didn't really see much," he said quickly as he pulled his head in and slammed the window shut. After a couple of seconds, the lights went out in the apartment.

Mack pulled out his phone and dialed 911.

"Nine-one-one, what's your emergency?"

"My truck was stolen," Mack said.

"Were you carjacked?"

"No."

"Was there anyone in the car when it was stolen?"

"No."

"Did you see the person or persons take your car illegally?"

"No, I …"

"Then this not an emergency. Hang up and call your local precinct. This number is reserved for actual emergencies and you can be fined for using it in a non-emergency." The line went dead.

"Local precinct? How the fuck would *I* know the local precinct?" Mack ratcheted his arm back and channeled his rage into the phone as he lobbed it in a high arc across the street.

"Maybe we need to—" Brigit started.

"Need to *what*? You suddenly have answers, Brigit?" He whirled on her. "Hey!" Mack yelled up at the window of the good Samaritan who'd watched his truck being stolen. "Hey! What's the local police precinct here?" He trotted across the street.

"Where you going, Mack?" Brigit asked.

"To get my useless phone. Hey!" Mack yelled to the sky at the top of his lungs. "Anybody know the local precinct here? Somebody stole my truck!"

"We could go back to Blackie's and ask," Brigit offered.

"Right! Let's go back to the bar! That will surely bring the truck back!"

"Maybe they can help."

"Your honey-dripping accent and pretty hair-flipping isn't going to help us out of this one, Brigit. These are not our friends."

"I know."

"Then quit saying such stupid things," he spat. "Do you know what was in that truck? My goddamn *life* was in there."

"Mack …"

"The peas! All the boxes of frozen peas!"

"What?"

"It's where I hid my money. Caleb must have taught you that lesson too. I grabbed them out of the freezer and hid them in the toolbox. All of them. All my money. Locked up safely. Because who'd be stupid enough to walk around New York City with so much cash?"

"Oh, shit, Mack," Brigit muttered.

"We have to get it back."

"They've got our bags, too, with all our clothes."

"Your clothes? Your *clothes*?"

"Well, I'm just saying …"

"You really don't know when to shut up, do you, Brigit?" He stuck his face right in hers as she cowered. "Do you know what else was in that truck? All the plans, the original plans for Maeve's Garden, all the drawings, years of work, and it's gone. It's all gone, Brigit!"

"That's what you're so upset about?" she yelled back. "The goddamn plans for your precious memorial. The one nobody is allowed to see anyway?"

"I should never have shown you! That was a mistake."

"When will you ever live among the living, Mack?"

"For what?" he snorted with laughter. "For my *family*?"

"Would that be so terrible? Isn't that why we're here?"

"Yeah, that's it," he answered sarcastically. "To find Kieran."

"What do you mean?"

"Wake up, Brigit! We are not going to find Kieran."

"Why not?"

"He doesn't want to be found!"

"What are you talking about?"

"Why didn't he ever come home?"

"Maybe—"

"We don't know if he's still in New York; he could have moved to Chicago or Atlanta or Armpit, Iowa for all we know. Christ, Brigit, we don't even know if he's still alive."

"Don't you say that!"

"Our family is a train wreck. *You* can't even stay sober for *one* night."

"Kind of hard to do when your brother cares more about the dead."

"Go have a drink, Brigit. Have several. Have them all, maybe you *can* join Mom."

She stumbled back, knocking into a metal garbage can and tipping it over.

"Hey! Cowboy! Get outta the street or I'm calling the cops!" A disembodied voice shouted from high. Mack whipped around, hoisted the fallen trash can over his head and hurled it into the street. The metal screeched on the pavement, echoing down the street as plastic bags of rotted food splattered across the avenue.

"Call them! Call the cops!" Mack screamed at the top of his lungs.

"Mack ..." Brigit put a hand on his shoulder from behind and he swung out, striking her hard in the face. He turned as she gasped, blood running down her face. Brigit struck back at him with both hands. He couldn't see anything but flying fists as she hit him again and again. Her hot, sour breath assaulted his nose and his head pounded. He placed his palms on her shoulders and shoved her to escape her onslaught of fury.

Brigit flew backward and crashed down into the street. Blood was spurting from her nose, and the scrapes on her arms had reopened. She sprawled there only a moment when a van came barreling around the corner toward her. She struggled up and threw herself back against a parked car just in time. She looked across the street at her brother.

"Brigit!" Mack yelled.

Brigit stared at Mack. They locked eyes for an instant and he saw not shock in her face but resignation. She suddenly whipped around and began to run. He bolted after her, sliding into an old carton of lo mein that had spilled out of the garbage can he'd thrown. He slipped to the pavement in the scattered trash. Rubbing his hands on his pants to wipe off the slimy noodles, he scrambled to his feet. He sprinted to the corner and looked right and left, but his sister was nowhere to be seen. Brigit had been swallowed up by the city.

CHAPTER 20

Mack paced like a panther in front of the liquor store. All the pretty colored bottles shimmered under the brilliant light inside, safe behind bars and bulletproof glass. The light blue of the Bombay Sapphire pulsed like a heartbeat, *drink me*, next to the dark emerald of the Tanqueray, tantalizing in her standoffishness. The luscious, deep red of a bottle of Absolut Raspberry beckoned, as the tall, thin, flaxen-haired Galliano stood pompously looking down on the rest. The cinnamon Fireball whiskey didn't care, she promised red hot and delivered, Mack knew this, could already feel the tickle going down his throat. The distinctive shape of the Crown Royal perched regally in its purple velvet sack; neither Irish nor Scottish but Canadian, of all things.

And there, at the end of the shelf, stood the shining silver bottle of Bourbon Sweet Tea, the juicy peach challenging him to take a bite. Mack closed his eyes and he could taste it, the smoky liquid untying all the knots in his head. It was a festival of relief, all within reach, all beckoning. He needed that clarity, that one hot smack to his brain. With just a shot, he'd know what to do. Just one shot. He'd buy the bottle, but have just one shot and then throw the rest away.

Brigit was in the wind. He didn't know how she'd disappeared so fast. She shouldn't be that hard to track, a wild-haired girl with a bleeding nose running down the street. But Brigit had been raised by an outlaw and knew how to disappear. He'd checked the motel and Blackie's, the only two places they'd been to with any sense of belonging. She'd probably run into one of these musty neighborhood bars with no windows and a heavy wooden door. He'd gone into as many as he could before feeling like she was getting even farther away from him. She could have jumped in a cab, hopped on a bus, scurried down into the bowels of the subway and gone anywhere. She wouldn't even know, or care, Mack thought, where she was headed.

She had no money and no ID. Someone would buy her a drink, listen to her sad tale of woe, and offer her a place to stay. Or worse, someone would cross her, just the smallest slight would set her off and there would be the fight he'd denied her earlier in the bar. He was going to find her beaten and broken in an alley stuffed behind a dumpster, surrounded by a team of New York detectives in dark raincoats shaking their heads at the tragedy. It was an accident, he insisted again to himself. He hadn't meant to hit her.

Mack's hand curled around the handle to the liquor store entrance and he pulled. The door was stuck. He shook it, still nothing. He looked inside. A small Latino behind the thick glass was shaking his head vigorously at Mack. Mack waved, but the head-shaking grew more agitated. He yanked harder on the door. It still wouldn't open.

"Everything okay here?" Mack turned to see a police officer, hands on hips.

"I can't get the door open," Mack said. "Officer."

"You're not gonna get that door open, buddy."

"Why? I just need—"

"We all got needs. You wanna argue with me?"

"No." He thought he'd hit bottom years ago, but apparently there was always a new low. Not a drink in three years, and he was groveling in front of a liquor store in Lower Manhattan.

"Luis here's been hit twice in the last month. Know anything about that?"

"Hit? Hit? Oh. No."

"You been pacing up and down in front of this store for twenty minutes, talking to yourself. Who you waiting for?" The cop took a step closer, putting one hand on the baton in his belt.

"Nobody. Well, my sister. Not waiting for her, but looking for her. I mean, I don't live here, I live in Virginia." Mack mustered all the sincerity he could. He knew he was babbling, and he wanted to stop; this is what guilty people did, and he hadn't done anything wrong. He pasted a fake half-smile on his face.

"Virginia, huh? Long way to go for a drink," the cop said, never taking his eyes from Mack. "Why don't you turn around and put your hands against the wall and spread your legs for me?"

Mack's hands were shaking now, which really pissed him off and made him need that drink. The assumption of wrongdoing was insulting. He slowly turned and placed his hands against the rough brick wall of the store. The cop grasped his wrists and pulled them farther up the wall, then thrust his heavy foot in between Mack's feet and kicked them wider. He grabbed Mack's forearms and squeezed, traveling down his arms, grasping him around the chest with a practiced and not gentle hand. He quickly patted Mack's crotch; Mack squeezed his eyes shut and put his head down.

"What are you doing in New York?" The cop stepped back, and Mack slowly turned around.

"I'm looking for my brother."

"Thought you said sister."

"I did. I'm looking for her too."

"Pretty clumsy, you losing your whole family here."

"It's complicated."

"I bet it is. They gonna help you rob the store?"

"I am not robbing the store, I swear. In fact, I was looking for the police station. Somebody stole my truck."

"Did they now?"

"Yes, and I called 911, and they told me to call the local precinct but I didn't know where it was."

"So you, what, thought you'd stop for a drink first?"

"No, that's when my sister took off."

"Sister, brother … anybody else? You gotta missing grandma too?" The cop crossed his arms but still looked ready to take him down if he had to.

"My sister came to New York with me, but then she ran away," Mack willed himself to shut up, but it was too late. He didn't know how cops did this, grew to such a judgmental size right in front of you.

"How old's your sister?"

"She's twenty-one."

"There a reason she might run away?"

"We had an argument."

"You hit her?"

"Yes," Mack sank deeper. "Accidentally."

"Maybe you should come with me to the station," the cop said. He put a hand to his shoulder and started to mumble into the radio clipped there.

"If you could tell me where it is, I will come and fill out a theft report, or whatever I need to for my truck. But I have to find my sister, she doesn't know New York," Mack said.

"Yeah, that wasn't really a request," the cop said. He took Mack's forearm in a surprisingly strong hold, and placed his whole body firmly in front of Mack. "Do I need to cuff you?"

Mack sat on the hard, wooden chair in the police station, silently willing himself not to pop his shoulder. He was riding a fine line now. The street cop had ushered him out of the cruiser, plopped him next to a desk, and disappeared. A tired doughnut eater, resembling every TV cop who never quite made it, took his statement about his truck, then about

Kieran, and then about Brigit. On the surface Mack was a mess. Right now he looked suspicious, unstable, but was not yet guilty of anything. But they wanted him to be. It was the middle of the night, even in New York, and he suspected they suspected he might conveniently wrap up this string of liquor store heists. Maybe there were other robberies too, and they could get him for those as well. His mind was ticking too fast without that drink to calm it. What the hell, maybe there was an unsolved murder, too. Maybe a whole slew of them. Lock him up for good.

Because he *was* guilty. He'd smacked Brigit. He'd hit her hard, made her bleed. He saw her face again from across the street where she leaned on the car she'd thrown herself against. The look was not horror, or surprise, but resignation. She looked as if that's what men did, and she was not surprised to find he was like all the rest. Brigit gave as good as she got, which probably made it worse; no teary victim, not her. She fought back. She kicked and yelled and lashed out with purpose, scratching and swearing. If nothing else, Caleb had taught her to defend herself.

Mack had Caleb in his very bones. Maeve had warned Mack of the McKinsey hair-trigger temper when he was a child. When Mack was old enough, by Caleb's standards, to drink, everything had changed. The bourbon soothed him. As a teenager, Mack thought he was using it sparingly, until he turned into the hopeless drunk people avoided. But he knew he didn't have a problem, even if there were holes in his memory. How could people be angry at him for things he couldn't even remember? After Lauren broke up with him he no longer cared. At the height of Mack's past alcoholic acrobatics, he'd passed out in bar parking lots, in the bushes by the grocery store, and on the pitcher's mound at the little league park. Once he'd woken up in the morning to a little kid kicking sand at him. He sat up only to smack his head on the bottom of a playground slide. But no one had ever called the cops, or rolled him, or, ironically, stolen his truck before. People in Touraine knew him.

More importantly, people knew his father. Caleb was strong, and he was rich. Mack wasn't sure which people feared more. Caleb could spend large, as long as he got to decide where it should go. He also insisted on anonymity, which was a joke in Touraine. He didn't want a line of bums at his door looking for handouts, Mack had heard him say more than once. Nothing pissed him off more than people asking for money. But there wouldn't have been a new firehouse without him, or the public swimming pool at the park, or the library restoration. What Caleb did not do was shower it on his kids. He wanted them to learn the value of money, and that "sure as shit wasn't going to happen with me throwing it around on you," was one of his favorite lines. They were on their own to learn that lesson, was another.

He stood up suddenly. The baggy-eyed cop looked at him.

"Are we done?" Mack asked.

"You got someplace else to be?" The cop leaned back in his ancient office chair with a creak.

"I've got anywhere else to be, unless you want to lock me up. I don't expect you to find my sister, or my brother, or even my truck. And I didn't rob the liquor store, as much as you'd like it if I had. So there's no reason for me to be here."

The detective stood, adjusted his gun belt, and sarcastically mock-bowed Mack toward the door.

Mack walked out into the night, which was quiet now. In a couple of hours the sun would rise, but this was the hour of the night when even New York could fall silent. He headed down the sidewalk, the numbers getting smaller until they turned into letters and the park loomed in front of him. It was now a dark hole that lured him in like a magnet. There were lumps of homeless people laid out on benches with their ragged coats over their heads despite the heat. Grocery carts of treasures were parked around them as their walls, reminders of a life they'd once had. A small group of teenagers huddled together by a tree, leaning against each other, sharing smokes. Mack made his way to the dog run. He sat on a bench and watched nothing. It was empty now, with not even a pit bull in a choke collar sniffing about.

Years ago, when he'd first gotten sober, Mack had exchanged denial for despair. During his first month in Alcoholics Anonymous, he'd been stripped down to nothing. He thought he'd sunk as low as he could go, only to find his bottom was much lower than he imagined. He was told, when he dared ask for the truth, what a bastard he'd been when he was drunk. Girls would leave bars in tears, and quite a few fights had broken out. He'd ended a childhood friendship by declaring his pal should not breed so he wouldn't have to teach his babies to dumpster dive for their dinner. He remembered none of this and wanted to deny it all. After thirty days clean and sober, he had to own the horrible stories from his blackouts.

But now, so many years later, he could still question his value in the world. He knew his comfortable blanket of self-pity was wrapping him once more in denial. The more he blamed himself for all the problems in the world, the more detached he allowed himself to become. He was simply existing, taking up space. His life had no point. The minute he took any sort of control, like bringing Brigit to New York, it all fell apart. The only place he felt alive was in Maeve's Garden.

He closed his eyes.

He was back in Touraine, at home with his family. Maeve was laughing and cooking her Irish sausages. Caleb was making the strong black coffee to which he'd undoubtedly add some bourbon, offering a cup to Maeve and chuckling at her grimace. Brigit was setting the kitchen table for breakfast and excitedly chattering about a date she had that night with Shooter Jackson, as Kieran sat in the corner searching for the right chord on his guitar to some unnamed song. Mack knew this was as illusory as a rainbow in an oil slick. He stood in the doorway to the kitchen and watched a scene that had never happened. He longed for the normalcy in front of him, and dreaded the despair that would descend when he walked in and destroyed it.

"Well, here's the birthday boy at last," Lonny said as he came up behind Mack and clapped a hand on his shoulder. "We thought you were gonna sleep all day." He offered one of his half-smiles, kindness in his eyes. All the faces turned to Mack then.

"Happy birthday, my boy," Caleb said, holding out a coffee cup with a grin. "Let's put a little hair on your chest, here. About time."

"You're still giving me a ride downtown later, right?" Brigit asked.

"Happy birthday, my love." Maeve crossed to him and put her hands on his shoulders and kissed his cheek. She swiped a lock of hair out of his eyes, before turning back to the sausages.

"There's the old man," said Kieran, looking up. Mack wanted to go back to his mother, the swipe of a kiss she'd just planted on his face, the touch of her hands on his shoulders. The gentle crinkle of lines at her eyes as she smiled up at her son.

"You'll always be an old man to me," Kieran teased. This was their running joke, since they were born less than a year apart. Mack was supposed to reply, "And you'll always be a little shit to me," then Maeve would chide him for swearing, and Caleb would laugh. But Mack couldn't reply. There was Maeve, her back to him now, the smell of the sausages wafting over to him. He couldn't move.

"Didn't you hear me, old man?" Kieran persisted. Mack turned his head to his brother; Caleb was gone, and Lonny had disappeared. His mother turned to him with the skillet in her hand.

"It's time to go, Mack," she said quietly.

"Is he all right?" Brigit asked. Mack glanced up at her, and then Maeve was gone, too. He had to get her back. He swirled around, desperate to find his mother.

"Mack. Mack!" Kieran reached out and grabbed his shoulder.

Mack shook his head; it was too bright. He sat up. The park. The bench. He looked up and blinked. A faint streak of sunlight was crawling through a tree branch in the park. And there, backlit like a saint in a movie, stood Caleb.

CHAPTER 21

He stood in front of Mack, hands shoved in the front pockets of his jeans, straight black hair and unforgiving blue eyes looking into Mack's without pause. Mack shook his head. It was not Caleb standing in front of him in Tompkins Square Park. It was Kieran. His younger brother had become a startling replica of their father. The previous softness of his face had given way to a rigid jaw and sharp cheekbones, one of which showed a scar across the top. New York had marked him.

He jumped up and grabbed his brother in a rough hug, wrapping his arms around him and clutching the back of Kieran's shirt in clenched fists to make sure he was real. Sobs rose in his chest. Kieran was alive. Mack had been terrified he'd be dead. He held his brother tightly, and this time, he wouldn't let him go.

Kieran remained stiff under the embrace, and finally put his hands on Mack's arms to disengage. He pushed Mack back and looked at him with a mixture of hunger and disappointment—a look Mack had seen far too often on Caleb's face. Mack did a half-stumble backward.

"It was Ghi who found him, can you believe it?" Brigit said.

"Brigit." She stood behind Mack. Relief and shame battled as he turned to see his sister. He winced at the lump of her nose shifting to the right and the matching bruise blooming under her eye. "Brigit, I'm so sorry."

"I went to Tess's apartment," she chattered on, "hoping maybe she'd let me clean up, and Ghi was out front waiting for, well, waiting, and he sent me straight upstairs. Tess was so nice, she let me wash my face and gave me this shirt, which I promised I'd send back to her, so I have to do that as soon as we get home. Then suddenly Tess says, 'he's on his way' and there he was, Kieran, walking in the door. Can you believe it?" She was babbling like a kid on Christmas morning.

Mack leaned back on the bench. Kieran was watching his sister talk with a smile, which is where the resemblance to Caleb left him. He stared at Brigit as if she had been the one who was missing, and maybe, to him, she had been. They looked so genuinely joyful to be in each other's company, he was afraid to ruin it. He'd never expected to see his brother again.

"So *you* found *us*. How?" Mack asked.

"You made a lot of noise," Kieran said. "You two are as pathetic as lost dogs on a freeway. People felt sorry for you. They reached out to me, once they knew you were for real. Tess made some calls, Hurley made some calls, my old friend Marshall even called me, and I haven't heard from him in a year. New Yorkers get a bad rap, but they really are nice people. They became my family." Kieran sat down at the other end of the bench.

It was still early in the morning, but the sun was blazing and promising a sticky, humid heat. A Black woman jogged past them in running shoes, unknowingly letting out snippets of music to the song in her headphones. Two young Asian mothers chatted as they pushed animated toddlers in umbrella strollers toward the playground. A teenager, male or female, impossible to tell by the baggy t-shirt and the droopy Rasta hat, searched through a trashcan for recyclable cans, or maybe breakfast. These were the people who owned the park in the morning. Apparently these were also Kieran's people now.

"Did you tell him about Dad?" Mack asked.

Kieran's face hardened. He tried to mask it, but the silence hung thick between them. Since leaving home, their youngest brother had not sent a word to Caleb. He had cut him out completely.

"I just told him Dad was in the hospital." Brigit sat down between her brothers. "But Lonny would call us if something changed, right? Do you think you should call him?"

Mack pulled out his cellphone and flipped it open to a blank screen. "My phone's dead. And the charger was in the truck."

"I told him about your truck," Brigit said. She turned to Kieran. "Hey, do you have a phone? Can you call the hospital?"

Kieran's eyes met Mack's, where secrets that had only existed between the two of them since boyhood still lived.

"No," he lied. Mack stared at his brother. "Not with me."

Mack still didn't know what had happened between Caleb and Kieran. He'd begged his brother to tell him what their father had done, but, for the first time, Kieran had refused to talk to Mack.

"His situation's serious, Kieran," Mack said. Even saying his name felt strange. "He's got lung cancer, and on top of that, he had a stroke."

"Yeah, on my birthday," Brigit said.

"He sent us to find you," Mack said.

"So that's why you're here," Kieran said with a small smile. "You came for him."

"No, we came for you, Kieran," Brigit said.

"We've been looking everywhere for you. No one would admit to knowing you, except for Tess," Mack said.

"I know. They were protecting me."

"Why, because your sister and brother are so scary?" Brigit asked.

"No, because I didn't want Caleb to find me."

"But we couldn't find you either!" Her voice was rising.

"I've been right here."

"And how would we know? We wrote to you, and the letters came back. You could have called, you could have even called me collect. I was seventeen, Kieran. I missed you. How could you not know that I missed you?" Brigit slapped his arm lightly.

"I'm sorry, Brigit. I really am. I missed you too."

"It felt like you didn't want us to find you."

"Do you two have a plan here?" Kieran asked.

The tantalizing smell of coffee slapped Mack, and his head whipped around like a cartoon dog sniffing a bone. A older man was ambling toward them, an open book in one hand, a blue Grecian urn cardboard cup in the other. The dark earthy aroma promised to make everything better. There was a cart at the corner of the park. He could fall back into old habits so easily.

"I didn't want to come," Mack said.

"Well, that's nice to know."

"I didn't mean it like that."

"Mack's not very good at expressing himself, Kieran, in case you forgot. No one ever knows what the hell he's thinking until he hits you with it," Brigit said.

"I am so sorry, Brigit. The last thing in the world I want to do is hurt you," Mack said.

"But you did, all the same." She looked away. "You wonder why I don't trust people."

"Brigit, you know that was an accident. I have always been on your side, always."

"You'd better tell me what you're talking about," Kieran said.

"My face," Brigit said quietly.

"*You* did this to her?" Kieran jumped up, his fury immediate, and grabbed Mack by the front of his shirt, hauling him to his feet. He curled his right hand into a fist.

"Go ahead, I deserve it," Mack said, arms dangling at his sides.

"Don't you get all high and mighty," Brigit said, wedging herself in between them and pushing both away. Mack slumped back on the bench as Kieran turned away. "Mack *has* always been on my side, which is why this hurts so much. But he's been there for me, he stuck around."

"I had no choice," Kieran said.

"Bullshit! You always have a choice. You left us, Kieran."

"I didn't leave you."

"We didn't even know where you were going!"

"*I* didn't even know where I was going, Brigit. Caleb threw me out."

"What?" Mack was stunned.

"First Roseanna, then me."

"What do you mean?" Mack asked.

"If you don't do what Caleb McKinsey wants, he gets rid of you."

"I thought you and Roseanna broke up," Mack said.

"One day she never showed up," Kieran stopped and faced them both with his unwavering, inescapable stare. "I went to her house and there was no one there. It was completely empty. The house was stripped bare, not that there was much to take in the first place. And I searched, Mack, everywhere. Then Simon from the gas station told me he saw Caleb driving out to Roseanna's house the week before."

"But Kieran ..." Mack stopped.

"When I asked him about it, he didn't even act surprised. 'None of us liked her, son,' he said."

"Why didn't you tell me?" Mack asked.

"Because he was right. I knew you never liked Roseanna."

"But I knew you loved her. I would have helped you look."

"I kept begging him to tell me where she was. After a week he said he was sick of listening to me and told me to get in the truck. I was sure he was taking me to her, but he drove to the interstate and pulled off. He threw a few bills at me and told me to get the hell out. He said he'd made sure himself I'd never see Roseanna again. That I'd better go off to find a place to turn me into a man. And if I came back as the whiny-ass crybaby that I was now, no one would ever see me again either."

"Christ, Kieran!" Mack said.

"Roseanna used to talk about this bakery in New York where a cake cost more than a hundred dollars. It was the only clue I had, so I followed it."

"Is she here?" Brigit asked.

"She's not anywhere, Brigit." A pigeon bobbled curiously toward them until Kieran stomped and it flew off. "All those rumors we heard about him as kids were true. The severed hand of the Franklin County thief wrapped around the tree with barbed wire, the nest of water moccasins Jimmy Legs Fitzpatrick woke up to in his kitchen. His own brothers killed on a bootleg run they'd made hundreds of times before. Open your eyes, Brigit! Mack knows it's all true."

"What are you saying, Kieran?" Brigit asked him.

"He killed her, Brigit. Caleb killed Roseanna."

"He's not a murderer!" Brigit said.

"He killed his own brothers to take over Bourbon Sweet Tea. You don't think he'd get rid of one nobody girl from the mountains?"

"What?" Brigit asked.

"People in Touraine disappear. Think about it," Kieran said.

Brigit did not want this image, but before she could close it down, her mind went back to Estelle, the librarian she'd adopted as a surrogate mother when she was six years old. Estelle had been sweet, saving her the best books, calling her a lovely girl, and listening to her stories about her family. One day, though, she'd overheard Estelle complaining that Brigit was 'like a stray cat you feed once and it follows you forever' and asking another librarian how to get rid of her. Brigit had bolted out of the library, tearing down the street until she tripped and skinned both knees. When Caleb asked that night what had happened, Brigit had told him Estelle didn't like her anymore. The next day Estelle disappeared. No one knew where she went, no one had ever talked about her again. Brigit hadn't wanted to see Estelle, but she hadn't wanted her to die, either.

"I never came back, because I didn't know what he'd do to me," Kieran said.

"Wait a minute," Brigit said.

"You think he'd *kill* you?" Mack asked. Kieran shrugged and shakily pulled a pack of cigarettes out of his back pocket.

"Could someone please explain about Caleb's brothers?" Brigit asked.

"You've heard the rumors," Kieran said.

"That's all bullshit," Brigit said.

"There were three of them; they were older and experienced, and they all wound up dead on the same night, shot point-blank," Kieran said. "It was a bootleg run they'd done many times before. Except this time, Caleb wasn't with them."

"But there's never been any evidence—" Mack started.

"People look as hard as they want to see," Kieran said. "Maybe that's why it took you three years to get here."

"You haven't seen him, Kieran. There's nothing he can do to you now," Mack said quietly.

"Besides, it's our turn. We're finally going to take what's due to us. We're going to take control of Bourbon Sweet Tea," Brigit said.

"You never will," Kieran said.

"We can if we stick together. Now that I'm twenty-one, I have voting rights, and if we combine our stocks, we have the majority."

"If Kieran still has his stock," Mack said.

"He does. He wouldn't sell it for the same reason you wouldn't, Mack. Neither of you want Caleb to have that kind of control."

"She's right, I would never sell it to Caleb. But I don't want it, either. I'll sell it to you. I'll sell it to you for a dollar."

"You can't, Kieran. It has to be fair market value. And I don't have that kind of money, and neither does Mack. And Caleb has first refusal."

"Why does it always work that way?"

"Kieran, look. The hell with him. Don't come back for him, come back for Brigit."

"Maybe I won't go back either," Brigit said. "Maybe I'll stay here with Kieran for a while."

"Jesus, Brigit. You were not even supposed to leave the state. I could go to jail for bringing you here," Mack said.

"What? Why?" Kieran stepped back to look at Brigit, who kept her head down.

"She got in a fight on her birthday and drove her car into Lickinghole Creek Bridge."

"The bridge ... where Mom died?" Kieran paled.

"Her car's totaled," Mack said.

"Jesus, Brigit," Kieran enfolded her in his arms, and she melted into him.

Mack wanted desperately to hug his sister too, but he knew she'd push him away as Kieran had. Neither of them wanted, or needed, anything from him. The lack of sleep coupled with the stress of handling the future for all of them beat down on him. He wished he could be in Maeve's Garden, but he had a feeling even Maeve didn't want him anymore.

"If Mom were still here, none of this would have happened," Mack said. "This is my fault."

"How is this *your* fault?" Brigit asked.

"When we were kids, she told me she was taking us to Ireland, and she made me keep it a secret from everyone."

"You never told me this," Kieran said.

"I wanted to, but she made me promise. Even Dad didn't know. But then I panicked, because I didn't know if we were coming back."

"What did you do, Mack?" Brigit was staring at him with suspicion.

"The day she died we got in a fight. I told her she was *stupid*, I told her I *hated* her. I told her she should just go away. Then she got in the car and drove into the bridge and she died."

"Oh, Jesus, Mack." Kieran looked away.

"There were questions, but it was *too* an accident. I know it was."

Mack was shaking now, walking around in tight little circles, clutching his ribs. He couldn't focus his eyes on anything. Now they knew; he'd driven their mother away and ruined their lives. He could smell his own rancid sweat under the grime of the city, and feel their revulsion.

"Mack, what—" Brigit started.

"I'm sorry, I'm so sorry. I know she wanted to get away from

Caleb, but she never wanted to get away from us. I know that. I did that. I'm sorry."

Two beefy gym rats in red berets walked up to the group. "Everything all right here?" asked the blond with the crewcut, nodding toward Mack.

"What?" asked Brigit, not taking her eyes off Mack endlessly circling. He had a stain from the lo mein on his jeans, his hair was sticking up and he smelled sour. But it was the look of dissociation in his eyes that scared her. Mack was not there. She glanced at Kieran, whose stoic demeanor had dropped into unease.

"Is he bothering ya?" asked the one with the shaved head. "We patrol the park, sometimes we have to relocate individuals if they're bothering people." A little ripple ran through his shiny left biceps.

Brigit moved in, grasping one of Mack's arms.

"It's okay," she said.

"Ya sure?"

"I'm sorry," Mack whispered.

"We can take him to a shelter."

"No," Kieran said, stepping in and taking Mack's other arm. "He's our brother."

CHAPTER 22

Kieran fidgeted in his airliner seat between Brigit and Mack. Both of them were asleep. He'd fallen back into his childhood habits, letting the needs of the family pull him into action. Though he'd imagined the moment of seeing his brother and sister so many times in the past three years, their jagged edges cut into the soothing reverie of the home he had created in New York. He knew there was no going back. But apparently they didn't know that yet.

When he'd first arrived in New York, Kieran had headed straight to Willow Bakery. There had been a long line outside. A succulent fragrance had wisped out the door and drawn everyone in. Roseanna had not been there, however; he had shown her picture but no one had seen her. He'd felt compelled to at least buy one of their whimsical cupcakes, though he'd eaten it without enthusiasm. He should have been eating it with her. He'd spent the first night wandering the streets after being prodded awake on a park bench and told to move on by a police officer. His happy demeanor had been summarily trampled into childish naiveté in Manhattan.

The next day he found more bakeries, but no Roseanna. A Vietnamese dishwasher at one restaurant had offered him a shower and a night's sleep on the floor of his apartment, which Kieran thought was the tiniest place a human could live. He had met other people on his search, one of whom had directed him toward an Irish bar where he might be able to play. Once he'd fallen in with other musicians, life had become easier. They were a nomadic bunch by nature, and understood his quest. He could be patient until Mack came, and Kieran had known his brother would arrive soon. Growing up, he and Mack had always worked out whatever nightmares Caleb had thrown in their path.

After one late night at a new bar, he was leaving by the back door, followed by a chattering redhead who'd been listening to him play all night. As they entered the alley, a fist covered in metal had met his cheek and he went down on the vomit-begrimed sidewalk covered in a thin layer of sleet.

A white guy in a tattered blue hoodie hovered over him, fist raised.

"Gimme your wallet," he demanded.

Kieran had hesitated a moment too long. The vicious kick to his ribs had stolen his breath and there was a crack when he flopped onto his side. The man leaned down and snatched at his pockets until he found Kieran's money and cellphone. The girl had grabbed Kieran's guitar to save it from falling, and he put a hand out to her. She'd paused for a moment before she turned to follow the thief, clutching the guitar.

"It'll be at John's Pawn tomorrow afternoon," she said over her shoulder.

Another dishwasher saved him that night, and introduced him to the pain relief he needed. Kieran found the crystal meth not only took away the sting, but it brought Roseanna to him. The images of the girl he loved right in front of him had been breathtaking. It hadn't taken long for his money to go up in smoke as he chased a phantom Roseanna around Manhattan. Each time he crashed, he couldn't scratch away the bugs that crawled under his skin, or escape the hallucinations of Roseanna just up ahead that disappeared around every corner before he got to her.

He'd been lucky to meet Tess, who'd taken him in to clean him up, as someone had done for her years earlier. Tess was patient, and kind, and Kieran had loved her as much as he could. But it had not been the same way he felt about Roseanna, and he knew it never would be. His sentimentality had been squeezed out by the reality of surviving on the streets. He still glimpsed Roseanna now and then in crowds, but he'd stopped running after her. He knew she was gone, and he knew his father had taken her.

Kieran had always known there were cracks in Caleb which he filled with moonshine. Kieran took the worst of the beatings, because he'd thought letting Caleb unload his rage without fighting back would make his father feel better. But Caleb's unhappiness was a vessel that never emptied. Kieran knew Roseanna would have fought back. On good nights, he imagined her escaping Caleb. On sleepless nights, he knew she never had.

Shortly after Brigit's second birthday, Kieran's arguing parents had woken him late one night. He'd snuck out of bed and crawled down the hall to their bedroom door.

"Please, Caleb. Let me go. It's been over ten years since I've seen them," Maeve had said.

"It's not a good time, Maeve," he had answered.

"They've never even met their grandkids."

"You send them pictures, don't you?"

"It's not the same and you know it."

"So let them come over here for a visit."

"He's too sick to fly. And you owe me." There had been the loud thump of something thrown on the floor.

Caleb's voice rose. "I owe you? That's a laugh."

"I've helped you for years. You know you'd never have gotten the government licenses without me. I wrote all those appeals for you, charmed those jackboot agents."

"Didn't seem to bother you much."

"You promised, you did. Do you think I would have come to America if I thought I'd never see my family again?"

"Is that a threat?"

"Da's dying, Caleb," Maeve said. "Please let me go."

"I said no!"

"It's my family!"

"Your family is right here in this house!" Another thump on the floor.

Kieran knew he shouldn't be listening outside the door, and if Caleb walked out right now he'd deserve the beating. It would be worse, though, if Maeve knew he was here; he wanted to help his mother but he didn't know how. There'd be trouble either way. Kieran held his breath. He couldn't move. He couldn't risk making a sound. Suddenly something clutched at the back of his collar. He swallowed down the squeak of terror and closed his eyes. It was pulling him down the hall, into his room. The door closed quietly and he looked up into Mack's face.

"What are you doing?" Mack whispered.

Kieran started to cry. Mack helped him up into bed and covered him, pulling the blanket up over his head. He tucked the blanket firmly around Kieran, snuggling him into a nest of quiet. Mack sat down on top of the covers, his hands at Kieran's feet, and held them through the comforter.

The next morning at the table Kieran had noticed Caleb's red eyes.

"I thought we could all go down to the diner for breakfast today," Caleb said from the doorway. Maeve glared at him and yanked her cast iron pan out of the cabinet. She cracked eggs into it with a vengeance. Mack sat sullenly, staring down at the table. Even Brigit was quiet. Usually Maeve gave in, but not today.

"I'm going to ride my bike down to the creek," Kieran said, mustering up all the sunshine he could find. "Maybe I'll find some crayfish. There's tons of them down there. They're easy to catch, too. I'll bring home a whole bucket full. We could make a pond out back and keep them as pets. Wouldn't that be cool?"

"Don't bother," Caleb said. "You take them out of their home they'll die."

Maeve whirled and pitched an egg at Caleb, which landed at his feet. Brigit laughed and pointed to the egg on the floor.

"Better clean that up," Caleb said as he walked out. Maeve ran after him.

"Jesus, Kieran, can't you ever learn to shut up?" Mack hissed.

Kieran was floored. Mack never yelled at him. He'd been trying to make it better, and somehow he'd made it worse.

After Maeve's death, ten-year-old Kieran had watched his family splintering, barely looking at each other. Mack was rarely home now, and when he was he and Caleb growled at each other like lions claiming territory. Brigit wandered woefully around, calling for her mother as if this were an elaborate game of hide and seek. Most nights it was Kieran who rocked her to sleep through her tired wails for Maeve.

Four days after the funeral, Kieran made a pile of grilled cheese sandwiches as the sun was throwing out the last rays of the day. Brigit jabbered away in her chair to the sound of the sizzling butter and the smell of melting cheese. Lonny poked his head in the kitchen.

"I'm making grilled cheese, want one?" Kieran asked.

"Okay," Lonny said.

"Could you cut one up for Brigit so I can make some more?" Kieran asked him.

Lonny cut a sandwich into four triangles and put it on a plastic Peter Rabbit plate in front of her. He sat down with his own plate as she grabbed a piece and stuck the whole thing in her mouth.

Mack came in.

"Can I have one?" he asked.

"Here," Kieran said, sliding a hot sandwich on a plate and holding it out to Mack. "Could you fill up Brigit's cup?"

Brigit banged her plastic cup on the table as Mack pulled a gallon of milk out of the refrigerator. Lonny rescued her cup and handed it to Mack, who poured.

"Uh-oh," Brigit cooed.

"Oh, Brigit," said Mack, picking up the triangle of sandwich she'd thrown on the floor.

"Can you make her another one?" Lonny asked.

Kieran started to make more when he saw Caleb heading unsteadily toward the kitchen, a jar of shine in his hand.

"Dad, want to eat with us?" Kieran asked.

"Not hungry," Caleb said. He leaned in the doorway and watched.

"I'm making grilled cheese, but I could make eggs, too, if you want," Kieran felt his nerves fluttering with his need to fill the uncomfortable silence in the room.

"That what we're eating now, samiches and eggs?" Caleb asked.

"I can make spaghetti, too. I mean, I can if we have a jar of sauce in the pantry."

"Ain't you just Betty damn Crocker," Caleb said.

"We have to eat. Brigit has to eat," Mack said.

"Daddy!" Brigit called, holding up her arms to Caleb.

"Lonny, that Deere ain't gonna drive itself into the shed," Caleb said, ignoring his daughter. Lonny left the room, half a sandwich on his plate.

"You could have let Lonny finish his dinner. If you're not hungry, you could have put the tractor away," Mack said.

Caleb crossed the room in two quick steps and smacked his son across the face with the back of his hand.

"It ain't gonna be like that, boy, you ain't in charge," he said as he turned and left.

Mack's face was turning red, but he continued to sit and eat. Brigit began to wail, and Kieran picked her up out of her chair.

"How about some ice cream?" he asked. He picked a carton of strawberry from the freezer, along with a bag of frozen lima beans, which he handed to Mack for his face.

The next day Roberta had come to work for them. She was a farm woman of few words, who came in the afternoons, cleaned just enough, and cooked big dinners with leftovers. It took Kieran a few months, but he'd finally charmed her enough to teach him to really cook. That turned out to be the talent that would save him from starving in New York. He'd eventually graduated from living at the Bowery Mission to cooking for them. Restaurants paid more, but he preferred working at the shelter. He liked to see the heads of the people nobody had wanted bent over food he had made for them.

The in-flight announcements began as the plane descended into Virginia. Kieran looked out the window at the wooded hills he never thought he'd see again. He tamped down any excitement he'd see Roseanna, irritated at himself for that small slice of hope. Caleb had stolen her, and Kieran didn't know why. He was sure his heart would break all over again, hearing the truth about her death. But if Caleb was dying, this would be his last opportunity; he had to know where she was buried, and the only person who could tell him was his father.

Brigit began to stir, her breath a fetid booze cloud. She'd grown into a mess that Kieran would bet had to do with bourbon. Mack seemed to have withdrawn into himself, more severe now, taking the weight of the world upon his shoulders. They were different people than the ones Kieran remembered, as Caleb had continued to leave his mark.

But this was all the family he had left, his sister and brother, and they could at least see each other through this nightmare. It might be his closing move, if Caleb were to make good on his last promise to Kieran. He wasn't sure if Caleb would consider him a man yet, but Manhattan living had taught him some hard lessons. If he and his father ended taking a final midnight ride on an unmarked bootleg road, Kieran knew only one of them would be coming back.

CHAPTER 23

Lonny shuffled down the hall toward Caleb's room. The nurses had insisted he leave last night because they had tests to do, they said, and he should go home and get some sleep. He wanted to stay, but the cows needed him, too. He'd tended to the livestock and now he was coming back. Maybe Caleb had perked up some and they could figure all this out together.

Entering Caleb's room, he saw immediately that things were much worse than when he left. He squeezed his eyes shut but it was too late to erase the wreckage of Caleb's ruined arms. They looked like a fresh battlefield; red, wet holes, a round bubble of blood sticking up over one that no one had bothered to wipe off. It had hardened into a dome. The needle holes were surrounded by deep purple flesh rings, working their way out through the rainbow of bruising. Lurid blue and green and finally pallid yellow ran from Caleb's now deflated, saggy biceps to his bulging-veined wrist. Lonny opened his eyes to see Caleb staring at him, taking in the disgust that Lonny felt; not for Caleb, but for whoever had done this to him.

"I'm sorry," he said as he moved to the old man's side, grabbed a tissue and burst the blood bubble, wiping it away.

Caleb winced when Lonny touched his wound.

"Luuh …" He looked up at Lonny. His face was split, muscles in a spasm on the left side as he tried to speak, while the right half remained completely still.

"Caleb? What happened?" Lonny squeezed down the panic in his chest. He never should have left Caleb's side.

"We had a rough night, didn't we, Mr. McKinsey?" chirped a skinny little Asian nurse who flittered in. "We had another stroke, didn't we? That makes it hard for us to talk, doesn't it?" She picked up his chart from the end of his bed and began to read, finally acknowledging Lonny. "You're sure here bright and early."

An older nurse with pink mottled skin and iron-gray hair cut short like a boy entered after her and went straight to a side table to fill a syringe.

"Luuh …" Caleb pleaded from his twisted mouth.

"I don't think he wants no more shots," Lonny said.

"Just a couple," the skinny nurse replied brightly, as if he were five years old.

"He needs these to help him get better," said the nurse with the gray hair.

"Yeah, but he don't want them," Lonny said firmly. He pulled Caleb's blanket up over his arms to his chin. Both nurses stopped and looked up at him. Iron gray raised her head.

"That's not up to you," she said.

"Luuh …"

"See? He don't want no more shots."

"Until he can make that clear, we have to proceed." Iron gray stood firmly as the skinny nurse stepped out.

"Maybe you don't know, but I know. He's telling me."

The skinny nurse was back now, with a stern-faced doctor Lonny guessed was probably the same age as him, and that's all they'd ever have in common. The doctor's nose wrinkled at Lonny's barn smell and his smooth face furrowed.

"And you are …?" he asked, while looking at Caleb's file.

"Lonny Allen."

"I'm Dr. Reeves, and unless you can produce a power of attorney, Lonny, we will treat Mr. McKinsey," he said into Caleb's chart. "Can you do that?"

"No, but he don't want any more shots."

"Please step outside while we administer his meds."

"Can't I stay with him?"

"His visitors should be family only," Reeves replied.

"His family left town," said the skinny nurse.

"What a surprise," Reeves said, snatching the syringe. He finally turned his head to Lonny. "Step out now, or I'll have to call security." He turned back to Caleb.

Lonny walked out into the hallway. He paced up and down outside Caleb's room, flexing his hands. Caleb was trying to curse the doctor and nurses; his voice was slurry but Lonny knew what he meant. Something crashed to the ground, and Reeves issued a warning to Caleb. Lonny paced faster. He wished for Mack to walk in that door right now. Mack wouldn't know what Caleb wanted no better than them doctors, but he'd listen to Lonny. Mack knew the order of things. For the first time, Lonny cursed Caleb's son.

"Luuuuhh …" Caleb howled like an old dog abandoned by the side of the road. Lonny pushed back through the door. Reeves was leaning over him with a needle. Caleb's arms were stretched straight out to his sides, a nurse holding down each one.

Lonny grabbed the doctor by his collar and yanked him back. The needle went clattering to the floor. Lonny turned and shoved Reeves out in the hallway. Lonny stepped back in, toward the skinny nurse, who jumped away and ran out. Iron gray slowly eased back to the wall. Caleb reached out awkwardly with his left arm, flailing around in front of him. Lonny took his hand firmly and stood there.

"Security!" Dr. Reeves was now screaming in the hallway.

"I'm sorry," Lonny said.

"Sorry is not going to cut it," Iron gray said.

"I wasn't talking to you," he said to her as he bent over Caleb.

There was the look.

Lonny gently placed the worn fedora back on Caleb's head. He looked at Caleb, who nodded. Lonny pulled the I.V. needle out of the back of Caleb's hand, then bent and gathered him up in his arms and carried him out.

In the fresh air outside, Caleb closed his eyes against the bright sun and smiled with the half of his face that still could. The doors swooshed shut on scurrying nurses insisting that he return immediately. Lonny didn't turn around. He'd never, ever treated someone the way he had that doctor today, but he did what he needed to do.

Lonny managed to get Caleb buckled into the truck in a mostly upright position. Caleb's eyes were still closed, but Lonny could hear him breathing. Shade from the pines and black walnut trees dappled the road on the way to Touraine, cooling the heat of the day.

Back in town, Lonny slowed to a crawl when he got to the dirt road leading to the farm. He could hear Caleb wheezing now. The road was kicking up a lot of dust, so he rolled up the windows and turned on the air conditioning, something he hated to do. It was artificial air, but it did seem to ease Caleb's breathing. As they approached the house, he looked over to Caleb. His eyes were open and he grunted and waved Lonny on.

Lonny drove out to the barn. He'd only let the cows out an hour ago, but a lone cow was striding toward the barn, head bobbing purposefully. Lonny pulled the truck into the hayloft and tugged the heavy doors closed behind him. He didn't know what he'd do if those government guys showed up now, but he guessed he'd be in a heap more trouble than he already was. He gathered straw and carried it through the milk house. He fashioned a bed in an empty stall and unrolled an old horse blanket.

He went back to the truck and unbuckled Caleb, carrying him into the stall and laying him down carefully, tucking the blanket around him. Winnie, the oldest cow in the herd, lumbered in and shook her head with a soft huff before settling down to offer her flank to Caleb.

Lonny adjusted Caleb's fedora, and sat in the straw at his feet.

"Luh," Caleb sighed.

"Caleb," Lonny replied.

Winnie turned her head, soft brown eyes gazing at Caleb through long lashes. Caleb's breath came out in long, rattling gasps now. This was Lonny's truth, then, for the one person who had always taken up for him. He didn't know how to explain the bond between himself and Caleb, and he guessed he didn't have to.

Winnie lifted her head. Her mournful lowing echoed, calling the herd home. In the distance, Lonny could hear their cries, mixed with the faint wail of sirens, growing louder as they traveled up the mountain.

CHAPTER 24

Lonny watched the bedraggled gang of McKinseys trudging out of the airport's arrivals gate like prisoners on their last walk of freedom. He couldn't tear his eyes away from Kieran, who was now the twin for the Caleb that had rescued Lonny as a child. There'd always been a resemblance, but now it was more than physical. Lonny could see Kieran had been kicked now, too.

Mack was heading toward the green Enterprise car rental counter. Something had happened in New York with his truck, Lonny guessed. He felt a familiar pang of loneliness. Why wouldn't Mack, or any of them, call Lonny and ask him to pick them up? Because it never occurred to them, he knew. The McKinsey kids had always included Lonny, when they thought about it.

He stayed by the door, hands in his pockets. Mack would know what to do now. He was good at being in charge. Just the thought eased Lonny's tension.

"Mack?" Lonny said.

"Lonny!" Brigit said. "What are you doing here?"

"I come to get you."

"How did you know we'd be here?" Mack asked.

"The credit card people called on Caleb's phone. Said they had to make sure it was you buying plane tickets in New York. I told 'em it was. Not too many flights from New York to Charlottesville, was hoping it'd be this one." That was a lot of sentences in a row for Lonny, and they were all staring at him.

"Thanks for doing that," said Mack.

Lonny shifted from foot to foot. "You don't need no rental car. I brought Caleb's truck, so we got enough room."

"Good to see you, Lonny," Kieran said.

"Kieran," Lonny shuffled his feet, staring at Kieran. "You, uh, you sure look like your pa now." He looked down. "We should go."

They followed him out to the truck and piled in, Brigit and Kieran in the back of the extended cab and Mack in the front. Lonny had jumped in the driver's seat without a word, which was fine with Mack. He filled Lonny in on his stolen pickup.

"Think you'll get it back?" Lonny asked.

"I'm sure it's just spare parts by now," Mack said. He wondered what the thieves had done with his painstakingly drafted plans for Maeve's Garden. Probably floating in the East River by now, with the frozen peas. He hoped his cash was floating in the river too, instead of in their pockets.

He noticed they were headed out of Charlottesville, toward Touraine.

"Lonny, I think we should head straight to the hospital," Mack said.

"I done something, Mack." Lonny looked straight ahead.

"What did you do?"

"I brought Caleb home."

"He's home?"

"Is he better?" Brigit asked.

There was a long silence in the truck.

"Lonny?" Brigit persisted.

"He's home, anyway," Lonny said.

When they pulled up the drive, Brigit jumped out and started quickly into the house. Mack followed her.

"Mack," Kieran called to him. He stopped to light a cigarette. "What's going on?"

"I don't know, but I don't want Brigit walking into a disaster by herself." He picked up the pace to catch up to Brigit. She faltered by Caleb's bedroom door, letting Mack enter first.

Caleb was a form on a bed, outlined by a thin blanket. His eyelids fluttered as if he were trying to fight his way out of whatever dream he was currently battling. They could hear him wheezing as he tried to draw breath. Kieran walked in behind them and stood at the foot of the bed, staring down at his father.

Lonny slowly made his way to Caleb's side and picked his hand up.

"Caleb? They're all here now. Mack and Brigit are back, and they brought Kieran, just like they said they would."

"I can't believe they let him go home," Mack said. "Is there medication, an oxygen tank? Do we need to get a nurse? Did they send instructions on what we should do?"

"They didn't exactly let him leave," Lonny said.

"Then what—" Brigit started.

"Lonny, you have to tell us what happened," Mack said.

"It was rough, Mack. He was all full of drugs, on account of another stroke, and he didn't want to be. He wasn't talking too good, so I told them nurses he didn't want no more shots, but they said...." Lonny stared miserably down.

"What?" Mack asked.

"They said it wasn't up to me, because I'm not family."

"Lonny," Brigit said.

"And they made me leave so's the doctor could give him another shot, but Caleb was wailing, so I busted back in and stopped them. He wanted to come home. I could tell. So I unplugged him and put him in the truck and brought him here."

"He's not breathing very well," Kieran said.

"Mack," Lonny pleaded. "I don't know what to do now."

"I'm calling an ambulance," Mack said, leaving the bedroom.

"There was one here, but we were hiding in the barn," Lonny said.

"Jesus, Lonny!"

"He didn't want no more shots, Mack."

"Why can't we drive him?" Brigit asked.

"Listen. He needs oxygen and the EMS people have it."

"But—" Brigit started. Mack was already on the phone, giving the address.

She hovered uncertainly over Caleb, listening to his labored breath. She was concerned and detached at the same time. She didn't know how she was supposed to feel. She wished she could ask someone, but the very fact of her wondering how she should feel about her sick father made her sound like a cold, hard bitch. Which, coincidentally, she'd been called by Caleb on more than one occasion.

Think of something nice, she willed herself. She remembered when she was little, four maybe, and Caleb would scoop her suddenly up off the floor and plant her on his shoulders, then pretend he didn't know she was there. She'd grasp his hair in her little fists to hang on, as he walked around the room, asking, "Where is Brigit? Where did that girl get to?" They'd come to a doorway and he'd pretend he was about to walk her right into it, then duck at the very last second and she'd giggle uncontrollably.

She could see this Caleb, young like Kieran was now, so clearly. He'd laughed with her. That's what she wanted to think of, what she wanted to remember about her father. But when she closed her eyes, instead she saw the furious Caleb, the one who burst into her bedroom one night and started to sweep the toys from her shelves with his arm, throwing them violently to the floor, staggering and cursing that she was a spoiled brat who had too much goddamn shit and didn't deserve any of it. She'd covered her head with a pillow, making herself small under the covers as he threw things at her. Mack had run in and grabbed her up in a bundle of blankets and escaped to Kieran's room. Kieran slammed the door as soon as they got in, and the boys pushed his dresser in front of the door. They huddled together in the corner, listening to Caleb rage outside, pounding and yelling until he finally passed out.

This, too, was her father. One couldn't live in her head without the other.

When the ambulance arrived, Mack climbed in the back without a word to anyone. It took off down the driveway, lights flashing. Lonny stood on the front porch step, pulling on his hands, watching the ambulance speed away. Kieran sat in the rocking chair, smoking, looking too much like the old man for Brigit's taste. She ran down to Caleb's truck.

"Let's go," she said, climbing in the driver's seat and starting the engine.

Both men hesitated.

"I'm in a mess of trouble," Lonny muttered.

"Get in this goddamn truck right now!" Brigit bellowed.

They both jumped in. Brigit gunned the engine and sped off after the ambulance. She managed to stay right behind it, hazard lights flashing, blowing the traffic lights along with it, all the way into Charlottesville. She squealed into a space at the hospital as the emergency technicians unloaded Caleb and rushed him inside.

Brigit ran toward the hospital entrance, only to realize she was alone. She whirled back to them.

"Come on," she said. Neither of them moved. Her face tightened in rage. "Kieran, don't you chickenshit out on me now! Whatever you have to say to him, I'm sure Mack and I have said worse. Lonny, you are too family and you should have told them so." She stomped through the door, once again followed by Kieran and Lonny.

They found Mack standing outside a room while nurses and doctors hurried in and out. One nurse stopped at the sight of Lonny. "You need to get out," she snapped.

Lonny stood firm now as Mack walked up to her.

"I'm Mack McKinsey, Caleb's my father. Lonny knows better than anybody who what Caleb wants, and he needs to be here. I know you had a misunderstanding, but we've brought him back and cleared that up." Mack spoke with a calm he did not feel.

"But he—" she pointed at Lonny.

"I know what he did." Mack lowered his voice. "Look, you know who Caleb is. We are all family here. We all want the best for him, you included, I'm sure. You don't want to have us all thrown out."

"There's a sweet headline," Shooter Jackson appeared suddenly behind them. " 'Hospital Denies Dying Man His Family' will look nice at the top of the *Daily Progress,* don't you think? One of his sons lives in New York, so we'll make sure it gets in the news there, too. So many social media sites are dying for good content. I forward a sad photo of grieving children denied entrance, University of Virginia Medical Center sign in the background, and it goes viral."

The nurse looked away.

"You know he's not going to be here much longer," Mack said quietly.

"I'll have to call the doctor," she said, retreating to the nurse's station.

"You should do that," Shooter said. "And we'll go see Caleb." He put his arm around a surprised Brigit.

Lonny watched them rise to his defense and felt safer. Now that Caleb was all hooked up again, his breathing was quieter. Lonny snuck in his room and sat next to him, holding his hand. Caleb's hand was still warm, and as long as that was the case, Lonny was okay being back here. He didn't suppose it much mattered where it happened, really. The floury scent on Caleb's skin was still there, though the doctors kept trying to cover it up with all the medicine, which, in Lonny's opinion, smelled worse. But he'd seen the look in Caleb's eyes before he took him home. Caleb had finally smelled it too.

CHAPTER 25

Mack stepped outside the hospital to get a moment alone, relieved to let Shooter take over. There would be a lot of questions for which he had no answers.

"Mr. McKinsey?" Agent Peterson approached him out of nowhere.

"Jesus," Mack said, turning away. "I have nothing to say."

"I'd like to apologize for my partner the other day." Peterson said. "I'm very sorry to hear about your father. Is there anything we can do? The U.S. government has great doctors."

"You have got to be kidding!" Mack turned to confront him.

"We can help each other. I know you want to break away from Virginia. You've been trying, but there are a lot of roadblocks."

"How do you know?"

"Think of Brigit. She could go to jail. But we can make that go away."

"Brigit isn't part—"

"Everything's connected, Mack. Look, we have a drone going out today. Give it up now, we can fix a lot of your problems. But once we find it on our own, there's nothing I can do to help you."

"Find what?" The tension in Mack's arm was building.

"Why are you talking to him?" From the parking lot Agent Miller was hustling up to them, sweat stains blooming under his arms. "He can't help us. Send Kieran out, we know he's here with you."

"Kieran knows even less than I do," Mack said.

"See, that's where you're wrong. Tell him we can make that deal now." Miller panted.

"What?" Mack asked.

"Excuse me, Mr. McKinsey?" A young Black man in a white coat stepped out from the hospital. "Can we speak, please?"

Mack joined the doctor inside, looking back over his shoulder at the ATF agents, standing there as if they'd wait forever.

The physician said, "Mr. McKinsey, I'm Dr. Howard. I'm an oncologist from Johns Hopkins. I flew in to consult on another patient and Dr. Reeves said I might want to take a look at your father. I've looked over his chart. His cancer is quite aggressive and it doesn't look like there's been much treatment."

"Caleb's not big on doctors," Mack said.

"There's a new steroid I think might help. We could give it a try, but there are side effects. It could cause clotting, so we'd have to give him a stronger blood thinner than the one he's on for the stroke. But that has the potential for causing internal bleeding. We won't know if he can handle it until we give it to him, but if he stabilizes, we can proceed with chemo and radiation."

"What if he doesn't take it?"

"Well . . . then all we can do is make him comfortable."

"And this blood thinner?"

"The coumadin he's on now is administered more slowly. The new drug's given in one shot. But once we give it to him, we can't stop it."

"So it might kill him?" Mack asked.

"We'd know in the next few hours. You should talk to your family. I think it's his best option for treating the cancer, but if it doesn't work, it could accelerate things."

"Those are my options?"

"I'm sorry, Kieran. I know this is difficult."

"I'm not Kieran," Mack shook his head. "I'm Mack."

"Oh. I apologize. I had a note that his son Kieran has power of attorney."

"That's my younger brother."

"Is he here?"

"I'll talk to him," Mack paused. "We have a sister, too. Brigit. If that matters."

He headed back to Caleb's room. This was not the decision he wanted to make, giving permission for the shot that might kill his father. But for once, he wasn't in charge. Caleb's future was up to Kieran. His brother, who was apparently cutting secret deals with the ATF.

Shooter was standing guard outside Caleb's door. "Kieran? Brigit?" Mack called softly from the doorway. "Lonny? We need to talk." Mack waited in the hallway, next to a cart with metal dinner trays that smelled like canned vegetables and boiled meat.

"Shooter, could you give us a minute?" Mack asked as they all filed out of the room.

"Sure, I'll be right here." He gave Brigit a half smile.

Mack glimpsed a small waiting area. He led them down to sit in the thick wooden-armed chairs with the soothing blue cushions.

"They want to give him a new drug. It's a shot," Mack started.

"He don't want no more, Mack. Please, don't let them keep him all doped up," Lonny said.

"This is supposed to help. Get him stable, so they can treat the cancer."

"So, okay," Brigit said. "Let's do it."

"But it's risky; it might cause internal bleeding that they won't be able to stop."

"Well, that don't sound good," said Lonny.

"But if they don't give it to him, there's no other treatment," Mack said slowly.

"So wait—he might die if we do and he might die if we don't?"

Brigit asked. "What are we supposed to do? There must be something else. Can't we get another opinion? There have to be other ways, other medicines." Her voice was rising. "We just got here, they can't fling shit like this at us. We don't know anything right now."

"Calm down, Brigit. We'll figure it out," Mack said.

"I say no. No! I don't want to do this," Brigit said.

"Me neither, it don't sound good at all," said Lonny.

"So we vote. Mack? What do you say? You can't be in favor of this," Brigit said.

"It doesn't matter what I say," Mack sighed.

"What? Why?" Brigit said.

"It doesn't matter what you say, either. Does it, Kieran?" They all looked to Kieran. "Caleb designated Kieran as his power of attorney."

"Give him the shot," Kieran said. He stood and walked away down the hall.

Brigit gasped. Lonny's head fell into his hands.

"Are you sure, Kieran?" Mack called after him.

"Oh, that's great! Just give Dad a death sentence and then fucking walk away!" Brigit yelled.

Kieran whirled on them. "Why do you want to save him so badly? For what? Has he changed somehow? Has Caleb McKinsey had his come-to-Jesus moment?" Kieran shook his head. "Maybe you're all *afraid* this will work, and he'll actually live. Is that it? Are you all sitting there secretly wishing he'd die?"

"Who the hell did you become in New York?" Brigit said.

"I became *me*, Brigit. I'm not the always-happy good boy anymore. Caleb made sure of that."

"So your revenge is ratting him out to the feds?" Mack asked.

"What are you talking about?" Kieran said.

"I was just cornered by an ATF agent outside who said they'd very much like to talk to you so you can finish cutting your deal with them."

"What?" Brigit cried.

"And if *I* don't talk to them, they can throw you in jail, Brigit."

"Mack?" It was the first hint of fear Mack had seen in his sister.

"I have no deal with anybody. But thanks for having my back, brother," Kieran said.

"Then why would they say it?" Mack asked.

"Because it's what they do, Mack. Divide and conquer, don't you know that?"

"They tried to talk to me, too," Lonny said. "They're trying to get to Caleb."

"Do you see? They've got all of us turned against each other now," Kieran looked at Mack. "Confusion makes people act out, make mistakes. That's what they're counting on. This is why Caleb told us to never talk to them."

"I wasn't talking to them," Mack said. "They just … they say things they can't know, but they *do* know."

"What're we gonna do, Kieran?" Lonny asked.

"We need to think about Caleb right now. The doctors put it as nicely as they can, but Caleb *will* die without the shot. If this is his only chance, we have to take it."

The four of them were ushered into the cancer ward's private lounge to wait while the doctors administered the medicine to Caleb. They were sheltered by thick glass doors from the hospital's hallway with the alarms and bells and overhead announcements for emergency codes. There was a long dining table with plush chairs around it, and a kitchen with recessed lighting and soft curtains on the windows. The mini fridge was stocked with juice and fruit, and there was a basket of imported crackers and Danish cookies on the table. No one wanted to eat, however. Mack figured it was always that way in the death lounge. He wondered if the hospital had considered that irony.

"Did you know Mack had to drag me into the hospital to see Caleb from jail?" Brigit asked Kieran suddenly. "We're way more messed up than when you left."

"It's not as bad as it was," Mack said.

"That's because none of us have talked to each other in three years," Brigit said.

"Three years? Since I left?" Kieran asked.

"Since my graduation."

"I am so sorry I missed it, Brigit."

"You missed a great fight at my graduation party. Mack and the old man went at it like vipers and got my entire class to attack each other."

"You fought with Dad?" Kieran asked.

"He fights dirty," Mack said. "Broke my foot."

"You should have seen it, the old man begging for mercy. Mack took him down good."

"This making you feel better, is it?" Lonny asked loudly. "Could you not spare a kind thought for the man?"

This silenced Caleb's children.

"I'm sorry, Lonny," Brigit said, after a moment.

"Me too, Lonny," Mack said.

"He weren't mean on purpose," Lonny said. "Caleb didn't have a great time of it growing up, but he wasn't never gonna tell you that. His brothers beat him, and I know he did the same to you. He thought that was what you were supposed to do, to make you tough. But he was so proud of you." Lonny stopped. Usually he was a one-sentence-at-a-time guy, but today he'd broken all his records. "I'm gonna wait outside for now," he muttered as he left the room.

"Caleb wants you to take over Bourbon Sweet Tea," Mack said to Kieran.

"The only thing I want is for him to tell me what he did to Roseanna."

"It should be me anyway. Taking over. You both need to tell him it should be me," Brigit said.

"Okay, Brigit," said Mack.

"No. Do not humor me, Mack." There was no uncertainty in her eyes now. A strong, calm reserve emanated, and both brothers looked at her in surprise. "Neither of you want to run it, but I do. And I have plans. We can make Bourbon Sweet Tea something to be proud of."

"I used to think so, growing up. But now I just want to get away from it," Kieran said.

"Yeah, you'll have your work cut out for you there," Mack griped.

"I can do it. We can do it," Brigit insisted. "As long as we stick together."

A nurse opened the door and stepped in. They turned toward her. "Good news. Your father's awake," she said, smiling. "We administered the shot, and he's rallied in a big way. His speech has even improved. We see this sometimes, they just wake up and start talking like no time has passed at all."

She escorted them back to Caleb's room, where they could hear their father holding court. His speech was slurred but unmistakable. Behind the curtain around his bed, Dr. Howard laughed.

"Christ, there, doc, she coulda been Sophia Loren. Warn me next time before you wake me up, so's I can at least cop a feel," Caleb said.

Howard pushed through the curtain and ran into the trio of Caleb's children hovering in the doorway. "He's doing well," he said, smiling. "I've adjusted his morphine so he'll be more alert."

"So he's better?" Brigit asked.

"We'll monitor him to make sure, but he's responding very well at the moment. He's alert and lucid. His speech is still affected from the stroke, but the improvement is tremendous. I'll be back to check on him shortly." He continued down the hall with a confident step. They could hear Caleb's gravelly voice, and see Lonny's feet under the curtain.

"This is ridiculous," announced Brigit. She fidgeted, then burst out, "We have to go in."

Mack had been certain Kieran would lead the way, and they'd follow his lead. "Kieran? Are you ready?" he asked.

"No," Kieran said, shaking his head.

Mack stepped back, popped his shoulder, hard, and felt the rush that came with it. He stepped up to the curtain, yanked it back, and stepped aside.

"Well, son of a bitch," Caleb said softly, looking past him. "Kieran."

For a long minute no one spoke. Kieran and Caleb stared at each other, past looking into future. Lonny stood by Caleb's side, looking beseechingly at Kieran. Brigit was staring up at the ceiling, blinking hard. Mack just wanted to leave. He'd fulfilled Caleb's request and brought Kieran, and now he was done.

"We're all here, Dad," Mack said, the words catching in his throat. Caleb frowned.

"I can see that. Took you long enough." He attempted to hitch himself up on the bed, awkward with his weak right arm. Lonny reached out but Caleb waved his hand away.

"What you been doing up there, partying in the Big Apple?"

Kieran stood quietly looking at Caleb, as he had when he was a child and Caleb was baiting him. Mack knew this made Caleb more angry. Maybe this was what Kieran wanted.

"We had a hell of a trip. Mack got his truck stolen," Brigit blurted.

"What you go and do that for?" Caleb growled, he and Kieran still locking eyes.

"Couldn't find a parking space," Mack answered.

"Always the smart ass, ain't you?"

"You sound a lot better than the other day," Brigit said.

"I sound like a drunk old sway-bag with a mouth full of marbles," he muttered. "Hell of a thing, ain't it?"

Still Kieran remained silent.

"Can we get you anything?" Brigit asked.

"I don't want nothing."

"Are you hungry? We could go get you some real food," Brigit said. "Anything you want."

Mack could see she needed to offer him something, but Caleb wasn't going to take it.

"I said no, now quit pestering me. Bad as your ma," he mumbled.

Red spots flushed up on Brigit's cheeks. "We went through hell to get Kieran here for you. We drove all the way to New York City, Mack's truck was stolen, all his money too, and he gave me this beautiful black eye. But I'm okay, *Daddy*, thanks for asking," She headed for the door.

"Don't get yourself all worked up, girl," Caleb said.

She turned back to him.

"Now that I'm twenty-one, I have voting rights. I have ideas for the company. Neither of your sons wants to run it, but this *girl* does. Know this, old man. You will no longer have the majority votes. If Mack and Kieran and I work together, we can take you down." And she barreled out of the room.

"What is she ... aw, hell. Let her go," Caleb said as Mack started after his sister. "She needs to burn it off like your ma used to."

Mack stopped. He could see the concern in Caleb's eyes, despite what he said. Mack stared at him. He didn't think Caleb had meant to be so gruff. For the first time, his father seemed frightened.

"You ever gonna talk to me, or jes' stand there like a deaf-mute?" Caleb asked Kieran, who hadn't moved since walking in the room. Mack wouldn't be surprised if Kieran suddenly rushed over and clamped a pillow over Caleb's face.

"Sorry, Kieran. He was a lot nicer the other day," Mack said. "Well, 'nice' for him. Which doesn't mean actually nice, just slightly less of an asshole."

"Kind words from my son," Caleb said.

"What did you do to her?" Kieran asked suddenly.

"Who?" Caleb frowned.

"What did you do to her?" he asked again. There was no pleading in his voice now, as there had been years before. It was firm, unyielding. His eyes probed into Caleb's, just like the ones looking back.

"What the hell're you talking about, boy?"

"What did you do to her?"

"Her? I didn't do nothing to her."

"What did you do to her?"

"Jesus, I can't believe you're still pining over that piece of low county trash," Caleb said, his eyes narrowing. "I don't know where she went."

"What did you do to her?"

"Mack, can't you get him to …"

"What did you do to her?"

"What did I do? I paid her off! Okay? I gave her the goddamn money to leave and she did!" Caleb snarled.

"You gave Roseanna money to leave me?" Kieran shook his head.

"I had to know, boy. You had that settling-down look, I could see it. But I had to know if she really loved you." He shuffled in the bed, twisting the sheets around himself. "I offered her an envelope full a' money. Told her she could keep that, or she could keep you. She did not even wait to think it over. She just grabbed it, son. Took the money and got the hell out of Dodge. Spit on my shoes before she left, if that makes you feel better."

"You . . . *paid* Roseanna to leave Kieran?" Mack asked.

"I didn't think she'd take it! She followed him around like a goddamn puppy!"

"What did you think she'd do?" Kieran walked slowly up to the side of Caleb's bed. "You knew she was poor. You knew she came from a family who didn't care about her. She'd never had any money. What did you *think* she would do?"

"She had a choice."

"A choice?" Kieran leaned down over Caleb, who was trembling.

"She could have had you instead," Caleb said.

Kieran backed away like he'd been slapped.

"I should have told you, maybe. But you'd a chased her down, and brought her back. It were already wrecked, don't you see? I thought you'd get over it. Figured you'd mourn her and come on back. Better for you to think I broke your heart, instead of her. Then you could go on and find somebody worth it. You gotta let her go, son. She weren't worth it. I know. Your ma was worth it. Ya gotta find that."

"I thought you killed her."

"Jesus, Kieran! That's what you been thinking about your old man all this time?"

"Why wouldn't I? You killed your brothers."

"Who told you that?"

"Everybody in town knows that."

"And you believe them?" Caleb turned to Mack. "That what you think, too?"

Mack hesitated, not wanting to add up all the evidence but unable to stop. "Yeah, I do. I saw the car, when I was a kid. Hidden in the barn, with all the bullet holes."

"Jesus," Caleb said wonderingly. "Jesus."

Kieran turned and walked out. He headed toward the exit, hands shaking.

He stepped outside and lit a cigarette. There were hard memories everywhere he looked. Littered scraps of Roseanna stuck to buildings and trees and street signs. They poked and prodded at him. She was everywhere and nowhere, always right behind him, or right in front of him, but never with him. He'd convinced himself that Caleb had killed her. His father was violent, he knew this firsthand. But he had no reason to lie, not now.

Roseanna had left him for money. She hadn't even talked to him first. She'd made a choice, and it wasn't him.

Back in the room, Caleb struggled to sit up.

"Lonny, you go make sure he's all right. Tell him he needs to visit the mountain, that's what he's here for. He'll know. And make sure he don't do nothing stupid."

When Lonny left Caleb leaned back into his pillow and closed his eyes. Mack could see how much more sunken his eyes were, just in a few days. The flesh had started to hollow off his cheeks as well. His silvered hair was brushed back from his face, but thinning, with the shiny scalp poking through. The knucklebones in his hands were almost poking through the thin, scarred skin. His fragile skin looked ready to split open and let him slip to the floor.

"I'm going to go," Mack said.

"I ain't done with you," Caleb said, eyes still closed.

"I'll see you later," Mack said.

"Might not be a later, and we both know it."

"Look, I don't need ..."

"You don't know what the hell you need," Caleb said. "That's your problem."

"Oh boy. Here we go."

"I want you to do me a favor," Caleb said.

"A *favor*? I just did you a huge favor! I brought you Kieran, which is all you wanted in the first place. You are really pushing it, old man."

"Put my ashes in your garden when I'm dead."

Mack froze. "You've been to Maeve's Garden?"

"That what you call it? That's nice. Put that gardenia in the middle for her, did you? She'd of liked that."

"How did you find it? How did you know?" The violation felt visceral.

"Oh, I been watching it for years. I kept an eye on you after your ma died. Know you had a tough time of it, I do know that." Caleb's voice was quiet now.

"That was mine," Mack whispered.

"It *is* yours, son. I only went in a few times. I can see the whole family there, like we was all plucked out of your head. You got a way with nature," he said. "But I gotta tell ya, you have to let it go."

"What?"

262

"McKinseys, we got tempers. We're stubborn, but we ain't got strong hearts. Your ma took mine. Your brother's been pining for years over someone don't deserve it. And you think you ain't deserving, but ya are."

"You have no right—" Mack started.

"But you do. Find somebody. You gotta live for the living. Your sister and brother gonna need you more than ever. You gotta hang on to 'em. You think you ain't up for it, but you are."

A shadow moved quickly through the doorway as Brigit strode up to Caleb's bedside.

"So here's the thing," she began.

"I know—" Caleb started.

"No, you listen now. I'm gonna say this before you can piss me off again and make me leave. Because I'm really tired and confused and all these bruises are starting to hurt. I need to tell you some things the boys won't. You are *not* a good father. Sometimes you were fun, but most of the time you made us feel like we were no better than the cow shit stuck to your boots. And we are better than that, all of us. So I'm not sitting here trying to make you feel bad, I'm just telling you like it is because it needs to be said and you need to do better."

"You're right."

Brigit faltered at this, but only for a moment.

"And I *will* run Bourbon Sweet Tea, even if you try to stop me."

"You're a good girl, Brigit."

"I...stop it," Brigit said. "You're supposed to yell at me."

"I'm proud of you," Caleb said. Tears slid down his cheeks. He did not try to wipe them away. "You're tough and you don't take no shit. You are just like your ma, and that's the best thing I can ever tell you. Now quit bothering me and go get Lonny—"

Caleb started to cough, deep, rumbling gasps, and spasms shook his frail body. His left arm flailed around and he grasped at Brigit. She took his hand and helped him sit up. Mack rushed over to his father and pounded on his back. One of his monitors was beeping loudly.

Blood was spurting from his mouth with each wet, hacking cough as Caleb looked into his children's eyes and beyond, with fear.

"Help! Somebody please help us!" Brigit screamed. Blood, dark, red and viscous, was pouring down his hospital gown. He was choking on it, as it rumbled up out of his chest where there should have been air.

Mack let go of Caleb and ran to the doorway. "We need some help here!"

Dr. Howard burst into his room with two nurses, one of whom pushed Brigit roughly out of the way as they laid Caleb out and turned him on his side. Alarms buzzed as the doctor yelled and pounded on Caleb's chest, again and again. Brigit was frozen against the wall, unable to look away. Mack crossed over and scooped her up, once again, and carried her away from Caleb.

CHAPTER 26

Caleb was sliding backward, but it was not painful. Seamus O'Hearn was there, and he was telling Caleb he needed to go back to Ireland, like the trip so many years ago that had changed everything.

It was winter, and they were young men on the side of the mountain in the middle of the night, scouring the forest for the revenuers. Seamus had been by Caleb's side while he'd grown Bourbon Sweet Tea like a favored child. The years of hard work had paid off, and Caleb had stacks of money hidden away in the secret cavities of his basement; enough to walk away and leave the risk behind.

"Caleb, you ever take a vacation?" Seamus asked him.

"This here's my vacation," Caleb answered, lighting another cigarette.

"Hell, you're sitting on a rock in the woods."

"Watching my product, that's all."

"That ain't no vacation. You oughta go to Ireland."

"What the hell'd I do that for?"

"Don't you want to see where you came from?"

"I came from right here." Caleb pulled up the collar on his coat against the wind.

"You ain't curious 'bout your past?"

"I know all the past I need to know."

"Too bad," Seamus said as he rose to go. "With all this, over there you'd be a goddamn king." Seamus stood quietly, pausing to listen through the dark night. When he was reassured by the sounds of the crickets and tree frogs, he disappeared down the hill.

A king, Caleb snorted. He did work hard, but no one here considered him anything but an outlaw.

Seamus O'Hearn had gone to Ireland a few years before and gotten himself an Irish bride. He sure was proud of that, too, though there were rumors she might be a distant cousin. She was shy, Orla was, and looked to Seamus before answering any question put to her. Seamus grew plump on her baking, his face taking on a self-satisfied look as she bore him four sons in a row.

"Find yourself a quiet girl from a big family, mousy even; a middle sister's best. She'll be so damn grateful for her own home and family, especially in America, she'll fall right in love with you," Seamus had told him.

The idea of Ireland ate away at Caleb for months after that. What little he knew of his heritage came from his father insisting on spelling whiskey with an "e" so as not to be mistaken for a damn Scotsman. Caleb had been alone for a long time, though. He'd known a couple of women, but he was dedicated to the business of bourbon and he had no room for compromise. Seamus didn't seem to have made much of a sacrifice, though, and it was a big house for just him and Lonny to rattle around in. Come spring, he found a plane ticket in his hand.

His first night in Galway, he'd tried a local pub, a wooden-floored and salty-smelling place, and bought a round of drinks for the bar. This earned him the nickname "Yankee." Caleb tried to enlighten them on the Confederacy, but learned that if you were from America, you were a Yankee no matter how far south your roots extended. His reputation preceded him, as on the next night he met Maeve.

"So you're the Yankee, are ye?" she asked him, sidling up to his barstool, tucking a long messy wave of copper-streaked hair behind an ear. She was rather forward, not something he was used to. "And what is it you are doing in Galway?" Maeve asked. She looked right at him, with a pouting mouth that turned down at the corners in a challenge.

"Looking for a fine Irish lass," he answered. "But you'll do."

She threw her head back and laughed with her entire face, cheeks dimpling and eyes crinkling, and Caleb found he wanted to make her laugh again and again.

"And what do you do in America, Yankee?" she asked him as she took the stool next to his.

He sat back and gave her the stern look, as he did anyone in Touraine who asked him questions. But she did not flinch.

"My name's Caleb McKinsey. I make whiskey," he answered.

"Do you now? So's me da."

"A noble profession," Caleb said.

"Is it then?" she asked with a twinkle in her sea-green eyes. She leaned into him then, and with a straight face, told him a dirty joke. "Doesn't matter what size, as long as it fits a camel," she ended solemnly, then howled again with laughter. She took in his shocked face, patted his cheek and rose to leave.

"You're a saucy wic, is what you are," he said to her. Maeve stopped, all laughter suddenly still. Caleb didn't see the insult here. She was white, Irish and probably Catholic, he assumed. She signaled the bartender.

"Johnny, this man here is feeling the need for poitín, he says," she called out. The bartender reached far under the bar and pulled out a clear bottle without a label and poured two shots, setting one in front of each of them. He stood back and crossed his arms, waiting.

Maeve lifted one and looked at Caleb. He lifted the other glass. Maeve stared, unsmiling, into his face.

"Here's to women's kisses," she began, "and to whiskey, ever clear; not as sweet as a woman's kiss, but a darn sight more sincere. Sláinte." She downed the shot.

Caleb brought his glass up to his lips and felt his eyes water slightly as the sharp odor of pungent smoke rose in his nose. He was only one second behind her, but worlds away when the sour liquid burned down his throat. He gagged for a moment, which made everyone at the bar laugh, before he swallowed. Christ, this made his Sweet Tea taste like church lady lemonade.

"The name's Maeve Donegal. And that's how we "wics" do it in Galway, Mr. McKinsey," Maeve said. She tossed her head back and sauntered out the door. Caleb hesitated for a second before throwing too much money on the bar and following her.

"Can I buy you dinner?" he called at her back.

"I've eaten, thanks much," she answered, moving swiftly down the sidewalk.

"How about another drink?" He hurried after her.

"No, thanks." She waved, but did not turn.

"Breakfast tomorrow?"

"Never eat it."

People were turning to look now, smiling at his public humiliation as he pursued her. Glints of the day's last golden rays danced off the River Corrib and into his eyes.

"This is your famous Irish hospitality?" That stopped her. "You'd leave a lost Yankee standing alone in the street?"

Maeve turned and walked slowly back to Caleb.

"What is it you want from me, Mr. McKinsey?"

He wanted to stick both his hands into that cloud of hair, pull her close and kiss that mouth.

"A tour of Galway?"

"I'm not a tour guide."

"That's okay. I'm not a Yankee." There was the smile again; he couldn't let it go, so he smiled back.

"Tomorrow noon. Meet me at the Galway City Museum," she said. The smile stayed in her eyes as she turned to go.

He watched her walk away until he couldn't see her anymore, people slipping around him on the sidewalk like sunfish down the river.

Caleb was outside the City Museum well before noon. Maeve came walking up and caught his eye; he could swear there was a hint of lipstick today.

"I see you made it, Mr. McKinsey," Maeve said, stopping in front of him.

"I did indeed, Miss Donegal."

"Anything in particular you want to see?" There was that twinkle again.

"Can you tell me about the arch?"

"Not much you can't read from that guide book in your hand."

"I want to hear your story."

"The Spanish Arches were built to protect the bay, after the Irish helped the Spanish against the English. Which is our very favorite thing to do, helping anyone against the English." She looked up, straight in his face again. "This is where the likes of you come in, black Irish with the black hair and blue eyes."

"You telling me I'm really Spanish?"

"So they say. That's where the temper comes from, too. Do you have a temper, Mr. McKinsey? I think you probably do."

"You can call me Caleb."

"Can I, now?"

"Not too many get to do that. I'm a big deal in America."

"Now why would you tell me that?"

"How else you going to know?"

"It's pretty clear, actually."

"Is it?"

"Well, it's clear you think you are." There was the smile again, the quick sparkle. She was not a bit afraid of him. She was just on the edge of insolence and for whatever reason, he loved it from her. People didn't talk to him like this in Touraine. His past with his brothers, the

business he'd learned out of cruelty and then built to a great success—
she didn't know anything about that at all. She had nothing to gain, and
nothing to fear.

Over the next week, he pursued her like a bottle of Pappy Van
Winkle 25-year-old bourbon. He waited outside her office in the
mornings and sometimes she'd let him buy her coffee. He waited
patiently at noon, hoping she'd grant him a lunch date. She was usually
busy after work, yet there he stood, waiting. She worked for the *Tuam
Herald* newspaper writing obituaries, which she took very seriously.

"Why do you want to write that stuff?" Caleb asked.

"Every person deserves to have something nice said about their
life at the end," she replied.

Caleb wasn't sure this was true, but he could see she believed it.
"What would you write about me?"

"A forceful yet witty Yankee left this Earth today. Poor Caleb
McKinsey was crushed to death under the wheels of a market lorry for
asking too many questions. A wild-haired woman was seen walking
swiftly away."

At the end of the week she was waiting for him after work for a
change.

"I've got something special for you tonight," she said.

"How do you know I don't have plans?" Caleb asked.

"I don't care if you do, this is better."

"You don't know what my plans are." He stood firm.

Maeve looked up at him with just a second of uncertainty in her
eyes, then grinned it away.

"Are you coming?" She started down the street.

She took him to the Corrib Princess for a dinner cruise up the
river. It was a large, flat boat with sparkling glass windows lit from
inside. Climbing aboard they found elegant white tablecloths and
gleaming polished wood.

"So. There's Irish whiskey and Irish coffee. There will be Irish music later and Irish dancing as well. If you weren't Irish when you got to Galway, Caleb McKinsey, you surely will be when you leave."

"So this's where the Yankee becomes a Paddy?"

"With that accent? Not bloody likely."

They drank wine at dinner, Caleb letting her take the lead. He was content to sit back and watch, for once, instead of calling all the shots. She led him to the upper deck for the sunset, pointing out an old ivy-covered castle fallen into disrepair.

"They say the ghost of Ian McAndrew walks those walls, and haunts any lovers that get too near by tossing loose stones on them."

"I'm guessing you haven't been too close."

"I don't get too close to things, Mr. McKinsey. It's dangerous."

"That it is."

"Like this river. Did you know the Corrib is the fastest-flowing river in all of Europe?"

Her hair was blowing back from her face, the long curls winding around each other as she stared up at him with those clear green eyes, taunting mouth turned down.

Caleb quickly put both hands behind her head and pulled her toward him until they were inches apart. He felt a shudder down his entire body that he was sure had started in hers and he gently, softly leaned down and kissed her. He kissed the mouth that had been begging him for days. This was what it meant to kiss someone, and he knew now he wanted to do so much more than make her laugh.

"Caleb ..."

"Sh. Listen," he said. Joe Cocker's "You Are So Beautiful" floated up from below.

"The band must be on break," Maeve whispered.

"Doesn't he ..." Caleb started, then broke off.

"Doesn't he what?"

"Doesn't he sound like he'll die without her? In an honest, 'this is all I got to offer' way?"

"Did you know he never says 'love' in the song?"

"He doesn't have to." Caleb held her hands up to his face and kissed the palms. "I won't let you fall in the river, Maeve. I give you my word."

Three weeks later, he stood at the altar of the small church out in the country where everyone in Maeve's family had been married. He waited anxiously for her to appear. He'd had no sleep the night before and had smoked through an entire pack of cigarettes already that morning. He was marrying a woman he'd known for less than a month, and what made him sweat through his shirt was not wondering if he was doing the right thing, but the desperate fear she'd change her mind and not show up.

Then she was there, filling the doorway, sunlight streaming around her and lighting up the amber glow of tiny leaves on her shimmering midnight blue dress and igniting her hair. Caleb let his breath out at last. She was here, beaming at him, and he had all he ever wanted.

Maeve's father, on the other hand, was doing all he could not to glower at Caleb as he escorted his only daughter down the aisle. He figured Caleb was a scoundrel, that he was taking his little girl away. Caleb was old enough to understand there wasn't a damn thing he could do about her da's disapproval but show him how well he would take care of Maeve. Only time might make her father smile, and he vowed to make that happen.

"You son of a bitch!"

Caleb whirled at this outrage. A repetitive thumping came from outside. No one could take this day away from him. Scowling, he strode out the door, and there was Jeb, in the trunk of the old coupe.

"Get me out of here," Jeb said. He twisted over to his side, but couldn't seem to get his feet to work.

Caleb backed away.

"I … I wasn't even there, Jeb."

"They told us. You set us up."

"I didn't, I swear."

"You killed your own brothers." Jeb managed to push himself up on one elbow. "There ain't nowhere far enough away for you to hide now, boy."

Jeb would hunt him down for the rest of his life. Loyalty was valued far above the law, and he would never outrun this betrayal. Jeb pulled himself weakly up to the edge of the trunk but fell back with a groan. Caleb raised his rifle, rushed forward and shot his brother in the head.

Caleb scrabbled hard now to knock away the hands clutching at him, but only one of his arms would respond. Furious at his body's refusal to defend himself, he pulled inward and stilled. The manic activity jarred his bones as he was yanked up and manhandled. Arms and hands snatched and grabbed at him and he squeezed his eyes shut hard. Not even Caleb McKinsey could fix it this time. He would ride that pale horse now, straight up to the big rock candy mountain.

CHAPTER 27

The wake unfolded at Caleb's house. Brigit knew he would have hated all these strangers parading through his house, but she also knew it no longer mattered what her father would or would not hate. These things were never for the dead, but for the living.

When the doctor had come out and told them he was gone, Shooter had enfolded Brigit tightly in his arms as she sobbed. The only parent she'd ever really known was gone, taking all her secret hope for a family reconciliation with him. Lonny had stood stoically, letting a few tears run down his face without making a sound. Kieran had slid down the wall to rest on his haunches, face in hands. Mack had gone into crisis mode. He answered the questions, signed the papers, called the lawyers. He gathered everyone in the truck and drove them to Caleb's house, where they remained silent. There were precious few sweet memories of their father to share. The king was dead, long live the king.

Many people showed up for the wake out of curiosity to see how the king of bourbon had lived, disappointed not to see walls of gold-plated bottles. Some proceeded cautiously, suspicious the infamous moonshiner was not really dead. A few came to genuinely mourn the man.

"He's in a better place, praise God," said Father Byrne to Brigit. Caleb had never been to church, and the local Catholic priest, Father

Gallagher, had refused to perform the service. Mack had called neighboring towns until he found Father Byrne, who did not demand but would accept a donation to the parish. The padre unsuccessfully wiped the powdered sugar from a bakery cookie from his mouth.

"Thank you," said Brigit.

"The Lord has a plan for us all," the priest said, taking her hand. At the service, he'd spoken in very general terms about flocks of sheep coming home at the end of the day. Mack had supplied him with a cheat sheet of the important facts, like who Caleb's children were and his late wife's name. The priest didn't mention bourbon. He also didn't mention Lonny, though they had specifically asked him to.

Brigit had been afraid no one would show up, like a shy, unpopular five-year-old at a hopeful birthday party. She was surprised to see so many here. Everyone sought her out, and she managed to remain quietly, soberly gracious with Shooter by her side. She glanced at Mack, his face wretched with guilt. She and Mack had needed each other in New York, and he had let her down. She'd already forgiven him; she would hold no more grudges. She hoped he would soon learn to forgive himself.

She leaned into Shooter, her feet aching from the heels she felt gave her the look of solemnity for the situation. Shooter took her hand and stood forceful as a sentry. He'd been staying here at the house with all the McKinseys since the night Caleb died. He slept on the couch like a faithful watchdog, and adopted a bristly look if he thought anyone was tormenting Brigit, including her brothers. Today Annamae also hovered over Brigit, as did her boyfriend Thad. Many of Brigit's friends came to hug her and offer words of consolation at losing a father. Brigit knew they would be shocked by the emptiness in her heart.

Lonny held up, though he left the house from time to time, walking out to the fence to have a word with the cows, who had gathered around the fresh bales he'd dropped early that morning. Each time Lonny left the house, Winnie would turn her great head and amble up to meet him at the fence. Brigit was glad Lonny found comfort where he needed it most.

Mack stood not too near Caleb's plain brass urn, so people could speak to him but not feel obligated to do so. Faithful landscaping clients conveyed their condolences, as well as a few co-workers from Sunshine, minus Pete the manager. Brigit recognized people who'd shunned him when he was drinking, people he had wounded deeply and hadn't spoken to him since, who were now offering sympathy. They came in peace, holding out their hands to him. For this day at least, all was forgiven.

Kieran stood in the corner like a totem, a pained look on his features. People would start forward to speak with him but hesitate and turn back when there was no welcome in his face. Many seemed unsettled by his resemblance to his father. The ever-present smile that had defined him in his previous life was gone.

"Good Lord, don't he look like his papa now," an old woman in a faded housedress with a floating cloud of sparse white hair exclaimed upon seeing Kieran.

"Hush, Viola," shushed a middle-aged woman in a plain black dress holding her arm. The old woman stopped short, as if afraid of getting too close to Kieran, and would go no further.

Seamus O'Hearn shuffled in, alone. He seemed to expect to see Caleb's double in Kieran, and made a beeline for him, grabbing him in a rough hug and patting him hard on the back.

"I was too late," Seamus mumbled.

Mack crossed the room to them.

"Thanks for coming, Seamus," Mack said.

"Can't tell ya how much I miss him."

"How are things over at your place?"

"Not good. Seems a run of bad luck is flying through this part of God's acre. They took off the monitor, though. Offered a plea, just like Caleb said they would."

"Seamus," Brigit said softly. She embraced him, the kind of father she had always hoped for.

"I'm so sorry about your dad, Brigit," he said into the top of her head.

"I'm sorry about your friend, Seamus."

"If there's anything we can do to help, let me know," Mack said.

"Like to hear old Caleb make a raunchy joke, have a good laugh and take a nip or two, is what I'd like. Guess them days are gone."

Most of the people in Touraine, and all the employees of Bourbon Sweet Tea, came out to pay their respects to the man who had put the town on the map, even if it was for moonshine. Townsfolk straggled through, paying respects and indulging in plates of honey baked ham and biscuits with a glass of lemonade. Mack had insisted on no alcohol at the wake, and no one had disagreed. This, too, would piss off Caleb, although many flasks were being sipped in secret.

Suddenly Kieran lunged for the front door. The car carrying the ATF agents approached, raising a cloud of dust. They'd barely made it out of the car when Kieran stomped down the steps toward them.

"This is a private event. Get back into your car and leave before I bring the sheriff out to escort you," he said.

"Mr. McKinsey, Kieran, I wonder if—" Peterson started.

"You spread lies about me to my family," Kieran said.

"We don't appreciate that around here," Brigit said, joining her brother.

"We have nothing to say to you," Mack added, with Lonny next to him.

"Brigit, you are in a lot of trouble," Miller started.

"You do not get to threaten my sister." Kieran strode forward until they were face to face.

Shooter had come to stand just behind Brigit, as had Seamus O'Hearn. Annamae burst out the door with Thad in hand. People started to filter out onto the porch, steady looks of determination on their faces. Here on Bucks Elbow Mountain, sheltered by the Blue Ridge and fortified by generations of tradition, they formed an alliance against the outsiders. One of their own was being attacked, and they would stand together.

"Nobody in this town will ever be on your side," Annamae said.

"Gentlemen, I know you are not intending to cause trouble," said Sheriff Donald Bartholomew, purposefully settling his gray campaign hat on his head, his shield glinting in the sun.

"Officer, don't pretend you don't know what these people are up to," Miller said. He tried to walk around Kieran but Kieran stepped quickly in front of him.

"Family means something around here," Kieran said, directly into Miller's enraged, pink face. "You had best leave if you want to see yours again. I will make it my mission to drive you into the ground. At the end of the day, I am Caleb McKinsey's son."

Kieran reached into his pocket and flicked a piece of metal to the ground at Peterson's feet. He bent to pick it up.

"Miller," Peterson said, a warning in his voice.

Miller turned to see his partner holding out the palm-sized piece of white metal with two blue stripes running through it to the cracked, jagged edges. He took the remnant of the ATF drone gently into his hand, like a favorite toy left outside overnight that had met its fate under the wheels of a semi.

"Souvenir," Kieran said.

Peterson backed away and got into the car, followed by Miller. As they turned around, Donald Bartholomew climbed in his cruiser to escort them out of Touraine. This seemed to be the cue, as townspeople got in cars and pickup trucks to follow. A long line of vehicles would surround and accompany the agents all the way to the interstate, just in case they'd forgotten the way.

The next morning, Brigit padded into the kitchen, still in her pajamas. Mack was at his usual place at the coffeemaker. He'd gotten into the habit, over the last few days, of making a big pot so it would be ready whenever people woke. They wandered in and out of the kitchen at strange hours. A month's worth of casseroles began arriving the day after Caleb's death. They were stacked in the freezer like bricks. For all that food, however, they existed primarily on caffeine. Mack pulled out a filter and dumped in coffee. Just a week ago, Brigit remembered, he'd told her coffee was another addiction. Now none of them could get through a day without it.

She went straight to the sink and started washing her hands. She was obsessed with keeping them clean after the last day in the hospital. Blood had covered everything, her arms slick as if they'd been submerged. She had thrown away both her shirt and Shooter's, because she would never lose that blood-stained vision. She'd scrubbed her hands red and raw that night, unable to get all the blood off her palms, under her fingernails, in the creases of her knuckles.

"Good morning," she said as she wandered over to the coffeepot.

"Where's Shooter?" Mack muttered.

"Sent him to the store for more coffee," she yawned.

"Morning," Kieran said. He appeared quietly and sank down at the kitchen table. He didn't look as if he'd slept much. They both heard him, late at night, pacing in his room.

Brigit got out cups and poured for them all. Mack heard Lonny outside and waved him in through the kitchen window. He made his way in the back door, stopping to bang the mud from his boots with a rhythmic thump on the cement steps in anticipation of the clean house and the people in it. Brigit had missed that sound.

"We have some things to talk about," Mack said. He cleared his throat. "The house, the land, Bourbon Sweet Tea. The lawyers are reading his will tomorrow, but it'd be nice if we could just talk first. Because we're still McKinseys, and we're still a family. So I'm going to make breakfast." Mack turned to the refrigerator and took out the eggs.

"You're going to cook?" Brigit asked.

"Unless you want to do it?" Mack asked her.

"I serve it, but I don't cook it."

"I'll do it," Kieran said.

"Really?" Brigit asked.

"That was my job in New York."

"You're a cook?" Lonny asked.

"For a homeless shelter."

Brigit looked at Mack; they didn't know, they'd never asked. They might have been suspended in the timeless amber of a small town, but Kieran hadn't been.

Kieran stuck his head in the refrigerator. "Are these what I think they are?"

"Irish sausages. Remember?" Mack said.

"The ones your Ma used to make?" Lonny asked.

"Yeah," Mack said. "Seamus brought them."

"I loved these," Kieran said, grabbing the cast iron pan.

"It's been years since we all sat around this table," Mack said.

Brigit cleared her throat. "Can I ask you guys about my court appearance?"

"We'll be there," Kieran said. "I talked to Caleb's lawyer, he'll represent you. He thinks he can get you off with community service and a fine, but you'll lose your license. They'll go over everything when we go in tomorrow about the will."

Mack lowered his cup. "You talked to his lawyers?"

"You had a lot going on, I thought I'd help."

"Kieran … I'm sorry about the ATF," Mack said.

"I know." Kieran kept his back to them while he fried, the scent of hot grease filling the kitchen.

"You're going to stick around now, right?" Brigit asked.

"You were always the one with the hope," Lonny said.

"Please stay," Brigit said. "We could finally be a family again."

"Breakfast," Kieran said. He loaded up plates with mountains of fluffy eggs and crispy skinned sausages, and they all sat down together.

"Kieran, this is good," Brigit said.

"Thanks."

"Yeah, it's great," Mack said.

"I can get you a cooking job here," Brigit said. "You like it that much?"

"I do. I also like feeding people who might not eat otherwise."

"Can I say something? Seems like now's a good time." Lonny stood. "I got some stuff from Caleb." He pulled out a ring of keys and went to the office, unlocking it and returning with a sheaf of papers and Maeve's Donegal jewelry box from Ireland.

"Mom's jewelry box," Brigit said. "It was here all along."

"I knew you were looking for it, and I'm awful sorry, but Caleb asked me to lock it up." Lonny set the papers and the box on the table. "This ain't coming from me, so's you know." He cleared his throat. "There's an emergency meeting of the board of Bourbon Sweet Tea tomorrow, but I gotta tell ya, it doesn't look good."

"Why?" Brigit asked.

"Over the last couple of years, Caleb gave most of the profits away." Mack frowned. "He did *what?*"

"He set up a foundation, he said for tax purposes, and he donated almost everything that came in. Schools, small fry ones in little towns. But a lot of them."

"Dad gave all his money away?" Kieran said. Caleb had never been generous with his own kids, and even in the end had found a way to leave nothing for them.

Brigit was shocked. Mack had told her Caleb was only dangling the promise of money in front of them again to get what he wanted, which was Kieran. Caleb hadn't understood that they wanted their brother back more than they wanted to be rich. But a hint of hope had remained, and Brigit saw the same conflict in Mack's face.

"So there's no profits to build on," Brigit said.

" 'Fraid not. There's likely to be offers to buy, though."

"I don't want to sell it, I want to run it," Brigit said. "That was the whole point."

"I know it's hard to believe, but Caleb meant well," Lonny said.

Brigit looked at the ceiling. "Are you *shitting* me?"

"Brigit, you have to let it go," Kieran said.

"Oh—you carried him around as a murderer, but I need to let it go?"

"You don't have to forgive him, but you do have to stop living in his world," Kieran said.

"There's, uh, there's more," Lonny interrupted. "Lawyers don't have this, so we oughta keep it to ourselves."

"No," Mack said, watching the freedom he'd just grasped flying away.

"The reason the ATF was hassling him wasn't for Bourbon Sweet Tea. That was only their hostage. Caleb's been running a secret still site for years."

"Wait, what?" Brigit asked.

"Caleb was making *illegal* moonshine too?" Mack asked.

"He was."

"But—why?" Mack rubbed his face.

"He liked the challenge," Lonny said.

"Is it up and running now?" Mack asked.

"He does one run a year," Lonny said, "but it's a big one."

"No wonder the ATF agents were all over," Mack said.

"They weren't looking for Seamus," Lonny said. "They were looking for this."

"Seamus lost everything," Mack said.

"Your dad took care of Seamus. Paid for everything. His lawyers."

"Seamus knew about the secret still?" Mack asked.

Lonny nodded. "Helped him build it."

"But ... is it ... did they find it? Are we in trouble?" Mack was spiraling now. "We had no idea he was doing this."

"I did," Kieran said. Brigit and Mack turned to him. "I followed him once, very carefully. It's literally underground, inside the mountain."

"You never told us," Brigit said. Kieran shrugged.

"We need to get rid of this," Mack insisted.

"Well, that's the other thing," Lonny said. "Caleb wasn't going to go to prison neither. The explosives are already set."

"What?" spat Kieran. *"Explosives?"*

"Jesus Christ, are you kidding me? Who did that?" Mack said.

"Caleb asked me to," Lonny said. "But there ain't no detonators. Yet."

"Did he tell you to blow it up?" Kieran said.

"Not exactly. He told me to tell you-all about it, so's you could think on it."

"This is why he wanted you back, Kieran," Brigit said, "to be his outlaw."

"Sorry, I ain't quite done yet," Lonny interrupted.

"There can't be more," Brigit wailed.

"This here jewelry box, there's numbers carved inside the top of it. Account numbers. Caleb couldn't keep the illegal money in the regular bank, see. He told me this when you guys went off to New York. Made me promise to keep it to myself. I called on 'em yesterday."

"Well, if Caleb left us anything, which would be miraculous, I think we need to give it to Mack towards a new truck." Brigit said.

"Well. Here's the thing. There's four accounts, one in each name," Lonny said. "They're pretty big. I mean, you could quit waitressing if you wanted to."

Brigit looked skeptical. "For how long?"

"Forever."

Forks hit plates as they all stared at Lonny.

"No shit?" Brigit asked.

"You sure?" Kieran asked. "Maybe for you, Lonny, but not us."

"Nope. He made 'em all equal," Lonny said. "You can give it away, spend it, set it on fire, if you want. Or..."

There was quiet as they looked at the papers Lonny passed out. Absorbing the enormous numbers in what looked very much like offshore accounts.

"This much, it can't be real," Brigit whispered.

"It's illegal," Mack said.

"Could you, just once, give us a minute to dream?" Brigit said. "Jesus, Mack. Remember how we grew up, never asking Caleb for anything because we knew the answer would be no? Everybody in town thinking we were the lucky rich kids, and our father wouldn't even buy me a goddamn *Babar* book of my own. 'They're free at the library.' Come on, Mack."

"There's nothing wrong with—" Kieran started.

"We can't keep it," Mack stated with finality.

"What, do you want to give it to the government?" Kieran said.

"We *can* keep it. And we can keep Bourbon Sweet Tea," Brigit crowed.

"There are ways, Mack, before you shut me down again," Kieran said.

"I am not going to jail," Mack said.

"Neither are most of the wizards of Wall Street, and their tactics are highly questionable," Kieran said. "You meet more than just poor white trash in court-ordered rehab in New York City. These finance sharks were at the top of the heap once, but drugs'll eat anyone's money. Their friends and families'd abandoned them, and they were happy to tell you about their glory days of shell corporations and trusts. We need to find a sharp financial manager to protect the assets. That's all."

"How did you learn all this?" Mack asked.

"I listen. People need to talk about themselves, either to prove their worth or bare their souls."

"Right now I think we need to listen to the lawyers, and find out what happens to Caleb's shares of Bourbon Sweet Tea. What if he gave them away, too?" Brigit said.

"He did," Lonny said, shifting in his seat and staring down at the floor. "He gave them to me. I told him not to. But he did."

"This is great! Now we have more than enough!" Brigit said.

"Wait, Brigit. Maybe Lonny doesn't want them. He could sell them, and even if we have right of first refusal, he now knows how much money we have at our disposal, legal or not. Caleb may have left us a windfall, but it's nothing compared to the billions of a corporation like Anheuser-Busch. There's always a bigger fish," Kieran said kindly.

"Lonny would never do that to us, he's family," Brigit said.

"The board will contest this, too," Mack said. "We could be in court for years, trying to unravel Caleb's schemes. We need to think about this, Brigit."

She shook her head so hard her hair flew. "No, we need to *act* on this now, before it gets out. A lot of people only identify Bourbon Sweet Tea with Caleb. The board's always fought him. They're likely ready to cash it all in to Anheuser-Busch and be done." She pounded the table and stood. "All the cards on the table! This company was founded on illegal liquor in the first place. What better use is there for the offshore accounts? I know I'm young. Caleb didn't believe in me, I know that too. But my ideas are solid, even fiscally conservative, believe it or not. I will lay everything out for you, and you can ask me anything. If we present a united front to the board, they'll listen. They'll have to, we're the owners now. But we have to do it together! Tell me you support me. Tell me, right now."

"I'm on your side, Brigit," Lonny said, rather meekly. "Like to keep it all together if we could."

"But what do we do with the illegal still?" Mack asked.

"You oughta think on that some. I'm guessing those federal boys will stay away now their fancy drone got shot down," Lonny said.

"They didn't seem to appreciate their souvenir," Kieran replied with a slight grin.

Brigit's head swiveled between Lonny and Kieran.

"There was a *drone?*"

"Coulda been," Lonny said. "Coulda been one of them golden eagles. Them big ones that go after deer?"

"Lonny's always been an excellent shot," Kieran said.

"I was just protecting my herd."

"Maybe we could keep the still running," Kieran said. Mack saw the first trace of life in his eyes again, that old do-or-die attitude.

"You should talk to Seamus," Lonny said.

"First we gotta get those explosives out of there," Kieran said.

"Mack? What about Bourbon Sweet Tea? You could make it remarkable," Brigit said.

She knew if Mack helped her save Bourbon Sweet Tea, he'd feel stuck in this town. There would be even more McKinsey moonshine, which he'd been running from his entire life. But he could start his landscaping design business right now. Starting with beautifying the grounds around the distillery, turning it from a drab black box into an inviting space with exotic blooming bushes and spreading shade trees in a surrounding garden, with benches to sit and sip bourbon. Brigit had dangled this enticingly in front of her brother, with the promise of the hotel, horse farms and golf course to come, all under Mack's artistic eye.

He hesitated, then dropped his gaze. "I'm...I'm in, Brigit. I'll stay."

"Kieran?" Brigit asked, with more assurance than she felt. Caleb had been right about one thing; Kieran had always been meant to be the heart of the business. The road was going to be bumpy, and he had the genuine warmth, the honesty, and the integrity that gave people faith.

But he was shrugging. "What do you need me for, Brigit? You'll be fine on your own."

"No. I won't." She stood. "We have to do this *together*. We can finally make the McKinsey name mean something *good*. We are a family, and no one's ever going to believe in you as much as we do."

"You still have that baby-sister stubborn streak, don't you?"

"When I know I'm right, yeah."

Kieran smiled at last. "Then I guess I have no choice. Let's run with it."

Brigit got up and went over to the sink, opening the cabinet and reaching underneath. She moved some dish soap aside and came up with a dusty old jar. She wiped it on her sleeve until they could see the clear liquid inside. She brought it back to the table and opened it.

"To family," she said. She put a hand on the table, put her head back and took a long gulp. She sputtered, just a bit, and handed it to Lonny. He took a small sip, blinked, and handed it on to Kieran. Kieran looked at it for a moment, then put his head back and drank. He choked and bourbon ran down his chin. They all laughed as he wiped his face and handed it to Mack.

Mack took the jar and held it to his nose. The smell was Caleb, and it was family, too. He looked at them all, then set the jar down on the table.

"I'm going to pass," he said. "I have to drive."

"Drive? Where are we going?" Kieran asked.

"We're taking Caleb for one last ride. Come on. I have a garden to show you."

They all started toward the front door together. But Brigit turned back.

"I'll meet you at the truck," she said.

She watched the men leave. With Caleb's death, the sense of family had come flooding back to them. The lonely journey they had all trod separately for the past few years was finished, and now they belonged together again. The abandonment she'd felt was melting slowly away. They would move forward, and though she might always be the little sister, they'd walk alongside her now.

Brigit picked up the jug of moonshine and stared through the clarity of the bourbon. She tried to imagine a hint of ginger, a whisper of jalapeño. And for the first time, the possibilities were endless.

ACKNOWLEDGEMENTS

A debt of gratitude to Lenore Hart and David Poyer for seeing the true story. Thank you to writers Selçen Phelps and Tony Kapolka, who were kind enough to read this too many times. Thanks to Bob Mooney for hearing the poetry and Kaylie Jones for finding the power. Praise to my insightful and honest writing group, Aurora Bonner, Vicki Mayk, and Francisco Tutella. Many thanks to Nancy McKinley, Jeff Talarigo, Taylor Polites, Mike Lennon, Phil Brady, Ross Klavan, Dawn Leas, and Laurie Loewenstein for keeping me afloat. Thanks to Lauren J. Sharkey for being my publishing partner in crime. For all the nights of imbibing bourbon as research, thanks to Wendy, Kayleigh, Joe, and Kristin—sorry about the hangovers! To the Tunkhannock Book Club: Karen Bracey, Terri McCloskey, and Dottie Kupstas, thanks for wining with me. I am deeply indebted to John Amato, who showed me mountain still sites where I did not get shot.

Family is at the heart of this book, and with love and appreciation I thank my daughter, Emma Douthett, and my sister Joy Jenkins, for being here through all of this, and my friends Nora McGillivray and Carla Ingargiola, who wanted to be. Thanks to my brothers for kicking my ass. And thanks, Dad, for telling me that I could write this book.

READY FOR MORE APPALACHIAN NOIR?

If you enjoyed this novel, check out *Deep River Blues*
by Tony Morris, also from Northampton House Press.

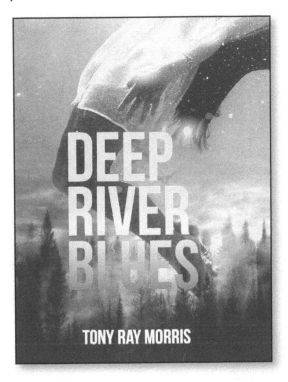

When a body's found in the French Broad River, Cord McRae, newly
elected sheriff of Acre County, Tennessee, suspects the death might be
connected to the Glad Earth Farm, a commune outside the small town
of Falston. Cord suspects they may be growing something more profitable
than sorghum cane up in the hills. The mystery's complicated by Cord's
investigation into a second recent murder of an Afghan vet; the power of
a local "hillbilly" mafia; and his own marriage, teetering on the edge over
Cord's on-again, off-again love affair with liquor. With echoes of Winter's
Bone and the novels of James Lee Burke, Deep River Blues is a worth-
while addition to the regional crime genre. Available online or through
any independent bookstore.

CPSIA information can be obtained
at www.ICGtesting.com
Printed in the USA
LVHW041352020621
689145LV00009B/130

9 781950 668090

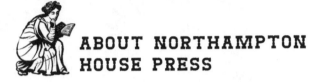

ABOUT NORTHAMPTON
HOUSE PRESS

Northampton House publishes carefully chosen fiction, poetry, and selected nonfiction. Our logo represents the Greek muse Polyhymnnia. Check out our list at www.northampton-house.com, and follow us on Facebook ("Northampton House Press"), Instagram (@nhousepress), or Twitter (@nhousepress) to discover more innovative works from brilliant new writers, for discerning readers of all ages.